A Perilous Pal

A Perilous Pal

A FRIEND FOR HIRE MYSTERY

Laura Bradford

BERKLEY PRIME CRIME
New York

BERKLEY PRIME CRIME
Published by Berkley
An imprint of Penguin Random House LLC
penguinrandomhouse.com

Copyright © 2022 by Laura Bradford

BERKLEY and the BERKLEY & B colophon are registered trademarks and
BERKLEY PRIME CRIME is a trademark of Penguin Random House LLC.

ISBN: 9780593334782

First Edition: July 2022

Printed in the United States of America
1 3 5 7 9 10 8 6 4 2

Book design by George Towne

For my Bradford's BFF group—you make this whole journey I'm on all the more fun. Thank you!

Chapter One

———✦———

Exhausted, Emma Westlake slid the paperback mystery across the wrought iron table and slumped back against her chair. "Part of me wants the next one in the series, and part of me wants to refrain just so I can get to sleep before 3:00 a.m."

"You can sleep when you're dead, dear." Dottie Adler ran her age-spotted fingers across the book's detailed cover almost reverently. "It was a good one, wasn't it?"

"My favorite one so far."

A smile that rivaled the afternoon sun spread the octogenarian's thinning lips wide as she reached for her Limoges teacup atop its matching plate. "You've got five more to keep you busy over the next few weeks."

"And then?" Emma asked, ricocheting forward against the table's edge. "Tell me she's writing more."

Dottie's sage-green eyes disappeared behind heavy lids for a moment before returning to meet Emma's across the rim of her cup. "I wish I could."

"But what do I do then? How will I know what's going on with these characters you've gotten me attached to?"

"You reread. And you pray."

Emma plucked a cookie from her plate, broke off a piece from the top, and held it below the table's edge, the answering wetness across the tips of her fingers . . . and her palm . . . and her wrist stirring a smile to her lips. "Pray for what?"

"A series reprieve." Dottie took another sip of her tea, followed it up with a bite of her own cookie, and narrowed her gaze on Emma. "I have to say, dear, aside from the raccoon circles under your eyes, your incessant yawning, and the fact that you really could stand a lesson or two in ironing, you look rather content."

Emma's laugh echoed in the still summer air. "Um, gee . . . *thanks*? I think?"

"Mind you, I had nothing to do with your decision to leave your house without applying concealer or consulting a mirror. That's all you. However, in regard to the looking content part, you're welcome." Dottie wiped the edges of her mouth with the cloth napkin from her lap and then summoned the third member of their weekly tea party out from under the table with another cookie. "The career path I've set you on is proving quite ingenious, isn't it, dear?"

"If by *career path you set me on* you actually mean your off-the-cuff suggestion as to something I might consider as a job, yes. It seems to be working."

Dottie bent forward, nuzzled her nose against Emma's golden retriever, Scout, and then released the brake on her chair's wheel and rolled a few inches back from the table. "I wasn't aware that coming up with the idea of being a paid friend, pushing you to try it, and procuring your first two clients was akin to an *off-the-cuff suggestion*, but that's okay, I'm not looking for credit."

"Cue the martyr music." Grinning, Emma pushed her own chair back from the table, gathered their empty cups and plates onto the serving tray she'd set off to the side, and made her way around the table to plant a kiss on top of the woman's snow-white head. "A Friend for Hire is showing promise, yes. A *lot* of promise, in fact. And while I may pretend otherwise just to yank your chain a little, I'm very aware of the part you played in making it happen."

"The *part* I played?" Dottie echoed.

"Oh. Right. My mistake. Let me try again. I'm aware of the starring role you played." Emma left the patio just long enough to set the tray inside the kitchen for the woman's housekeeper to attend to, and then returned to the patio and her chair. "Funny thing about my new business, though. I'm becoming real friends with everyone who's hired me thus far. Which makes it a little hard to take a check from them, you know?"

"You didn't make friends with Mr. Hill . . ."

She stared at Dottie. "Brian Hill *died*, remember?"

"While you were in his employ," Dottie drawled.

"Gee, thanks for the reminder." Propping her elbows on the table, Emma dropped her head into her waiting hands and shuddered. "Because, you know, I *have* been meaning to put that little fact on my website . . . Maybe even add a testimonial from the grave or something . . ."

"There's no need for sarcasm, dear. It's most unbecoming."

Emma popped her head up and sighed. "Sorry. That whole thing still wigs me out a little. But the good stuff that's happened so far? That makes me feel a little weird sometimes, too. Just in a different way."

"Weird, how?" Dottie transitioned her finger scratching into more of a petting motion, much to Scout's tail-wagging delight.

"I don't know. I think it's what I just said. Taking money for what essentially amounts to being nice feels wrong somehow."

Dottie nudged her chin at Scout. "It's enabling you to

keep feeding this one, right? And it's also allowing you to remain your own boss, yes?" Answering Emma's nod with a shrug, the elderly woman continued. "Besides, you've been accepting money from me for the same thing for more than eighteen months, so what's the difference?"

"I really wish you wouldn't go there about this." Emma spread her hands wide to indicate both the table and the teapot she'd forgotten to add to the tray. "It's about tradition more than anything else."

"A tradition you get paid handsomely to continue, compliments of my dear Alfred's estate, I might add."

"Semantics."

Dottie's left eyebrow arched, followed closely by her right. "Oh?"

"I mean, technically, yes. In the beginning I came because Alfred arranged for me to do so."

"And he paid you."

"Yes. But over time, I've come to look forward to our Tuesday afternoons because of this—the friendship we've built."

"A friendship for which a sizable deposit is still made into your checking account each week," Dottie mused.

Emma shifted in her chair. "Would you stop saying that? Please?"

"Why? Is that not the truth?"

Emma leaned back against her chair, then forward against the table, and, finally, back against the chair once again. "Yes, Alfred's attorney sends me a check for being here every Tuesday and has since Alfred passed. And yes, in the beginning, that was why I came—that, and because I knew how much you missed him. But"—Emma glanced across the table at Scout's face lying atop the armrest of Dottie's wheelchair—"so much more has come out of this than I ever imagined."

"Such as?"

"Well, for starters, Scout has become quite partial to the dog treats you slip him under the table while I'm getting the table ready each week."

Dottie pulled a face. "I don't know what you're talking about, dear."

"O-kay . . . So the whole *Shhh, don't tell* that always precedes the sound of Scout crunching something with his teeth while I'm making our tea is what? My imagination?" Emma rolled her eyes. "Please. You two are anything but sly."

"Fine. So it's the fact you get a check and I feed your dog that makes our teas valuable for you?"

Emma's laugh brought Scout to her side, tail wagging. "I thought you didn't feed my dog . . ."

"Oh, and lest we forget, these afternoon teas have also made you *literate*," Dottie said, plucking a crumb off her shirtsleeve.

"I knew how to read, Dottie."

"Yet you didn't."

"Because I was working morning, noon, and night as the travel agent I always wanted to be. And I was pretty darn good at it, I might add," Emma argued. "Or, rather, I was until people started booking their own travel instead of having me do it."

"Still, a thank-you is surely in order."

Oh, how she wanted to remain silent, if for no other reason than to watch the normally calm, cool, and collected octogenarian turn six distinct shades of red, but she couldn't. So much of her life *had* changed because of their Tuesday teas. Scout, her new business venture, and maybe even the first thing resembling a grown-up relationship in a very long time had all come into her life because of Dottie. So while teasing the elderly woman on occasion held some amusement, truth was still truth no matter how many times she might have said it in the past.

"You're right, Dottie. I *do* owe you a thank-you—you and Alfred," Emma said, her voice growing heavy with the same emotion that was beginning to take over Dottie's face. "To Alfred for asking me to continue these teas with you after his death. And to you for pushing me toward the animal shelter that gave me Scout. For coming up with this crazy business idea that shows signs of actually working. And for the people that same crazy business idea has brought into my life in just the last few weeks."

Blinking against the misty sheen clearly born on Emma's words, Dottie cleared her throat once, twice. "By *people*, do you mean Deputy Jack Riordan?"

"Perhaps," Emma said on the heels of a swallow.

"You're blushing, dear."

"It's summer. It's hot."

"Has he taken you on a proper date yet?" Dottie prodded.

"He's a single dad, Dottie—a *working* single dad. And, hello? His department is just now on the backside of its first murder investigation and everything that brought with it." Emma buried her growing smile in Scout's fur for a few moments and then gave up and put it on full display for Dottie to see. "*But* he dropped soup off on my doorstep last week when I was dealing with a cold, and he set a dog treat next to it for Scout."

"That's not a date."

"But it's a sign that he's thoughtful."

"It's not a date."

Her smile fading, Emma pinned her tablemate with a well-deserved glare, only to stifle it in favor of her phone and the chime signaling a new email. "Do you mind if I check this real quick?" she asked, pointing at the still-lit screen at her elbow. "It's my inbox for A Friend for Hire, and it could be a potential client."

At Dottie's nod, she keyed herself into her mail service and noted the bold name and subject line of the lone unread message.

I have no life!

Intrigued, Emma opened the email and began to read . . .

Ms. Westlake,

I've started and erased this inquiry half a dozen times in the past forty-eight hours after seeing your ad in the *Swoot Falls Gazette* on Sunday. The writing was out of desperation; the erasing was out of embarrassment. But it appears the desperation may actually win out this time around.

I always thought I had friends. But they were really just friends by way of my kids. And now that my kids have both graduated from college and are off doing their own thing (including forgetting to call every day like I always thought they would!), those friends have fallen away. I have no hobbies, no career, and no interests. My hobbies and interests were my kids' hobbies and interests. And the traveling I thought I might do at this point? Well, that went out the window when my husband of thirty years announced he was leaving me for a newer, hipper version of me.

You're probably wondering why I'm telling you all of this. And, honestly, I'm not sure. If my daughter would just come around to the fact that one call a day isn't the same as smothering, and my son's new live-in girlfriend didn't have such an issue with me dropping in on occasion, and my husband would wake up and realize that I look the way I do because I devoted my life to him and our children, everything would be fine. *I* would be fine.

But none of those things are happening, and I just feel completely rudderless. Maybe hiring you as my friend would help. If nothing else, it would give me something to think about besides my poor, pathetic existence and my overwhelming desire to murder my husband.

I have no schedule, so if you're interested in possibly taking me on as a client, you can email me back or call me

at 555-2324. Maybe we can meet for coffee and see if I'm
someone you'd even want to take on.

Friendless & more than a little pathetic,
Kim Felder

"Wow," Emma murmured. "This is absolutely heart-
breaking. This poor woman sounds so sad, so alone, so . . .
pitiful."

"Oh?"

"Yeah. Her whole world has just imploded. Her kids
have graduated from college and flown the nest, leaving her
at a loss for what to do with her time. Her husband of"—she
looked back at the email, skimming her way down to the
second paragraph—"*thirty years* up and dumped her for a
younger woman. And it sounds as if she doesn't have any
real friends with whom she can vent."

"Or plot the louse's demise."

"And then there's that," Emma murmured as she reached
the end of the email once again. "I feel so bad for this
woman."

"Then what are you waiting for?"

Glancing across the table, Emma met Dottie's pointed
gaze across the top edge of the woman's glasses. "*Waiting for?*"

"We're done with our tea for the week, yes? So call this
woman, or email her, or do whatever you do to sign a new
client in this day and age."

"Are you sure?" Emma asked. "I was planning on staying a little longer . . ."

At Dottie's nod, Emma returned her attention to the top
of the email, read it silently a third time, and then pushed
back her chair and stood. "You're right. If there's anyone
who needs my services, it's this Kim Felder."

Chapter Two

Emma filled Scout's travel bowl from her water bottle, watched him splatter half of it over the sides with his always-eager tongue, and then sat back, waiting. In hindsight, she wished she'd collected a few visual cues—car driven, hair color or style, height—rather than going into a first meeting blind, but at least she'd managed to secure the suggested park bench closest to Sweet Falls' beloved town gazebo.

To her right, in an area often dotted with picnic blankets, a squirrel hastily nosed his way across the grass, looking for something resembling food. Just beyond him, a town employee was emptying a trash can into the back of a golf cart. To her left, not far from the thicket of flowering bushes lining the eastern edge of the town square, she took in a trio of women about her own age, chatting over to-go cups from the local coffee shop while gazing down, every few seconds, at their respective offspring sleeping soundly in matching designer front packs.

"It was like I blinked and that part of my life was over,

you know?" Startled, Emma looked up just as a woman in her early to mid-fifties slid onto the bench beside her and released a heavy sigh. "And oh, what I wouldn't do to be able to blink it all back into being right now."

And just like that, there was no need for visual cues, or even a prearranged meeting spot. No, the tangible pain emanating from the stranger told her everything she needed to know.

"I don't know," Emma said, following the woman's gaze back to the young mothers. "It seems to me that every stage in life has something special to offer if you give it a chance."

"Said someone who can still read a menu without cheaters, likely cartwheel across the grass without feeling like their wrist is going to snap off, and still has that"—the woman nodded at the pack-riding babies—"to look forward to in life."

Emma shrugged. "You're not being woken at night by a crying baby, anymore . . ."

"Nope. Just my bladder."

"You can eat without noise."

"Just the sound of my every chew against a backdrop of utter silence."

"You"—Emma, again, visually swept the grouping of mommies—"can wear cute clothes people can actually *see*."

"No one is looking."

She tried again. "Your time is your own."

"To stare at the walls . . . to watch reruns of shows I can recite from memory at this point . . . to twiddle my thumbs . . ." The woman turned to Emma and extended her hand. "I'm Kim Felder, by the way."

"I'm Emma—Emma Westlake. And this"—she said, nudging her chin toward the golden retriever now licking Kim's knees—"is Scout. My dog."

Kim watched Scout for a few moments and then sank back against the bench. "I'm surprised you came."

"I told you I would when I called you yesterday."

"I know. But I'm still surprised. I'm not sure I would've if I were you."

"Why?"

"My email made me sound really pathetic." Kim held up her hands. "Which, I'll admit, is a fair representation of the facts."

"You didn't sound pathetic, nor are you."

Kim's answering laugh held no sign of humor.

"You're not," Emma persisted. "You've just hit a rough patch, that's all. But we're gonna figure a way out."

"We?"

She met Kim's tired eyes and noted the hope that flashed, albeit briefly, within them. "My business is called 'A Friend for Hire.' That means, should you hire me, it's *we* for however long you need me."

Kim's throat moved with a hard swallow. "I . . . I don't know what to say. Or—or what to ask you to do for me."

"Then just tell me about yourself and maybe we can figure it out together."

"There's nothing to tell. I'm fifty-three. My career was being a stay-at-home mom. Now, my kids are both grown and living lives that seem to have little to no room for me in them. I have no real friends because my world, my *life* was my kids."

"I'm sure that's not entirely—"

"Oh, and lest I forget, the man I gave thirty of my fifty-three years to, up and decided to ditch me for his much younger secretary—a woman with a far better body and the energy to stay up past 11:00 p.m. on any given night."

"You gave him two children," Emma said.

"I did."

"How old is this secretary?"

"Thirty-five."

"How old is *he*?"

"Fifty-five."

"But—"

"I picked out some really awesome gifts for her—on his behalf—for the first two years she worked for him." Kim blew out a tired breath. "A jade necklace that matched her eyes . . . one of those purses that was all the rage last year but was nearly impossible to find . . . a first edition of her all-time favorite book . . . and so on, and so on."

Emma tried to cover her "Nooo" but was too slow.

"She was also"—Kim touched the base of her neck and mimicked the squeaky voice of an animated mouse—"*so incredibly touched* by Roger's giving nature on the charity front."

"Charity front?"

Kim dropped her hand to her side and lifted her gaze to the sky. "I've always believed that success should be shared with those who are less fortunate. So I encouraged Roger to spread the wealth whenever his company surpassed its year-end goal. He balked the way most men would at first, but when I pointed out the tax benefit and the fact that it might also earn him and the company some good-guy press, he conceded. Every year I picked out a handful of charities, and he wrote the checks and fielded the accolades they brought."

"So what you're saying is that *you're* the reason his secretary fell for him?" Emma murmured.

"Yep."

"Wow. I don't know what to say."

"There's nothing *to* say. I am the ultimate clichéd fool, aren't I? Pathetically laughable, in fact. Only I seem to have lost all ability to laugh—or smile—about anything."

It was a lot to take in, a lot to absorb, and Emma allowed herself a moment to do so. "I'm a big believer in dealing with things in manageable chunks. It's less daunting that way, and each thing you get off your plate enables you to see more and more clearly. So, first things first . . . What you did, raising your kids the way you did, is admirable. You should be proud of yourself."

"I want to be. But it's like they don't need me—or the things I've always done for them—anymore."

"I doubt that. I think it's just that they need you in a different way now."

"When they were little, my peers would comment that parenting should come with a roadmap. I never really got that because it just sort of came naturally for me. But *this* part? This empty nest stuff? This suddenly single thing? I'm lost."

Emma eyed Scout eyeing Kim. "While I admit it was on a much smaller scale, I've been lost a time or two myself."

"Oh?" Kim asked, abandoning her view of the mommies. "In what way?"

"Well, for starters, when the last of my unmarried friends got married and the majority of my already-married friends started having babies, I felt a little sorry for myself."

"No special guy for you?"

"At the time, no. And while I adore living here in Sweet Falls with all of the best small-town feels, I was still the owner and sole employee of a home-based travel agency in a place I didn't really grow up in. Which means it was pretty much just me—twenty-four/seven. No one to go for walks with, no one to go for spontaneous coffee runs with, no one to gab with on the phone after work, et cetera, et cetera. Everyone I managed to meet soon moved into a different life stage than I was in. I felt pretty alone, truth be told, and I started spending a lot of time watching TV and bemoaning my loneliness until even I was sick of myself." She nudged Kim's attention toward Scout. "And that's when I went to the shelter and we picked each other out, isn't it, boy?"

Aware of his sudden spin in the spotlight, Scout wagged his tail so hard Emma couldn't help but laugh. "Best. Decision. Ever. Because now, I have a ready-made companion for all walks and a willing partner for any new adventures I happen to seek. *And* he's an amazing listener."

"But you have someone now, right?" Kim asked, glancing between Scout and Emma. "I mean, besides the dog?"

At what must have been a tangible manifestation of the confusion Emma felt, Kim rushed to clarify. "Because just now, when I asked if you had a special guy, you said *At the time, no.* Which sounds like—"

"I met someone recently, yes. He seems like a nice guy, but . . . you know."

"It's too early to know for sure?" Kim prodded.

"Exactly."

"I wish I could say you'll know soon, but clearly I'm not exactly an expert on reading cues, seeing as how I thought my husband was happy with me."

Emma waited the appropriate beat for commiseration purposes and then continued. "Getting Scout helped with the loneliness, for sure, but then the slow death of my business became impossible to ignore and I found myself feeling lost in a very different way. Fortunately for me, a friend made a suggestion and, well"—she spread her arms wide—"I'm following a new path that is looking pretty promising so far."

"How so?"

"I'm feeling hopeful for the first time in a long time, and I'm meeting some really great people at the same time."

Kim stilled her hand on Scout's head and managed a sincere smile. "I'm glad. It's nice when things work out for people."

"As I'm confident they will for you, too, Kim. You just have to put yourself out there in new ways."

"I don't think so."

"Which is what I said to my friend when she suggested the very business idea that had you reaching out to me by way of email yesterday. Fortunately for me, that friend didn't let me get away with *I don't think so.*" Emma turned so quickly her knees bumped Kim's. "Which is why I'm not going to let you get away with it, either. You've spent decades putting your kids and your marriage first, and now it's time to put Kim first. To pursue *your* interests and *your* dreams."

"What interests?" Kim echoed. "I have no interests. And as for dreams, I only have two: for my kids to be little again, and for my marriage to get back to what it once . . ." She waved away the rest of her sentence.

"Then we'll find you some interests."

"How do you propose doing that?"

Emma reached inside the tote bag at her feet and retrieved the notebook and pen she'd placed inside. "We're going to make a bucket list with all the things you've ever even thought about doing. You know, cafés you've always wanted to try but never did, hobbies you've always thought looked interesting but never had time to pursue, projects you've wanted to tackle but never had time to actually do . . . those sorts of things."

"But why? What's the point? There's no one to do that stuff with."

"This is why you reached out to me, right?"

"You'd do that with me? Go to cafés and try hobbies and stuff like that?"

"I'm a friend for hire, remember? That means we do things together." Emma clicked open her pen. "So, what should we put on the list?"

Kim looked from Emma to the empty page and back again, her shoulders lifting and falling with a shrug. "I don't know."

"Do you like plants? Trees? That sort of thing? Because I get a charge out of digging in the dirt. It's a great stress reliever."

"Not really, no. That was always Roger's thing. He took care of the outside of the house; I took care of the inside and the kids."

"Do you like to cook or bake? Because I've heard cooking classes can be a lot of fun."

"I like to eat. Baked goods, in particular."

"Okay, that's a start." Emma looked down at the paper. "We could see if there are any cool bakeries within, say, a thirty-minute drive and check them out . . . That could be fun."

"I read something somewhere about a woman who runs her bakery out of an old ambulance. Calls it the Emergency Dessert Squad." Kim's hand returned to Scout's head for another scratch, another pet. "I remember thinking, at the time, that it might be fun to go and see it one day."

"Oooh! Good one!" Emma wrote it down. "Do you remember where it was?"

"Ohio, I'm pretty sure."

"I'll look it up. Maybe we can make a weekend out of it."

Kim drew back, her eyes rounded with surprise. "You go away on trips with your clients?"

"I haven't yet, but I would if that's what someone hired me to do with them," Emma said, tracking Scout over to the edge of the gazebo with her eyes.

"What kind of stuff *have* people hired you to do with them?"

"Go to the gym, attend a dance, be a wingman at a party, look in on someone's elderly father while the son was on a business trip, that sort of stuff."

"Wow," Kim murmured. "So there really are others, besides myself, who are this pathetic . . . Who knew?"

Emma's gaze traveled back to Kim. "Actually, I wouldn't consider any of them pathetic. In fact, they're all incredible people—every single one of them. Just as I'm sure you are."

"My husband doesn't seem to think I am."

"Then have fun proving him wrong until it no longer matters to you, one way or the other." She looked again at her notepad and its single entry. "So, we're going to track down this Emergency Dessert Squad. And let's add trying as many cute bakeries as we can find in our own immediate area . . . So now what else? Maybe learn a sport? Take up hiking? Maybe try your hand at a new craft, or one you used to do but stopped when you were busy with your kids? Or maybe pursue something you've always been good at?"

"I'm good at raising kids. I'm good at making cookies. I'm good at hosting themed birthday parties. That's it."

Emma abandoned her pen long enough to squeeze Kim's hand. "I doubt that. Very much. You just haven't had the time to explore other things until now."

At the woman's answering silence, Emma flashed what she hoped was an encouraging smile. "It doesn't have to be anything big or flashy, Kim. Just something that intrigues you on some level."

"There is *one* thing I've been thinking about lately. Mostly when I'm lying in bed alone at night . . ."

Leaning forward, Emma reclaimed her pen. "Tell me."

"I think of all sorts of ways I can kill Roger. And some of them are pretty creative, if I do say so myself."

Emma felt her eyebrow rise along with the corners of her mouth. "This is a bucket list, remember? It's made up of specific things you want to do."

"Fine. Write this down," Kim said, pointing Emma's attention back to the notepad. "I want to make Roger's favorite cookie and lace it with something deadly."

"Kiiiiim . . ."

"Then how about push him in front of a bus? Or . . . wait—I had a good one last night! I string him up in the garage—piñata style—and hit him with his favorite baseball bat until there's nothing left of him." Kim giggled. "And if I stuff his pockets with candy before I start, it can feel like a party, too."

Emma's laugh brought Scout back to the bench, his tail wagging and his eyes bright with anticipation. "Maybe we could start with something a little smaller and a little less illegal. For now, anyway."

"Killjoy."

"I try." She studied Scout for a moment and then turned

back to Kim. "You said you're good at making cookies, right?"

Kim held up her hand. "Trust me, Emma, my daughter doesn't want me bringing by any more cookies. She's made that perfectly clear."

"I get that. But if you're willing to tweak your recipe to be canine-friendly, Scout and I know the perfect place to take them, don't we, boy?" She bent down, kissed the top of Scout's head, and then turned back to Kim. "And I can promise they'll be appreciated by every single mouth in the room."

It was fast, and it was fleeting, but there was no denying the hope that skittered across Kim's drawn face before disappearing, once again, behind the same fatigue and pain she'd worn on arrival. "I don't know, Emma. I—"

"You don't have to know, Kim. Not yet, anyway. But let's try this thing first and see if it lifts your spirits a little."

"The piñata-idea would definitely lift my spirits. As would the poisoned cookie, and the bus, and suffocating him with a pillow, and—"

"You didn't mention the pillow thing," Emma said, grinning.

"I didn't want to overwhelm you with too many things to write all at one time."

"Ahhh. I see." Emma tucked the notepad and pen into her tote bag and stood next to Kim. "Let's start with the dog cookies for now, though, okay? I can send the recipe you'd need to use to your email address. If you like what you see, we can arrange a day and time to drop them off and then maybe go out for a treat afterward to brainstorm some more ideas for your list."

"Oh, I've got more ideas. All entailing some measure of pain," Kim quipped before reaching down to give Scout one last behind-the-ear scratch. "But, yeah, send the recipe. It's not like I have anything else to do, you know?"

"You will. Soon. This just gives us a fun place to start. If, in fact, you even want to hire me."

Kim studied Emma for a moment, her expression unreadable. Then, with little more than a quick smile, the woman reached inside her back pocket, extracted a checkbook, and flipped it open. "You had me at your first *we*."

Chapter Three

Emma sank onto her favorite corner of the couch, waited for Scout to settle his chin on her thigh, and reached for the remote. Thirty minutes earlier, when she was just sitting down at her kitchen table, she'd had all the best intentions for a productive evening—culling through old travel agency files, expanding her marketing plan for A Friend for Hire, and updating her calendar for the upcoming week. Yet, by the time she'd taken the last bite of her meal, she knew none of that was going to happen.

Not tonight, anyway.

"It's okay to be a bum once in a while, right, boy?"

Scout lifted his chin, danced the upper ridges of his eyes up and down, and skimmed the entire width of the loveseat with his tail as her hand came down atop his head. "So, what do you say?" she said, resting her head against the back of the couch. "Game show, gardening channel, chick flick, police drama, or—"

The sudden ring of her phone hijacked her attention

from the still-blackened screen in front of them to the much smaller, illuminated one on the coffee table. A glance at the name displayed across it had her abandoning the remote in record speed.

"Hi," she said, pressing the phone against her cheekbone. "This is a nice surprise."

And it was. Very much. So, too, was the sudden disappearance of anything resembling fatigue from her mind and body.

"Hi, yourself. And to Scout, too."

Grinning, she looked down at her faithful companion. "Deputy Riordan says hi."

"Jack works."

"Right. Sorry. Deputy *Jack* says hi, Scout."

The laugh in her ear was rich, warm. "*Just* Jack. Please."

"No title?" she teased.

"No title."

"Jack says hi, boy."

Scout wagged his tail.

"Better." A sound that had her imagining the deputy stretching his toned arms toward the ceiling quickly gave way to his deep voice once again. "I was hoping I'd see you at the gym this morning, but no such luck. Still battling that cold you had last week?"

"Actually, thanks to you and that delicious soup you left on my porch, my cold is a thing of the past."

"I'm glad."

"That was really sweet, by the way," she said. "The soup, *and* the treat for Scout."

"It was my pleasure. Made the soup from a recipe of my mom's. Always worked like a champ when my sister and I had colds when we were growing up."

She allowed herself the smile stirred by the memory of the thoughtful gesture and the handwritten "Get Well Soon" note still propped next to her bedside lamp, and then got them back on track. "As for me not being at the gym this morning, Stephanie apparently hit the snooze button on her alarm clock one too many times."

"So what does that mean for you?"

"It meant a nice long morning walk with Scout, instead." She bent down, lifted the dog's chin off her leg, and planted a kiss just north of his wet nose. "Which isn't a bad way to start the day."

"I'm sure. But I meant more along the lines of you counting on that job and then not getting it at the last minute. That has to make things tough."

"With another client, maybe. But Stephanie pays me whether she shows up or not."

"That's good. For you."

"On paper, sure. But it's getting harder and harder to cash her check each week," Emma admitted, sitting back.

"Why is that?"

"Stephanie is becoming a real friend. A good one, in fact. And I *like* going to the gym with her."

"It's okay to like your job, Emma. Some of us actually do."

Swiveling her leg around Scout, Emma rested her bare cheek against the upright cushion. "I know. But it's not like Stephanie is the only one getting something out of this relationship at this point. In the beginning? When I didn't know her? Sure, getting up at five in the morning to meet her at the gym was work. And getting her to actually stay on the workout equipment for longer than five minutes was a task in and of itself. But now? I look forward to Monday, Wednesday, and Friday mornings. She's funny. She's quirky. And we get along really well. So much so, I've invited her here, to my place, at least a half dozen times in the last six weeks."

"Do you charge her for that?"

"For coming here?" At his grunt of assent, she continued. "Of course not. I invite her because I want to hang out with her. As a real friend."

"Okay . . ."

She searched for the best way to explain where her head was at, and settled on the straightforward. "I'm not paying her to be my friend, so why should she be paying me to be hers?"

"I hear what you're saying, but that's why she hired you, right? Why *everyone* hires you? For companionship?"

"Yes, but I don't know. I just genuinely *like* everyone who's hired me. There's something sweet about all of them—Stephanie, Big Max, John and Andy, and even Kim, from what I was able to tell in our limited time together this afternoon."

"You signed a new client?" Jack asked.

She nodded, then rushed to give voice to the gesture he couldn't see. "I did."

"That's fantastic, Emma!"

"Thanks."

"Tell me about her."

"Her name is Kim, like I said. From what I gather, she was the quintessential stay-at-home mom for her two kids—a boy and a girl. The cookie-baking, playdate-throwing, classroom-volunteering, scout-troop-leading, all-in mom everyone wishes they had. Only now her kids are grown and on their own and don't need her in the same way she wants to be needed."

"Ahhh, she's lacking a mission now."

"Pretty much, yeah. Her life was her kids. Her dreams were her kids' dreams. Her friends were the parents of her kids' friends. And now she's got nothing. Including her marriage of thirty years."

Jack's answering whistle was quiet yet laden with empathy. "Her husband died?"

"No, he dumped her. For his secretary."

"Oh. Wow."

"I know, right?"

"She didn't see it coming?"

"Nope."

"Wow," he repeated. "What a creep."

"You can say that again."

"Think you can get her back on her feet?"

Emma's thoughts traveled back to the park and the woman who'd flitted in and out of them ever since. "I'm going to give it my best shot, that's for sure. But she's in a tough place. The mom in her wants everything to be the way it was, for her kids to need and want her continued involvement in every aspect of their lives. And on top of that, the one person she thought would support her through it all took off for the hills, leaving her completely alone."

"I'm guessing you'll be carrying a box of tissues every time you get together with her."

"I'll have some, sure. But my goal is to help her rediscover—or maybe unearth for the first time—the real Kim. *Her* interests, *her* goals, *her* dreams."

"I like that," Jack said. "But how?"

"We're making a bucket list. And we're going to fill it with all those things she thought would be neat, or maybe always wanted to try if only she'd had the time. Worst case, she'll have some things to keep busy with for a while. Best case, she'll find a new passion she can throw herself into."

"So what's on the list so far?"

Her gaze traveled to the coffee table and her open notebook with the two items she'd written on the otherwise blank page. "She likes baking. And eating baked goods. So for now, it's just checking out local bakeries. I'm hoping I can track down some fun baking classes in the area that might interest her, but I have to do a little homework on that first."

"Sounds good. What else?"

"She mentioned reading something about some woman who runs a unique bakery business somewhere in Ohio. If we can track it down, we might make a weekend trip to check it out."

"Next . . ."

Emma scanned the empty lines that followed and shrugged. "Unless you count the various ways in which she'd like to kill her husband, that's it. For now, anyway. But we'll come up with more, I'm—"

"Oh, hey, Emma? Can I put you on hold for a second? I'm getting a call from the station."

"Absolutely."

She slid her attention onto Scout and ran a gentle hand down the back of his head. When she reached the base of his neck, she returned her hand to the starting point and repeated the motion, again and again and again.

One minute became two minutes.

Two minutes became three minutes.

And three minutes became four . . . five . . . six . . . and—

"Emma?"

Stilling her hand, mid-pet, she smiled. "I'm still here. Is everything okay?"

"No. I've got to go. There's been another murder."

Scout's chin popped off her leg at her answering gasp. "Where? When? How?"

"The body was found about an hour ago by one of the guy's employees. The deputies on scene are saying cause of death is strangulation, although the M.E. will be the one who has the final say."

"Wow. Of course. Go." She tightened her hold on the phone. "But be careful, okay?"

The answering silence in her ear had her checking the phone for confirmation he hadn't hung up. "Jack?"

"I'm still here. I guess what you just said threw me a little."

A mental replay of her words yielded no clues except . . . "Oh, Jack, I didn't say *go* because I was trying to get rid of you! I just said it because I know you need to—"

"It was the other part," he said, his voice husky. "About being careful."

"I don't understand."

"It's been a long time since I've heard those words directed at me."

At a loss for how to respond, she opted to say nothing.

"It was nice," he added.

She leaned her cheek against the couch again and stared down at her now-sleeping dog. "I meant it."

"I know." A shift in his voice let her know he was on the move, likely gathering his badge, gun, and car keys en route to the front door. "Any chance you'd like to catch a movie or go out to eat with me this weekend?"

"Are you asking me out on a date?" she teased him.

"I am." The smile she heard in his voice rivaled the one she knew she wore. "If you need to check your calendar and get back to me, that's—"

"I'm free and I'd love to go to a movie or out to dinner with you."

"Fantastic. I'll give you a call sometime tomorrow, and we can come up with an actual plan then. In the meantime, though, as much as I'd rather keep talking, I've got to help my guys figure out who killed this Felder fella."

His words were like ice water on her skin, making her draw back so quickly Scout nearly toppled off the edge of the couch. "*Felder* fella?" she echoed.

"That's right. Roger Felder, our victim."

She heard the squeak of his door, the latch of his lock, and her own gasped inhale. Felt Scout's chin leave her thigh in favor of a worried whimper. But really, in that moment, all she knew for certain was dread—bone-chilling, hair-raising, heart-slamming dread.

Chapter Four

S he paced . . .
She stared out the window . . .
   She paced . . .
   She stared out the window . . .
   And she paced some more, Jack's words playing on a continuous loop broken only by the click of Scout's nails moving between the same wood floors, the same throw rugs, the same strip of linoleum.
   She could feel his worry every bit as much as she could his breath on the backs of her legs, but still she paced.
   Roger Felder—a name she'd heard for the first time that afternoon—was dead. *Murdered*, Jack said.
   Pivoting, she headed back into the living room, Scout close on her heels. She needed to do something . . . hear something . . . know—
   She stopped next to the coffee table, her gaze traveling down to—and locking on—her open notebook, her mind's eye filling the empty lines with suggestions she'd thought had been in jest.

- *Make Roger's favorite cookie and lace it with something deadly.*
- *Push him in front of a bus.*
- *String him up in the garage, piñata style.*
- *Suffocate him with a pillow.*

Fisting her hand against her mouth, Emma made herself breathe. Jack said strangulation. Kim never mentioned anything about—

"Oh, I've got more ideas. All entailing some measure of pain."

Emma dropped back onto the couch and buried her face against Scout's waiting head. "Please tell me Kim had nothing to do with this. Please, please, please tell me that."

Instead of words, Scout answered with his tongue. On her cheek . . . on her chin . . . on her nose . . . and, finally, her hand, his large, dark eyes searching hers for some sort of clue as to what he should do to make her happy again.

"It's not you, Scout. I promise," Emma murmured, touching her forehead to his. "It's Kim—the woman we met at the park today."

The immediate wag of his tail let her know she'd lost him at *park*. And the rapidly growing knot in the pit of her stomach let her know she needed another set of ears.

With one last kiss on top of Scout's head, she reached for her phone, pressed her way into her client folder, and hit the call icon next to the second name.

One ring . . .

Two rings . . .

Three—

"I'm guessing, in addition to everything else you do well, you're also a master of telepathy now, too?" Stephanie Porter bit down on what sounded like a chip or a pretzel, chewed it for a beat or two, and swallowed. "I literally said—not more than two seconds ago—*Please, someone, make this stop* and . . . *Bam!* You called."

"It?"

"My mother."

"Ahhh . . ." Pulling her feet onto the couch, Emma wrapped her arms around her legs and closed her eyes against the sight of her notebook. "What's she on you about this time?"

"Apparently my biological clock is ticking so loudly, it's now keeping her awake at night."

She felt her lips rise up in a shaking smile. "That's a new one."

"No. Not really. This is part of a cycle with her," Stephanie explained. "The ticking keeps her awake for a few weeks, and *then* she's driven from a sound sleep every night for the next few weeks by the image of the grandchildren she'll never meet."

"Joy," she murmured.

"Everything you wanted to know about my neurosis in a nutshell, my friend." Stephanie chased down whatever she'd eaten with a gulp of something. "So a big thank-you to your telepathic self for getting me off that audible hamster wheel. That's a skill you might want to add to your website."

"If I actually had that skill, it might've behooved me to use it sometime between three o'clock this afternoon and"— she opened her eyes long enough to peek at the clock on the mantel—"about, I don't know, maybe two hours ago."

All crunching and gulping ceased in her ear. "Hey, are you okay? You sound a little funny."

"Where do I start?"

"The beginning is usually a good rule of thumb. Unless this is about the deputy and he's revealed himself to be a jerk. In which case, give me ten minutes to brush my teeth, put my hair in a ponytail, and head straight to his house to kill him."

Emma unwrapped her arms from her legs and stood. "Would you?" she asked. "Kill him, that is?"

"If he hurt you, yes. And when I was done, I'd kill him a second time."

"Seriously?"

"What did he do?" Stephanie asked.

"Who?"

"The deputy."

She wandered into the hall, let Scout's hopeful gaze lead hers toward the kitchen, and then crossed into her office instead, the only hint of light in the otherwise darkened room coming from the muted glow of her sleeping computer screen. "Jack didn't do anything. In fact, he wants us to do something together this weekend."

"You mean an actual date?"

She nodded.

"Emma?"

"Oh. Sorry. Yes. Like a date. Specifics as to the what and when still need to be worked out, but at least he asked."

"Dottie will be pleased."

Her answering laugh was quick, shallow.

"Spill it, Emma. What's going on?"

She ran her finger along the edge of her keyboard, across a framed picture from one of her many trips as a working travel agent, and down the stack of business cards for her newest business venture, her chest tightening along with her throat. "I signed a new client this afternoon."

"That's awesome, Emma! Congratulations! Word is really starting to spread!"

Oh, how she wished she could feel the excitement she heard in Stephanie's voice. Instead, all she felt was fear.

"Wait," Stephanie said. "How come I'm sensing absolutely zero excitement from you on this?"

"I was very excited. For the first few hours, anyway."

"What's changed?"

Slowly, Emma lowered herself onto her desk chair. "I think she may have done something really, really bad."

"Who?" Stephanie asked between crunches. "This new client?"

"Yes."

"And what is it you think she did?"

"There is a possibility she may have killed someone," Emma murmured.

"Ha ha! Very funny."

She dropped her head into her hands. "I'm not kidding, Stephanie."

"Okay, sure. And who, pray tell, do you think she may have killed?"

"Her husband. Or, rather, her ex-husband."

Stephanie inhaled sharply. "You're really not kidding, are you?"

"I wish I was." Emma stopped. Tried to steady her words. "But Jack got a call from the station while we were talking—about a body. A strangled body."

"Okay . . ."

"As he was getting off the phone with me a few minutes later, he mentioned the victim's name. And it's my new client's husband or ex-husband or whatever he is at the moment!"

"Oooh, do tell . . ."

Emma rocketed up and off her chair, her thoughts too scrambled to remain in any one place for long. "He dumped her for his younger secretary. She hated him."

"Rightfully so. But that doesn't necessarily mean she killed him, Emma."

"True. But what about if she *said* she wanted to?" Emma argued. "And had a veritable laundry list of ways in which she wanted to do it?"

The sudden cessation of all sounds on the other end of the phone only served to heighten her restlessness and the growing ache behind her temples. The eventual and partially hushed "Wow" Stephanie finally uttered propelled her down the hallway and into the kitchen.

"Maybe they were just figures of speech," Stephanie offered as Emma reached into the cabinet above the sink for the bottle of over-the-counter pain relievers. "Like what I just said when I thought you were upset over something the deputy did. I mean, I wouldn't really kill him. Maim him, sure, but *death*? No."

Emma popped off the bottle's lid, tapped two capsules into her palm, and tossed them down her throat. "Trust me, Steph, I want to believe that's the case with Kim, too, I really do. But what happens if it's not?"

"Then she goes to jail, and you're out a client. End of story."

"But I liked her. A lot." Emma closed and stowed the bottle, filled a glass with water, and drained it all with six big gulps. "I wanted to help her. Still do."

"There'll be no helping her if she did this. And if she did, it's her problem, not yours."

"I know that. I really do. It's just—"

"Let it go, Emma." Stephanie took another bite, another gulp. "Are you going to reach out to her? You know, as a concerned employee?"

"You mean Kim?"

"Uh-huh."

"You just told me to let it go!"

"If she did it, sure. But until that's determined one way or the other, it seems only natural you'd check in on her once you heard the news . . ."

Emma's answering laugh was met with a hard thumping against her leg. "Ahhh. I see where this is going. You want me to check in on her so I can pass on all the sordid details to you, right?"

"But of course. A gem like that would be a surefire way to get my mother on a topic other than me and the fact that I've yet to give her grandchildren." Noise in the background of the call was followed by a momentary muffling of Stephanie's voice, and then an exasperated sigh. "Please, Emma.

For the love of God, call this Kim woman and offer your condolences or celebratory words or whatever is proper when an ex dies. Then pump her for any and all details—the juicier the better—and then call or text or email me with everything you learn. If it does what I need it to do on my end, I'll write that testimonial for your website you've been wanting me to write."

Emma led Scout over to his food cabinet, liberated a treat from the bag on the top shelf, and watched him practically inhale it out of her palm. "Actually, there's something I'd like even more than that if we're going to resort to bribery and all."

"You want me to Scout-sit when you and the deputy go on your date?"

"Nope."

"You want to post *a picture* of me along with the testimonial?"

"Nope."

"Good thing. Because I'd have had to draw the line on that one. Out of respect for you as my friend, and for the long-term success of your business."

Rolling her eyes, Emma lowered herself to the floor next to Scout and draped her non-phone-holding hand across his neck. "I hate it when you do that."

"Do what?"

"Put yourself down like that."

"Why? Honesty is a good thing, isn't it?"

"If it was honesty, sure. But it's not."

"Says you."

"*And* a mirror if you'd actually look in one every once in a while."

"Nah . . . My mother is better than any mirror could ever be." Stephanie modulated her voice to sound older and like something out of a cheesy sitcom. "Do you know you have black circles under your eyes, Stephanie? You really should do something about those if you want to catch yourself a man. And maybe, while you're at it, you could try something other than a ponytail? Men like hair to flow around a woman's shoulders, dear. Flow, *like a riv-er*."

Emma's laugh echoed around the kitchen. "Like a river? Oh c'mon, Stephanie. Your mom doesn't really say stuff like that, does she?"

"Wanna come over sometime?"

She shook her head, sent up a silent prayer of thanks for parents who only meddled in her life on occasion and from a distance, and then rested her head against Scout while Stephanie returned to crunching. "Actually, how about you just agree to go with me on Sunday?"

"Go with you where?" Stephanie asked.

"I want to stop out and see my friend John."

"The old guy you looked in on last month while his son was traveling for business?" Stephanie asked.

"That's right."

"Why?"

Emma winked at Scout. "Why am I going, or why do I want you to go with me?"

"Both."

"I'm going because he asked me to. And I want you to go with me because he's a neat man."

"And . . ."

"There's no 'and.'"

"Emma, I *hear* the and."

She rested her head against the chair at her back. "Fine. You win. There's an and."

"Go on . . ."

"I think I told you his son, Andy, is an architect, yes? And a really, really creative one at that?"

"Maybe."

"Well, I thought you could maybe, um, talk to him and . . ." She cast about until she seized on something that would sound believable to a tried-and-true skeptic like Stephanie.

"And pick his brain for ideas on that house you keep saying you want to build!"

"And leave the fun I have here? Are you crazy?"

"No. I thought you said you *wanted* out. That it was time to find your own place and—"

"But who would point out my raccoon eyes every morning if I did that? Who would nag me about my lack of a life? My ticking biological clock? My messy room? How I parked my car too close to the sidewalk? How even so-and-so's fifth cousin once removed has a man in her life? How I'm never going to find anyone if I don't get myself out there?" Stephanie stopped, sucked in a deep breath, and then released it with a groan. "Okay, you're right. I need to do this. For me."

Emma smiled. "Now you're talking."

"But you know my workload at the VA. The patient charts, the crazy hours, and my not-so-charming boss who doesn't believe in work-life balance for anyone but himself. When on earth am I going to find time to track down house plans, settle on a lot, micromanage whoever builds it, et cetera, et cetera? Unless . . ." Stephanie's voice drifted in thought for a moment, only to return with a burst of determination. "Hey! I could hire you to do all that stuff for me!"

"I can't design your house for you," Emma protested.

"Of course you could. I hired you to go to the gym with me and you do that!"

"When you show up," Emma countered.

"Exactly! That's why you're the missing ingredient in me finally being able to live like a forty-year-old should. And your place is so cute . . . although, maybe I don't need so many flowers in mine."

"Your house should be a reflection of you, not me."

Another deep breath. Another groan. "And therein lies the problem. There's nothing to reflect."

"Just go with me out to Andy and John's place on Sunday," Emma said, returning her fingers to Scout's fur. "If worse comes to worse, it gets you out of the house and doing something for a few hours, right?"

Stephanie chewed, stopped, and chewed some more. "Fine. I'll go. But you need to hold up your end of the bargain and get me something I can distract my mother with for the next few days."

And just like that, her reason for calling Stephanie in the first place took center stage in her thoughts once again. "I'll see what I can find out. *Tomorrow.*"

Chapter Five

It was 3:15 in the morning when, at the urging of Scout's wet nose, Emma rose up on her elbow, felt around on the nightstand for her phone, and fumbled it into position against her drool-soaked cheek. "Hello?"

She waited a beat, maybe two, the only audible sound that of her own yawn. "Hello?" she repeated, her voice groggy. "Is anyone there?"

Again there was nothing. Just the sound of her own breathing in an otherwise silent and blessedly dark room. Lowering herself back down to her pillow, she—

"He—he's . . . *dead*, Emma!"

Rocketing upright, Emma reached for her bedside lamp and turned it on. "Kim? Is that you?"

The answering "Yes" in her ear was accompanied by a sniffle. "I know I shouldn't be calling you so late, but I have no one else to call. The—the kids are devastated. I-I'm numb. And—and so very, very angry."

Angry . . .

"I wanted him to suffer for a while! The way I did! I

wanted to make him pay for walking out on me after thirty years and two children together!"

She didn't need to be in the same room as Kim to know the tears that had started the call had morphed into gritted teeth and, likely, fisted hands. It was as plain as day. Or, more accurately, *night*, as was the case at the moment.

"But nooo . . ." Kim continued, almost hissing. "Just like everything else of late, I had no say. No control. No—"

Anger dissipated to sniffles and, finally, sobs so loud and so gut-wrenching, Scout's sleepy eyes shone with the kind of concern usually reserved for Emma. "Shhh . . . Shhh . . . I'm here, Kim. I'm here. It's going to be okay."

Seconds turned to minutes as the sobbing slowly subsided until the woman could speak again, her voice little more than a broken whisper. "Some . . . someone strangled . . . him, Emma. Someone . . . *killed* . . . Roger."

Someone . . .

As in not Kim . . .

Emma didn't mean for her sigh of relief to be quite so loud, but neither could she really help it. Client or not, she didn't want the person she'd met in the park roughly twelve hours earlier to be capable of something so awful.

"I fantasized about it. Many times," Kim said, clearly fighting back an encore of her earlier sobs. "There was something about the planning . . . and the plotting . . . and the imagining . . . and—and the thinking . . . and the writing it down in the same journal he'd always found so—so silly . . . and even occasionally sketching it out on old receipts and scraps of paper that made it so I could eventually fall asleep in this bed we were supposed to be in together. Forever. And now? I'm still alone, and there's nothing to plan, or plot, or imagine, or write as a way to get past the pain of what he did to me—to us—because he's . . . gone. Really, truly *gone*."

"I don't know what to say other than I'm so sorry, Kim." Emma switched the phone to her opposite ear and leaned back against the headboard. "Is there anything I can do for you?"

"You can tell me I'm not awful for not knowing what to feel. One minute I'm so sad I'm not sure how to breathe anymore, and then the next I'm almost relieved that I won't have to figure it all out. And then I realize how selfish that is and I get angry at myself. And then I get angry at him for making me feel angry. And then I want to rip his eyes out of their sockets. And then, the next thing I know, I'm back to sobbing all over again."

Emma closed her eyes and willed herself to breathe, to find the right words. "I would imagine what you're feeling is normal. Considering the circumstances."

"I feel really alone."

"Well, you're not. I'm here. Anytime. And I mean that."

"My kids? They have their whole lives in front of them—careers, relationships, babies, romantic getaways, family vacations, all of it. And me? I'm just here, taking up space, more or less. I have no career to fill my days . . . No friends to go here, there, and everywhere with . . . The love of my life walked out on me and now"—Kim's voice faltered—"there's no chance we'll make it out the other side . . . And if my kids see fit to include me in trips they take with their own families one day, I'll be there more as an observer and to take keepsake photos rather than as a necessary part the way I once was for them . . ."

Emma pulled the covers up around her neck and stared up at the ceiling. "You're only fifty-three, Kim. Your life isn't over."

"It feels like it."

"At this moment, maybe it does. But give me a chance—give *yourself* a chance—to see that it's most definitely not."

Another sniffle.

Another hitched breath.

"Your bucket list thing?" Kim finally asked.

"It'll be *your* list, actually. But yes."

Yet another round of sniffles gave way to a deep inhale and a slow, steadying exhale. "That's what I was thinking about when I got the call from my son about Roger. I'd even jotted a few things down while I was picking at my dinner."

Smiling, Emma patted the top of the covers to draw Scout closer. "Tell me."

For a moment, she didn't think Kim was going to answer, but after another few breaths and what sounded like movement, no further prodding was necessary. "I started dating Roger halfway through my junior year of college. And once I did, I lost myself in everything about him—his friends, his classes, his goals, and our dream to get married and have children. But before him? When it was all about me? I wanted to be a writer."

"What kind of a writer?" Emma asked, intrigued.

"All I knew was that I wanted to write fiction—maybe children's, maybe romance, maybe mysteries. Books had been such a huge part of my childhood, and I dreamed of having my name on a book jacket one day." The pain, the anguish of earlier, was gone. In its place was something that sounded like . . . *hope*? "I never did anything with it, but it was a dream at one time."

"So write now. It would be a wonderful distraction!"

"I think that ship has sailed. But revisiting that time in my mind led me to other things I liked back then."

"We're going to revisit this writing thing at some point, but for now, keep going."

She heard a quiet thump and then the distinct sound of pages turning. "Here it is . . . It's just a small list with a few things that maybe we could do together. If you're up for it."

"I'm listening."

"I thought maybe we could start a book club. I know it wouldn't be much with just the two of us, but maybe it could still be fun? That is, if you like reading?"

"It's funny you should say that, as I've just recently started reading again thanks to an elderly friend of mine who devours whole books on a daily basis. She turned me onto something called 'cozy mysteries' and now I'm working my way through her favorite series."

"So we can do that?" Kim asked.

"Start a book club? Of course. It's a great idea And who knows, maybe—depending on the genre we choose—we might be able to expand it beyond just the two of us." She made a mental note to add it to the list they'd started at the park and then hurried to stifle a building yawn. "What's next?"

"Next . . . next . . ." A strangled sob was followed, seconds later, by another round of sniffling.

"Kim? Talk to me. What's going on? Are you still there?"

"Yes. I-I'm still here. It's just . . . the next thing I wrote . . . was"—Kim blew out a shaky breath—"s-strangle Roger."

Emma squeezed her eyes closed.

"When he first left, all I could do was cry. Morning, noon, and night. What was wrong with me? What could I have done differently to hold his interest? That sort of stuff. And then, one day, the sadness shifted into anger—anger at Roger for throwing our life away, for ruining what was supposed to always be our children's home base, all of it. As a way to release some of that, I started concocting ways to exact revenge on him. At first, my ideas were what I would imagine is standard stuff when you've been dumped— slashing his tires, leaving him cookies that would make him sick to his stomach, and even sending out emails to all of his clients letting them know what a creep he was. And then one night, while I was waiting to fall asleep, I imagined messing with his car brakes instead of the tire thing. And how, if I did, he and his car would just disappear around a bend, never to be seen again.

"Next thing I knew, my thoughts moved from messing with his brakes to the piñata idea I told you about at the park. Soon, more ideas came, one after the other. Some of them made me laugh because they were so ludicrous, but at least I was laughing, you know? Others made it so I could put the hurt and the anger somewhere other than on me. And writing them down, on occasion, was freeing. For a little while, anyway.

"But, Emma? I didn't actually want anything to happen to him. I-I just wanted him to hurt the way he hurt me. And I wanted him to know—*and remember*—that walking out on me was the biggest mistake of his life."

She let Kim cry, scream, and cry some more, the hurt and pain over her husband's loss every bit as real as the hurt and pain from his betrayal. It was hard to listen to, from a distance, but it was what Kim needed in that moment—to feel her feels and to do so without being shushed or mollified.

Eventually, though, the tears subsided into a few hitched breaths and a hiccup or two. "Thank you, Emma. I-I guess I needed that cry more than I realized."

"Of course. What you're feeling makes perfect sense, Kim. You loved him once."

"Correction. I loved him *still*. He was everything I . . ." Kim's words trailed off, only to return a moment later etched with surprise. "Emma? Two police cars just pulled into my driveway."

Emma sat up, pulling the phone tighter against her cheek. "Police cars?"

"Maybe they're coming to tell me about Roger in case I haven't heard yet?"

"I guess that makes sense."

"They're coming up the walkway now. Four of them." Kim's ensuing silence didn't last long. "They're knocking now."

Emma ran a restless hand across Scout's exposed side. "Do you want me to stay on the line while you speak to them?"

"No. I've kept you on long enough, especially considering the time. I think I can deal with this on my own now, thanks to you."

"Are you sure? Because I don't mind waiting."

"I'll be okay. But thank you, anyway. I'm glad I saw your ad in the paper, and I'm glad I listened to my gut and wrote you that email."

"I am, too." Emma dropped back against her pillow. "Now go answer the door and then get some sleep. Tomorrow or whenever you're up to it, give me a call. You can tell me about the other things you came up with for our list and we can start strategizing what we're going to do and when."

"Sounds good. Good night, Emma."

"Good night, Kim."

Chapter Six

⊷⊶

She and Scout were waiting outside the senior center, facing east, when the sudden slowing of cars and pointing of cameras out passenger-side windows told her Maxwell Grayben, aka Big Max, was approaching from the west. What she could only guess at, though, was what she'd find when she turned around to greet the seventy-eight-year-old man who wore eccentricity like a badge of honor.

If he noticed the stares he so often drew or heard the callous comments of those who lived their lives making knee-jerk judgments, he never let on. Instead, her beloved client's joy for life was ever present, and his ability to live in the moment both admirable and enviable.

"Hey, old man! Where ya going? Halloween is four months away, dude!"

Jerking her head toward the opposite side of the street, Emma glared at the pair of teenagers pointing and laughing as if they were at a circus. More than anything, she wanted to yell back, to tell them to go home and have their parents teach them some manners, but it wasn't worth it. *They* weren't worth it. You either felt the pure joy radiating from Big Max, or you didn't. Plain and simple.

She closed her eyes for a moment, breathed away the rest of her anger, and then let the smile Big Max deserved power her turn to the west. And, just like that, the sleepiness that had been her constant companion all morning disappeared in favor of the gentle giant making on-again, off-again haste in her direction. Dressed in an ill-fitting plaid trench coat with a not-quite-matching hat, Big Max held a pipe in his right hand and a magnifying glass with his left. Twice, he stopped, bent at the waist, and took a closer look at something on the sidewalk before closing the remaining gap between them.

"Don't you look spiffy today, Big Max," she said, rising up on tiptoes to plant a kiss on the man's weathered cheek. "Very Sherlock Holmes–y."

Big Max nodded, then bent down, held his magnifying glass toward Scout, smiled still wider, and reached into the pocket of his trench coat for a Cheerio. "Here you go, big fella. I saved one from my breakfast this morning just for you."

Scout wagged his tail, looked up at Emma, and at her nod retrieved the tiniest of treats from Big Max's finger with a grateful tongue and a quick bark of thanks.

"So how are you, Big Max?" She patted the top of Scout's head. "Been keeping yourself busy?"

He nodded but didn't elaborate.

"Still working on fixing that ukulele you found?"

"It's all done," he said, proudly.

"That's great, Big Max! I can't wait for you to play me a song on it!"

Taking a few steps to her left, he held the magnifying glass to his eye and leaned over a balled-up napkin lying just outside a nearby garbage can. He made a few noises of curiosity, flipped it over with the toe of his worn black combat-style boots, and then returned to his full standing height with a shake of his head.

"Did you lose something?" she asked as he pulled a bundle of rubber-banded index cards and a stubby pencil from the front pocket of his coat.

"No."

"Did one of your friends"—she swept her hand toward the senior center's front door—"lose something?"

"No." He pulled off the rubber band, moved the top index card to the bottom of the misshapen pile, and drew what looked to be a circle and an arrow on the exposed card. When he was done, he secured the pile with the same rubber band and returned it to his pocket. "I'm investigating."

Scout cocked his head to the right, studied Big Max, and then looked up at Emma, waiting.

Winking down at him, she asked the question that was clearly on the tip of both of their tongues. "What are you investigating, Big Max?"

"Where my friend, the cookie lady, went."

Again, she swept her hand toward the brick building tasked with hosting bingo games, holiday gatherings, and quarterly dances for Sweet Falls' senior citizens. "We could go inside and ask about her. Or, rather, Scout and I could wait outside the door while *you* go inside and ask . . ."

"I don't know her name."

"Is she someone the senior center hires to bring in treats for events? Or is she one of the seniors, herself?" Emma asked.

Big Max looked beyond Scout's tail to a piece of gum stuck to the concrete. Stepping carefully around the dog, he again bent down, held his magnifying glass over the pink blob, examined it for what seemed like an eternity, and then repeated his earlier index card routine. Another circle and another arrow later, he shook his head. "She's not from the senior center. She's from my Wednesday morning walks."

"You take Wednesday morning walks, too?"

"I walk every day. On Saturdays and Mondays, I walk

down to the town square and wave to the little ones on the swing set. On Tuesdays, I walk by all those pretty apple trees."

"You mean Davis Farm and Greenhouse?" Emma asked.

"Sure do. They don't have apples on them trees just yet. But they will."

"That's a long way to walk, Big Max."

"Not for me," he said, as he replaced the rubber band around his stack of cards and shoved them back inside his pocket. "On Wednesdays, I walk around the lake with the flowers. On Thursdays I walk here, with you and Scout. And on Fridays and Sundays, I just walk until it's time to turn around."

"And you see this missing friend when you're walking around the lake in Camden Park?" she asked.

"I see her on the street, *before* I go into the park."

"And she gives you cookies while she's walking?"

"*One* cookie," he corrected her, as he locked onto another object he deemed worthy of his magnifying glass. When his inspection yielded nothing worth recording, he lowered the glass. "She doesn't walk; she drives. She always stops and gives me one cookie from her basket."

Emma studied her friend. "She sounds like a kind person."

"She smiles when she stops. But when I see her later, when she's getting out of her car to go inside her house, she doesn't have a smile. I always hope she will look up so I can try to make her smile again, but she just goes inside the door and doesn't see me."

"What door?"

"The door in the yellow house. On McGurdy Street."

Something about the name tickled at her subconscious, but when she tried to remember why, she came up empty. "I take it you didn't see her yesterday?"

"I saw her."

"Did she give you a cookie?"

Big Max nodded. "A butterscotch one. And then she asked me what my favorite cookie is and I told her."

"That's nice."

"But then she went away."

"Doesn't she always leave after you get your cookie?"

"Yes."

She gently squeezed his pipe-holding hand. "Then nothing is different, Big Max. Wednesday will come around again before you know it."

He crossed to a plant in front of the senior center and inspected a bug crawling on one of the leaves. When the bug failed to produce whatever Big Max was searching for, he returned to Emma and Scout. "I thought maybe I'd see the pretty blue lights flash and turn when she went by last night, but there was just white from the man in the moon."

"Pretty blue lights?" she echoed. "Man in the moon?"

"I always take walks when the man in the moon comes for a visit." Before she could formulate a response, Big Max adjusted his hat and moved on. "We were just one house away from the cookie lady's when she drove away in the back of that car."

"Big Max, please tell me you're not walking around at night by yourself. I mean, Sweet Falls is safe enough, but still . . . You could fall or get hurt."

He shrugged. "Even without the pretty blue lights, it wasn't dark. The man in the moon made sure of that."

"I don't know what blue lights you're talking about."

"The ones on the roof that are s'posed to go round and round. But they didn't last night."

She replayed Big Max's words in her head until she hit on something that fit. "These flashing blue lights you mentioned wanting to see . . . Do you mean the ones on top of a police car?"

"That's right."

"And the cookie lady was in the police car?"

"She was in the first one."

She drew back. "How many police cars were there?"

"Two."

"How many policemen?"

"Four." Big Max puffed out his chest beneath his trench coat. "I counted."

A shiver that had no place on a warm, sunny June day started at the base of her neck, traveled down her spine, and had her reaching into her back pocket for her phone. A few quick taps of her screen later, she stared down at the billing information associated with her newest client.

KIM FELDER
25 MCGURDY STREET
SWEET FALLS, TN

Swallowing hard, Emma looked up at Big Max. "Does your cookie lady have honey-brown hair like mine, but with streaks of gray?"

Big Max smiled his assent.

"And glasses?"

"I like her blue glasses best. But she had her black ones on when she went by in the car."

Emma closed her eyes. Steadied her breath. And then parted her lashes again to find Big Max making his way from one sidewalk seam to the next with his magnifying glass aimed at the ground. "Big Max?" she called, tugging Scout to follow. "You said there were no flashing lights, right?"

Big Max stopped, took a closer look at one seam in particular, and then abandoned it in favor of the next one. "Just the light from the man in the moon."

Relief flooded her body. "And the cookie lady? She walked *next* to the policemen when they came out of the house, right?"

"No, she led the way."

The fingers of dread spread out to her limbs. "Do you remember anything else?"

"She didn't smile when I waved." Big Max took another step forward and then turned back to Emma, his own smile dimming. "And she didn't have her cookie basket."

It had taken every ounce of restraint she'd had not to rush her walk with Big Max. But the moment they were done and she and Scout were back in the car, she was on her phone, calling the one person she knew could either confirm or deny her sinking suspicion.

"Hey, Emma, you must be psychic. I was just about to call you. How's your day—"

"Please tell me you didn't make an arrest in the murder of Roger Felder," Emma said, glancing between Jack's name on her dashboard screen and the active roadway she'd yet to pull onto. "Please, please tell me that."

"No, there's been no official arrest yet, but it's only a matter of time."

"Why?"

"Why no arrest?" Jack asked.

"No. Why the only-a-matter-of-time part?"

"Because I'm pretty confident we've got our person." The sound of papers being shuffled and stacked against a desk was followed, soon after, by the slow, steady creak of a chair. "Why? Did you know the victim?"

Lifting her gaze to the rearview mirror, she followed Big Max and his magnifying glass down the sidewalk for a few seconds and then blew out a breath as both disappeared around a corner. "Not the victim, no. Just the person I'm pretty sure you're looking at for his murder."

A quicker, louder creak let her know her words had caught his attention. "You know the ex-wife?"

"I don't *know her*, know her in terms of some great length of time. But I know enough—or, rather, my *gut* knows enough to say it had to have been someone else. *Anyone* else, quite frankly."

"I'm listening."

"I mean, this woman makes cookies and gives one to Big Max every Wednesday morning," Emma argued. "Has for quite some time from what I was able to gather just now."

A heavy silence gave way to a cough and an audible change in tone. "And making cookies is paramount to innocence?"

"No. Of course not. But it's part of it. I mean, I *met* her, Jack. And she was the quintessential mom—still is. Even with her kids being grown."

"Okay . . ."

"She wanted to find a way to move on, to reclaim her life in the wake of her husband leaving her for his secretary."

"Wait. This is the one you were telling me about on the phone yesterday? The one you were making the bucket list thing with?"

Emma nodded. "Yes!"

"I didn't realize."

"Kim called me in the middle of the night last night. After she found out about Roger's death. And, Jack, she was *devastated*."

"Showing emotion and making cookies doesn't mean she didn't do it, Emma."

She pulled her hands off the steering wheel and wiped them down the sides of her flowered pant legs. "You're not hearing what I'm saying."

"Then help me hear it correctly."

"It's not the making-cookies part. It's the ongoing gesture toward a man that other people are always so quick to . . ." She rested her head against the seat rest and stared up at the cloth ceiling of her car. "Look, we all say stuff we shouldn't sometimes. It's normal when you're hurt or angry."

A sound she took to mean his agreement had her rushing to get to her point. "But it's all just words . . . a figure of speech . . . a way to let off steam during a really, really difficult time. I mean, we've all done it at some point or another, right?"

"It?" he asked.

"You know, said we could kill someone who cut us off on the road, or did something awful to us, or just made us mad for one reason or another . . . But just because we *said* it didn't mean we were actually going to *do* it for real, right? And she always wanted to be a writer. So taking to pen and paper for some of that venting makes perfect sense, you know?"

She waited through a solid minute of silence and then looked back at the deputy's name on the screen. "Jack?"

"You do realize we have an actual dead body here, right, Emma? Because that makes all the difference in the world."

"It's a coincidence, Jack! That's all."

His answering laugh held no sign of humor. "A coincidence? Seriously? We've got a dead body, Emma! And a person of interest who had plans to kill our victim."

"Not *plans*," she argued. "Just . . . *thoughts*."

"That she wrote down."

"Some people work through things by saying stuff out loud. Others do it by writing. Case closed. Move on."

"Did you just say *move on*?"

"In terms of Kim, yes." She squeezed her eyes closed, only to open them as Scout's nose—and then his tongue—found her exposed ear. "So were your guys right? Was Roger Felder strangled?"

"He was . . ."

"Okay, but that's probably pretty standard for killing someone, right? I mean, besides using a gun or a knife?" She took the grunt he emitted to be a yes and kept going. "And it's not like that's the *only* way she said she'd do it, right? Kim had lots of ways she wanted to exact revenge on him—some crazy and a little far-fetched, sure, but there were other doable ways besides just strangulation."

Another creak. Another grunt. More shuffling. "Emma, I've gotta go."

"I understand. I know you're busy. I just hope what I said will keep you from having to waste a bunch of time looking in the wrong place."

"Oh, it will. Trust me."

Chapter Seven

———•———

She was two blocks away from McGurdy Street when the song she wasn't paying attention to anyway faded in favor of an incoming call. Glancing from the road to the dashboard screen and back again, she hit the green button.

"Hey, Dottie, would you mind if I called you back in about an hour or so? I'm in the car and I'm almost at my—"

"Did you hear the news?" Dottie asked, her voice breathless. "Sweet Falls is becoming the next Sweet Briar!"

Letting up on the gas, Emma took in the next street sign and turned left. A glance at the first two mailboxes let her know she was close. Dottie's repeated use of her name in conjunction with a growing agitation let her know she was being remiss in responding. "Sweet Falls is becoming the next Sweet Briar . . . Okay, I'll bite. Why?"

"There's been another murder!"

She pulled alongside the curb just shy of her final destination and slid the car into park. "You heard?"

"Of course I heard, dear! Do you think I live under a rock? It's been the top news story all day!"

"I-I didn't know. I slept a little later than normal this morning and then I spent some time with Big Max."

"The early bird gets the worm, dear. Remember that."

She resisted the urge to sigh and went for the less audible eye roll instead. "I'm aware, Dottie, thanks. But I was woken by a phone call in the wee hours of the morning and—"

"I didn't call to discuss your friends' lack of manners, Emma. That's for you to handle or not handle as you see fit. I'm simply calling to talk strategy."

"Strategy?"

"For getting this worm. With or without Stephanie."

"Worm?" she echoed, drawing back.

Dottie's exhalation was laced with a hefty dose of impatience. "If there's only one worm, Emma, the bird who gets there first gets it. It's an expression, dear. A very apropos one, in fact."

"I'm well aware of the expression, Dottie. What you lost me on is how my sleeping in has anything to do with Stephanie."

"Must you be so dense sometimes, dear?" Dottie hissed. "It's most unbecoming."

She tightened her grip on the gearshift. "I'm not being dense. I just don't have the time to try to decipher what you're saying and—"

Dottie's second, louder sigh drew her attention toward the rearview mirror and the answering lift of Scout's ears. "Another murder in Sweet Falls means another case for us to solve, Emma. With or without Stephanie."

"Whoa!" Emma held up her hand. "Stop right there. I'm a small business owner. Stephanie is an overworked nurse practitioner. You're . . ." She stopped, thought better of bringing age into the conversation, and after a deep breath picked up the ball farther down the field. "Anyway, this doesn't concern us."

"Margaret Louise Davis is a mee-maw of eight! Tori

Sinclair is a librarian! That didn't stop *them* from solving murders!"

It was on the tip of her tongue to remind the woman there was a difference between cozy mysteries and the real world, but good sense—and a desire to remain employed—won out in favor of tact. "Did you even *know* Roger Felder?" Emma demanded.

"Who?"

She lifted her eyes to the rearview mirror and rolled them at Scout. "The victim."

"No."

"Then let it go. This has nothing to do with you, or me, or Stephanie."

"But we have to *do* something, dear."

"Not with this we don't." Emma wandered her gaze down the sidewalk to Kim's mailbox and then up the accompanying driveway to the woman's front door. "But if you really want something to do, consider starting a book club with me and Kim. We could meet once a month and make some treats themed to whatever book we've read. In fact, if you want, you could pick a Southern Sewing Circle Mystery as our first selection. It'll be good for all of us."

"Who's Kim?"

"The victim's wife. Or, rather, his . . ." She let the rest of her sentence fade away as—with the help of Dottie's gasp—she realized her mistake.

"You know Roger Felder's wife?" Dottie echoed.

Emma buried her head in her hands and silently chastised herself for stepping into a trap of her own making. "Can we pretend I didn't say that?" she murmured, only to drop her hands to her lap with a sigh of frustration. "Don't bother answering that."

"I'm listening, dear."

"I met Kim Felder yesterday. In the park. She's hired me to help her find herself again."

A beat of silence was followed by another quiet gasp. "Is

that the one who wrote you the email you read during our tea on Tuesday? The one who was dumped by her husband of thirty years?"

"Yes."

"And now he's dead?"

Looking again at Kim's front door, Emma nodded. "Yes."

"That means it's only a matter of time, dear."

"Until . . ."

"She becomes a person of interest in the department's investigation." The excitement evident in Dottie's voice at the onset of the call was back. "Which means we *do* have a reason to work on this case! To keep our friend out of jail!"

Her gaze flew back to the dashboard screen. "Whoa. Whoa. Whoa. *Our* friend?"

"Of course. We're in a book club together, aren't we?"

Scout's tail wagged along with Emma's laugh. "A book club I merely suggested two seconds ago!"

"And to which I'm agreeing. So now I'm connected to"—a snapping sound filled the car's cabin—"what is her name again, dear?"

"Kim."

"Right. So now, because of our book club—"

"Which hasn't met," Emma tossed out, grinning.

"Because of our book club, Kim is now *my* friend, as well. And I will go to the ends of the earth to help a friend in need."

"Good to know." Emma reached out, stroked the top of Scout's head, and then shut off the engine. "That said, I talked to Jack about Kim. About the whole figure-of-speech thing and why she makes no sense as a suspect."

"So they're already looking at her?"

She waved aside the question and then plucked the key from the ignition. "For the first couple of hours, maybe. But that's just because they were at her house last night and saw her notebook. But now that I've explained the why behind it all, they'll be turning their attention toward finding the real killer."

"Notebook?"

Readying her hand on the door handle, Emma shrugged. "She wrote stuff in it. Stuff to help her blow off steam about her husband leaving her. That's all. It meant nothing."

"I see." Dottie paused. "Is she upset that he's gone?"

"She was last night when she called. But I think that's understandable, even with him dumping her for his secretary. They were married for thirty years, you know? And they had two children—"

"Perhaps it was the secretary, then."

She considered the possibility and felt the smile it birthed on her lips. "Can you imagine?"

"Of course, *our friend Kim* will want to see justice served for her children, if nothing else, yes?"

"I'm sure."

"And *as* her friends, we should do whatever we can to help her in that endeavor, yes?"

Emma's smile froze in place. "Oh no . . . I know where this is going, and I'm not interested."

"In what part are you not interested, dear?" Dottie countered. "Seeking justice for two heartbroken children or helping a dear friend during a trial?"

She didn't need to look in the mirror to know her cheeks were turning red. She could feel it just as surely as she could the sudden dampening in her hands. "They're not children, Dottie. They're completely grown and out of the house."

"He was still their father, wasn't he?"

"Ugh, Dottie, enough, okay? I don't have time for this conversation. I really have to go now."

"Fine. Go do whatever it is you have to do that is so much more important than helping a friend in her time of need. But know this, Emma Marie Westlake; I'm so very disappointed in you and your—"

With a quick pull on the door handle, Dottie's name disappeared from the screen. "C'mon, Scout, let's go see Kim."

S he paused her fist just shy of the door and looked over at Scout. "Lots of wagging, lots of licks, okay, boy?"

Scout cocked his head ever so slightly to the left and wagged.

"I knew I could count on you." Turning her attention back to the door with its cute, summery wreath, Emma started to knock but stopped at the last second. "I'm a good friend, right, boy?"

He tilted his head to the right and wagged again.

"That's what I thought. Dottie was just trying to guilt me into doing something we have no business doing, wasn't she?"

Shaking off the last of the funk brought on by the octogenarian's call, Emma rapped her fist against the wooden door and then stepped back, alongside Scout, waiting.

Seconds turned to minutes with not a sound nor any sign of life from inside the two-story home, despite the parked car in the driveway. She considered knocking again in the event her first attempt hadn't been heard, but abandoned the idea as her thoughts took her back to the reason behind her own yawn.

"After the night she had, I'm guessing she's sleeping," Emma said, glancing back down at Scout. "Which means we should come back later. Sound good?"

Scout's tail stopped, mid-wag, then sped up, his wide eyes leading her own back to the door in time to see the knob turn.

Slowly, hesitantly, the door cracked open to reveal a single amber-flecked brown eye as it narrowed and then widened on first Emma and then Scout.

"Hi, Kim!" Emma hooked her thumb down and to her right. "Scout and I wanted to check in and see how you're doing today. We heard your night went longer than we originally knew."

Kim pulled open the door the rest of the way and stepped back. "Emma! Come in! Please! Both of you!"

"Are you sure?" she asked, nudging her chin toward Scout. "We could just sit out here on your front porch if you'd rather."

"I'm sure. Come in." Kim waited for them to pass and then closed the door behind them, her whole body sagging in relief against the wall. "I'm so glad it's you and not the cops again. I-I just don't know that I can handle any more questions right now."

"I don't think they'll be back."

"I don't know, Emma. I didn't get that sense last night."

"Well, I'm hoping a little much-needed dose of clarity took care of that."

Pushing off the wall, Kim took in a deep breath and then motioned for them to follow. At the end of the hall they turned left into a large, airy kitchen with pale yellow walls and blue cabinets. On the countertop next to the six-burner stove was a series of baking canisters all boasting a duck wearing a chef's hat and holding a rolling pin in his webbed hands. The same duck made an appearance on a refrigerator magnet, the lower cabinet knobs, the valance on the window above the sink, and the octagonal placemats arranged atop the round farmhouse-style table.

"I know, I know. Ducks . . ." Kim gestured toward the table and made haste toward the center island and the glass-topped cake case sitting in its center. "I went with them because Natalie loved them when she was little. And now I just don't have the heart to get rid of them."

"You shouldn't. They're adorable."

Kim pulled two plates from a cabinet beneath the island, set them beside the case, and eyed Emma with a hint of wariness. "You don't have to say that."

"I know. But I like them."

"Roger used to say I was unable to grasp the notion of less is more." Kim shook off the visibly deflating memory and, instead, busied herself with cutting and plating two slices of cake. "How about a glass of milk? Or maybe some coffee?"

"Milk works great, thank you. And as for the rest, he should've seen *my* kitchen—or, I should say, my whole house."

Kim carried the plates to the table and then returned, seconds later, with two glasses of milk and a pair of forks. Reaching into a holder, she plucked out two duck-stamped napkins, her cheeks tinging red. "Don't tell me you have a thing for ducks, too?"

"Nope. Flowers. Daisies, in particular." She pointed at Kim's simple blue wall clock. "Even my kitchen clock is shaped like a daisy."

"Trust me. I found a clock, too, but Roger vetoed it the second he saw the box."

"I'm sorry."

Grinning, Kim stood, crossed to a door on the far side of the room, and pulled it open. "Don't be. I still bought it. See?"

Emma's gaze moved past the woman to the pantry wall on the other side of the open door. There, hanging dead center, was the chef-hat-wearing duck—his rolling pin serving as the clock's hour hand. "I love it!"

"It's great, isn't it?" Kim said, her smile fading. "I actually thought about putting it where everyone could see it when he first left me, but I just didn't."

Pressing her fingers to her lips, Kim stopped, shook her head, and then slowly closed the pantry door against her back, her very being seeming to deflate in front of Emma's eyes. Scout, who'd been nosing his way along the floor under the table, stopped and looked from Kim to Emma and back again, a quiet whimper lacing his every head turn.

"He thinks I'm a horrible host, doesn't he?" Kim asked.

"Not at all. He's just worried about you. We both are." She patted the spot opposite her at the table, waited for Kim to sit, and then pointed her own fork at the double-layer chocolate cake. "This looks incredible."

"It's my go-to recipe in times of stress. I made it last night. Or, rather, late this morning when I got back from the police station."

Emma stared at the cake and then Kim. "Have you slept at all?"

"Not really, no. After I baked and frosted this"—Kim swept her hand toward their respective cake slices—"I started cleaning. I mean, I know Natalie will likely choose a restaurant for Roger's repast, but just in case Roger's mother or stepfather wants to come here before or after the funeral service, I want things to be nice for them."

"Natalie is your daughter?"

"Yes. And Caleb is my son."

"I see." Emma forked off a piece of the cake she could no longer ignore and slid it into her mouth, the immediate explosion of decadence eliciting a moan she couldn't hold back if she'd tried. "Oh my word, this is absolutely *incredible*. You"—she took another bite—"actually *made* this?"

"I did."

"Wow. Wow. Wow." Emma took another bite and then pointed her empty fork at Scout. "Most of the time I think you've got it made, boy. But in this moment, knowing you can't eat this, I feel sorry for you."

Kim pushed back in her chair. "I'm sorry. I wasn't thinking. Can I get him a treat of his own?"

"No. Please. Sit. He's fine. See?" Emma pointed at Scout's tail. "He's happy to be here."

"It's not a problem. They're just inside the pantry."

"It's okay. He had a Cheerio before we got here, didn't you, Scout?"

Again, Scout wagged his tail.

"I have Cheerios if he'd like that better," Kim said, standing.

"Please. He's fine. In fact"—Emma looked through the

bay window to the backyard beyond. She searched the grass, the patio, the empty birdbath, and finally the tree before looking back at Scout. "Scout? Do you see him? He's climbing the tree—look!"

Scout merely tilted his head at Emma.

"Scout, look!" She pointed toward the window.

He looked at her finger and then back at her face, his tail picking up speed.

Shaking her head in mock disgust, she made direct eye contact with the dog. "Squirrel!"

Sure enough, Scout's attention and feet made a beeline for the bay window. Forking up another mouthful of cake, she grinned at Kim. "Now sit. He'll be happy watching that squirrel do whatever it's going to do for however long it's going to do it. Trust me."

Slowly, Kim lowered herself back onto her chair, her every movement a window into the exhaustion she clearly refused to acknowledge, even to herself. "I don't know how to navigate any of this—what's appropriate and what's not appropriate for me to do in regard to the service, the repast, the arrangements for his burial, any of it."

"Do you *want* to be involved?" Emma asked, pushing aside her now-empty plate.

Kim lifted her hands and then let them drop back down to the table with a sigh. "I don't know. I would've been. I should've been. But . . . I don't know. He walked out on me and our wedding vows."

"True."

"But my children are his children, too. And if nothing else, I want to do what needs to be done for them."

Emma took it all in, weighed everything, and then reached across the table to quiet Kim's restless hand. "Maybe the best thing to do is just be there for them. Which means you really need to get some sleep. Between getting and digesting the news, talking to me on the phone, going down to the police station, baking, cleaning, and now sitting here with me, I'm not sure how you're even still functioning at all."

"It's what I do." Kim blew out a breath and pulled a face. "Or it's what I used to do when I still had a life."

"You still have a life, Kim."

The woman pinned Emma with an unreadable expression for a moment, maybe two, and then gestured around the room. "I'm alone, Emma. The nest I spent thirty years fluffing for my family over the last thirty years is empty."

"No, it's not," she replied. "You're still in it, aren't you?"

Kim's laugh held such sadness Emma felt her own eyes mist.

"I get it," Emma said. "You think I'm crazy. But I'm going to prove you otherwise. But first, you need sleep. We can figure out the rest after that, okay?"

"I can't tell you how much it meant to me to be able to talk to you last night, and how much it means to me to have you here with me now." Kim stood up again, but this time she crossed to a desk tucked in a far corner of the kitchen and pulled a checkbook and pen from the top drawer. "What do I owe you for both last night and today?"

"Owe me?" Emma echoed, drawing back. "You don't owe me anything. I'm not here today because you hired me. I'm here because I want to make sure you're okay and so you know you're not alone."

Kim lowered the checkbook to her side. "We just met yesterday. After which I hired you to be my friend."

"And when it comes to doing the items on your list, you can pay me. But this is different."

Nibbling her lower lip inward, Kim shifted her weight from one leg to the other. "I-I don't know what to say. You're being so kind and—"

A loud knock startled Kim into silence and sent their collective gaze toward the hallway. Pressing her hand to the base of her neck, Kim worked to recover her breath. "That scared me."

"Me, too."

The knock was repeated, its volume louder, its tone more insistent.

Trading glances with Emma, Kim made haste in the direction of the front door. "Maybe it's Natalie or Caleb and they forgot their key in all the chaos."

Halfway down the hall, though, her pace slowed and then stopped. "Oh, this can't be good—not good at all."

"What's wrong?" Emma asked, only to find her answer looking back at them through one of the floor-to-ceiling sidelights flanking the front door.

Kim's hand flew to her neck, her chin, her cheeks, and back to her neck. "Wh-what do I do, Emma? Should I-I call an attorney?"

She took in the familiar face standing beside two of his peers on the front stoop and, after the briefest of hesitations, gathered her client's ice-cold hands inside her own. "Take a deep breath, Kim. It's fine. *You're* fine. I'm guessing that maybe they found the person who killed Roger and they want you to hear it from them instead of the local news."

Kim looked down, swallowed, and then lifted her eyes back up, first to Emma and then to the trio of deputies standing on the other side of her door. "Okay . . . You're right . . . I-I'm sorry. I-I guess I'm more tired and strung out than I realized."

"And that's completely understandable." Emma released her hold on Kim's hands and motioned toward Jack and the other deputies. "Do you want me to open the door?"

"No. No, I've got it."

Squaring her shoulders in time with a deep breath, Kim pulled open the door and mustered a smile. "Good afternoon, deputies. Do—do you have news on Roger's death?"

"No, ma'am, we don't." Jack stepped forward, an envelope in his hand. "Kim Felder, we have a warrant to search your home."

Kim staggered back into Emma. "A warrant?"

"Yes, ma'am."

"What is this about, Jack?" Emma asked, peering around Kim's shoulder as her heart began to thud. "I thought you heard me when we spoke earlier. That you got what I was saying."

Jack held the warrant out for Kim to take. "I heard every word."

"Then what's with this warrant stuff?"

"In light of what you said, the judge agreed that a search of these premises is warranted."

She felt Kim's eyes as they fixed on her face, but she was too stunned to meet them. "I told you it was just talk—like anyone might say in the same circumstances. How on earth did that add up to a search warrant for—"

And then she knew. He hadn't seen the notebook during his first visit to the house, didn't know anything about Kim's propensity for venting her anger in written form. Shaking her head against the memory of her own words, her own stupidity, she willed herself to breathe, to think, to keep from slamming the door in Jack's face. The Sweet Falls Sheriff's Department was there, on Kim's doorstep, with a warrant to search her property because of one person, and one person only: *Emma*.

"Kim?" Emma grabbed hold of the woman's hands with her own now equally ice-cold ones and squeezed. "It's time to call your attorney. Now."

Chapter Eight

It was just after eight at night when she pulled in behind Stephanie's maroon sedan and cut the engine. Part of Emma had wanted nothing more than to go straight home, feed Scout the dinner she knew he needed, and then collapse onto the couch for the cry she desperately wanted to have, but she couldn't. Not yet, anyway. Not until she'd briefed the troops she'd summoned to help right the horrible wrong she'd set in motion with her own reckless stupidity.

"Good thing the shelter didn't know I could be this dumb when I showed up looking for you, huh, boy?" Fisting her keys, Emma took in the pair of eyes looking between her and the stately home to their right. "Because if they had, I'd have missed out on the only completely trustworthy male on the face of the planet."

Scout stood, squeezed his way between the front seats to lick Emma's cheek and chin, and then propped his front paws on the passenger side window sill and wagged his tail, any disappointment he may have had over not going home to his food bowl paling against seeing the friend he knew went with this driveway, this house.

"You're right, Scout. We're here to fix things, not engage in a pity party over someone who clearly isn't worth it." Emma looked past her dog to the lights in her elderly friend's parlor windows. "So let's go inside, shall we? The troops are waiting."

Drawing in a deep breath, Emma opened her door, stepped out onto the grand circular driveway, and waited as Scout lumbered across the front seat and onto the pavement beside her. Together, they made their way up the front walkway to the massive arched door saved from being intimidating by the flowering bushes standing sentry on either side—bushes planted by a man who believed nature's beauty was the perfect tonic for almost anything in life, provided you took the time to notice and see.

"I'm trying, Alfred," she murmured as she stopped, inches from the door, and abandoned her view of the man's living legacy in favor of the darkening sky above. "I really am. But this? This is a real doozy. I'm pretty sure no flower or bird can—"

The front door opened, sans knock, to reveal a clearly perturbed octogenarian sitting in her wheelchair, arms folded across her chest. "We're in here, waiting, and you're standing out here talking to yourself?"

"Actually, I was talking to . . ." Unable to continue past the growing tightness in her throat, Emma instead scanned the flowers and trees to her left, and the flowers and trees to her right, as she worked to steady her thoughts and her breath. When she had, she looked back to find nothing but understanding waiting behind Dottie's stylish bifocals.

"Come in, dear." Dottie glanced down at Emma's tail-wagging counterpart. "*Both* of you. And we'll find a way to help our friend."

Swallowing back the instinct to question the use of the word *our*, Emma allowed herself the nod she needed far more, and stepped inside. "I'm sorry to invite myself over so late, but I didn't know what else to do."

"You did the right thing," Dottie said, leading Emma and Scout into the front parlor. "Isn't that right, Stephanie?"

"Isn't what right?" Stephanie parted her cheek from its resting place against Dottie's floral settee and yawned. Twice.

Just forty, Stephanie Porter was often mistaken as someone a good decade older, and it wasn't hard to deduce why. Between the woman's herculean workload at the VA, the endless patient charts that had her burning the midnight oil when she finally made it home, and the lack of anything resembling a healthy amount of sleep, it was a wonder she could string together a coherent sentence most days, let alone find time to address the ever-increasing infusion of gray in her otherwise cocoa powder–colored locks.

"I woke you up, didn't I?" Emma asked, mid-groan. "Stephanie, I am so, so sorry."

"If you saw the number of charts I have to go through before morning, you wouldn't be asking that question. But, since you are, no, you didn't wake me up."

Crossing to the settee, Emma lowered herself onto the empty cushion next to Stephanie. "Great. Even better . . . I interrupted your work, so now you'll get even less sleep than you already do."

"Actually, the only thing you interrupted was my mother's endless yakking, a feat in and of itself, for sure." Stephanie swiveled her back flush with the armrest and hiked her bent leg onto the couch. "So to that end, I say *thank you*. For saving me from my pathetic existence, if only for a little while."

"Stephanie . . ."

Rolling her eyes, Stephanie held up her hands in surrender. "I know, I know. Save the lecture. My existence is not pathetic. Just me and the way I'm living."

Emma held her disapproval steady. "You're making improvements."

"Right. I made it to the gym once out of twice this week."

"Come tomorrow morning, it'll be two out of three."

Stephanie's laugh was broken by a third and far bigger yawn. "We'll see about that."

"And this weekend, you're driving out to see John and Andy Walden with me, remember?"

"That was a conditional agreement, if you recall."

Emma slumped back against the couch. "Oh, I recall. And that's why I'm here."

All vestiges of fatigue gave way to intrigue as Stephanie leaned forward. "Uh-oh. She did it, didn't she?"

"She?" Emma echoed.

"Your client."

"And *my* book club member," Dottie said, engaging the lock on her wheel.

Stephanie leaned to the left to afford an uninhibited view of their elderly hostess. "I didn't know you had a book club, Dottie."

"It's *new*. Emma and I just started it."

Stephanie's green eyes traveled back to Emma. "*I* like books . . . Maybe we could swap out our gym mornings for that, instead?" Then, as quickly as the question left her lips, Stephanie slumped back against the corner of the couch. "Not that I'd have time to read an actual book, even if you did let me hire you for something like that."

"First up, there is no book club," Emma said, arching her brow at Dottie. "*Yet*. I simply threw the idea out there as something that might be fun to do and something that might be good for Kim."

"Oh."

She turned her full attention back on Stephanie. "No *oh* needed. If we'd actually gotten to the planning stage, we would have invited you," Emma said in a rush. "And not for payment, FYI. But rather just as something fun to look forward to once a month."

"I've always wanted to do something like that." Stephanie said, sighing. "But this job, and the hours, and living with my—"

Emma looked up at the ceiling. Closed her eyes. "I wouldn't spend too much time thinking about it, seeing as how I ruined everything today with my big mouth."

"Finally," Dottie drawled, "we get to the point."

"Said the woman who brought up the whole book club thing," Emma said, blowing out a breath she quickly drew in, once again. "Kim is in trouble. Big trouble. And it's all my fault."

"We're listening, dear."

Slowly, she opened her eyes, counted to ten in her head, and then pushed off the couch in favor of a little restless pacing. "I thought he already knew since he'd been there last night. I figured he saw her notebook while he was there and that's why he took her in. You know, so he could question her about what she'd written." When she reached the fireplace, Emma spun around and headed back toward the couch. "Which is why I called him this afternoon. So I could make sure he knew that it was all just a figure of speech—the kind any of us might use when talking about someone who'd betrayed us the way Roger did Kim."

A few steps shy of the couch, she veered off toward the hallway and then back to the fireplace. "But he hadn't seen it. Didn't know it even existed. He'd just brought her in because he knew she and Roger had been married, that Roger left her for another woman, that a divorce was in the works, and that Kim was not happy about any of it. Period.

"That is, until I stuck my foot in my mouth by going on and on about how a figure of speech—whether spoken or written—doesn't necessarily mean anything and—bam!" She palmed her face, staring back at Stephanie and Dottie across the tips of her fingers. "He took what I told him and used it to secure a warrant to search her house . . . find her notebooks . . . read the many ways she wanted to kill her husband . . . and arrest her right then and there!"

"By *he*, I'm assuming you mean Deputy Riordan?" Dottie asked.

Emma dropped her hands to her sides, fisting them as she did. "That's right."

Stephanie winced. "She wrote that stuff down?"

"Yes."

"Ouch."

"Ouch is right." Emma resumed her path around the parlor, restlessness quickly bowing to anger. At Jack and herself. "I went to him in an effort to help him, not hurt Kim. Yet hurting Kim is exactly what I did!"

"Wow," Stephanie murmured. "I don't know what to say."

Emma whirled around. "Don't bother. I'll say it for you. I am a certifiable idiot. I literally handed him the smoking gun with a bright, shiny bow on top. And now, because of it, she's sitting in a cell waiting to find out whether she can be released on bond or not. It's insane."

"Look at it this way, Em—if she did it, she's exactly where she should be. And Jack will have you to thank for it—not a bad hand to be holding, in my opinion."

"She didn't do it."

Stephanie pulled a face. "Hey, I get the whole just signing her thing. I really do. But there'll be other clients, Emma."

"It's not that."

"Then is it the fact he ran out on her? Because, I'll admit, that little nugget of information makes his demise a little easier to swallow."

A sudden and overwhelming blast of fatigue sank her onto the raised hearth. "No. It's not that, either."

"Then what?"

"I don't know. I just know she didn't do it."

"Okay, but may I play devil's advocate?" Stephanie paused for a moment. "You just met this woman, what? A few days ago?"

Emma dropped her shaking head into her hands. "Yesterday. Afternoon."

"Yesterday," Stephanie echoed. "Do you realize how many ditches are littered with the bodies of young women who thought the guy they just met at the bar was nice?"

She knew Stephanie was right, that her steadfast belief in Kim Felder was premature at best, but her gut wasn't wavering in the slightest. "I can't explain it, Stephanie. Call it a hunch, call it naivete, call it whatever you want. But I can tell you it's no different than what I felt about you at the end of our first meeting."

"That's good enough for me." Dottie released her brake, wheeled herself over to Alfred's rolltop desk in the corner, and rummaged around the top drawer until she found the notebook she'd been seeking. "Alfred, God rest his soul, had hunches about people all the time—hunches I didn't always subscribe to. Case in point: *you*, dear. Which means if he'd been swayed by my opinion at the time, you wouldn't be standing in my living room now."

"Um . . . *thanks*?" Emma said, lifting her head off her hands in time to catch Stephanie's grin just before it was coughed away. "I'm touched."

Dottie waved at Emma's response as if it was a pesky gnat. "What matters now is that Alfred taught me to give hunches their due. So if not the soon-to-be-ex-wife who believed in working through her anger by logging various ways to exact revenge on the weasel, then who?"

"Who? Who what?"

"Who *killed* him, Emma!"

She dropped her head back into her hands and moaned. "I can't answer that, Dottie! I never met the man! *Who* actually killed him isn't my problem. Getting Kim out of the jail cell I put her in *is*."

"Which will be tough to do on account of that bow-topped present you foolishly gave your young man."

Again, Emma's head popped up, but this time her full attention went straight to the notebook-holding octogenarian. "I thought he already knew! And Jack—I mean, Deputy Riordan—is not my young man!"

"Semantics," Dottie and Stephanie said in unison.

"No, not semantics! We may have been moving toward something before—before"—she rocketed up off the hearth—"today, but we're not now. No way, no how!"

Stephanie also stood, successfully stymieing Emma's third trip around the room. "C'mon, Emma, you can't mean that. The guy is just doing his job."

"Taking something I shared with him in confidence and using it to arrest an innocent woman?"

"He's a cop, Emma!" Stephanie countered. "You shared what could be vital evidence in a murder investigation with him! He can't just ignore that because it might hurt your feelings!"

"Stephanie is right, dear. You can't fault the young man for doing his job." Dottie wheeled herself closer to the pair, tapped her pen on top of the closed notebook, and locked gazes with Emma across the upper rim of her bifocals. "Which means if you want to get Kim out of that jail cell, we need to find the real killer."

"That's Jack's job."

"He thinks he's done his job."

"But he hasn't," Emma argued.

"Says who?"

"Says me."

"Do you really believe that, dear?"

"I do."

"Then we need to prove it to him by delivering the *correct* killer." Without breaking eye contact, Dottie opened the notebook across her lap and clicked open her pen. "And we'll do it with an even bigger, shinier bow to boot."

Chapter Nine

～•～

Emma had just pulled her phone out of her duffel bag to check the time when she sensed his approach. Jack Riordan moved with purpose. Always. It was one of many things she'd found appealing about the handsome deputy. Today, though, there were no butterflies taking flight in her stomach at the sound of his footsteps. No urge to tuck an errant hair behind her ear. No impulse to correct her posture or greet him with a big smile.

Yes, she'd heard everything Stephanie had said the previous evening about how arresting Kim was Jack's job, but she was still angry. And, maybe even more so, hurt.

"Hey, Emma."

Bypassing her phone's welcome screen, she pressed her way into the email inbox she'd already checked and didn't look up. "Hey."

"Stephanie bail again?"

"No. She'll be here."

"It's five forty five." Jack stepped closer, the tips of his sneakers invading her view. "Doesn't she have to get here at five thirty if she's going to get here at all?"

"She'll be here," Emma repeated, her voice void of anything resembling warmth even to her own ears.

"Are you okay? You seem . . . off."

"Nope. All good."

She saw his sneakers back away but knew he was still there, clearly trying to decide what to say next. After a beat or two of heavy silence, he cleared his throat. "About this weekend . . . I got a little sidetracked from the whole date-planning thing, but I was thinking maybe we could start with a picnic so Scout could be included? And then maybe catch a movie afterward, if that works for you?"

Literally twenty-four hours earlier, she'd have been beside herself knowing he'd not only spent time planning their date but was also thoughtful enough to include her dog. But it wasn't twenty-four hours earlier, and *thoughtful* wasn't the adjective uppermost in her mind when it came to the man clearly waiting for some sort of response.

"Emma?"

Squaring her jaw, she lifted her gaze from the screen she wasn't really looking at anyway and mingled it with eyes she didn't need the neighboring streetlamp to know were ocean blue. "Won't you be working on the case this weekend?"

"Some, sure. But we've got our killer."

"Your killer . . ."

"Thanks to you, that is." He hiked the strap of his own gym bag higher on his shoulder and leaned against the building. "You telling me about the stuff she wrote was huge."

She lowered her phone to her side. "Stuff I told you because I assumed you already knew and because I wanted to make sure you understood what it really meant. Not so you could turn around and . . ." She blew out a breath. Shook her head. "I told you that stuff in confidence, Jack."

"In confi—wait." He parted company with the brick wall at his back and turned to face Emma. "You're upset with me?"

Her laugh echoed in the early morning air. "*You think*?"

"Why?"

"Why?" she echoed. "Why? Really? Maybe because Kim was already having a difficult enough time getting back on her feet. Accusing her of something she's no more capable of doing than *I am* might well be the knock-out punch that keeps her on the ground forever!"

He stared at Emma, his expression moving between shock and . . . she wasn't sure. "She wanted to *kill him*, Emma. She wrote it repeatedly. In eight different places. I don't understand what you're not getting here. Or what you could possibly be upset with me over."

She sat with his words for a moment, the truth behind them warming her cheeks and further accelerating her already accelerated heartbeat. "Okay. I get that. I-I really do. And I know how all of the stuff she wrote must look. But sometimes the way things *look* and the way they really *are* don't always match. And that's why I came to you in the first place. In case you were overlooking that fact. Only you didn't even know about the stuff she'd written. *I* told you about it."

He strode to the edge of the sidewalk, raked his fingers through his dark blond hair, and then made his way back. "You're right, I didn't know about it. Not yet. But you did the right thing, Emma."

"Handing you the reason you needed to arrest her was the *right* thing?"

"Of course it was! A man is dead! Strangled in his own living room. Someone has to be held accountable for that, Emma. Tell me you know that."

His choice of words, and the irritation with which he spoke them, deflated her own anger into something more befitting the exhaustion that came with worry, regret, and a lousy night of sleep. "Look, I know justice needs to be served. I'm a big believer in righting wrongs, I really am. But that's not what you're doing here, Jack. In fact, you just created another wrong by arresting Kim."

When he said nothing, Emma plowed ahead, the memory of Kim's face while being handcuffed driving her emotions and her words. "I'm not trying to do your job, Jack, I'm—"

"That's interesting. Because that's how it sounds . . ."

"But that's not how it is. It's just—" She stopped, palmed her face, and groaned. "I'm sorry. I don't know how to do this, how to say this clearly enough."

His laugh was quick. Wooden. *Angry?* "No, you're being more than clear. Crystal clear, in fact."

"Jack, I—"

"I've wasted enough time out here as it is, Emma. If I don't go inside now, I'll barely get even a twenty-minute workout in. So . . . um . . . I guess I'll see you around."

She opened her mouth to ask about their weekend date, only to close it again as his parting words took root in her head. Squaring her shoulders, she blinked back the tears she refused to shed, and turned her attention in the direction Stephanie would come. "Right. Sure. See you around."

Stephanie picked up on the second ring, her voice heavy with sleep. "Um, hello?"

"I guess it's safe to assume you're not on the way?" Emma asked, slumping back against the brick wall.

"*Emma?*"

"Yup."

Sleepiness gave way to surprising alertness. "Are you okay? Has something happened?"

"Not really."

"I asked you two questions."

"My answer works with both."

"Where are you?" Stephanie asked, mid-yawn.

"Standing outside the gym. Waiting for you."

"Waiting for—oh! Whoa! It's six o'clock."

Emma nodded.

"And I'm still in bed."

Closing her eyes, Emma leaned her head against the hard brick wall at her back. "I was afraid of that."

Another yawn was followed by a quick stretching sound and a flurry of noises that suggested Stephanie was on the move—the creak of a bed's springs, the smack of what was likely slippers on an uncarpeted floor, and a slew of mutterings that were largely undiscernible. "I'm sorry, Emma. By the time I got home last night from Dottie's and finished my charts, it was after 2:00 a.m. I either slept through my alarm or never remembered to set it. But I'll still pay you for the week. Don't worry about that."

"A week that's supposed to include *three* trips to the gym. You only made it to one," Emma protested. "You can't keep throwing away money like that. It's silly."

"I want to go, Emma. I really do."

"You *want* to go to the gym? Huh! You and I both know that's not true. You hate every minute on that treadmill."

"With a passion," Stephanie conceded. "But the reason I hired you to go with me is still there—I need the exercise, I need to blow off steam, I need to be out in the land of the living, and I need interaction that doesn't include asking people to open their mouths wide or follow my finger."

"But you're not doing it."

"I will. All three days next week. I promise."

"And if you're up late working on charts the previous evening?"

"I'll be crabby when I come around the corner at five thirty."

Emma laughed. "So, in other words, status quo?"

"Exactly. Only I'll actually be there instead of calling you explaining why I'm not." A door opened and closed in the background of the call. "Can I put you on speaker while I brush my teeth?"

"No, it's okay. You need to get ready for work."

"Trust me, Emma, I'm able to multitask more than it may seem. So—" Stephanie's voice got quieter and then louder before a second noise—running water—entered into the mix. "So, is the 'tude I'm picking up just because of me or something else?"

Emma pushed off the wall and, after a moment's hesitation, turned in the direction of the parking lot. "There is no 'tude."

"Heres . . . a . . . ude."

"What?"

"Orry . . . Bwushing . . ." A sudden scrubbing sound was followed by spitting, then gargling, then spitting again. "There's a 'tude. Plain as day. Which isn't like you."

"I'm tired, I guess."

"You're never tired."

Shrugging, Emma turned at the corner. "I saw Jack while I was waiting for you."

The second round of gargling ceased as quickly as it began. "Uh-oh. That doesn't sound good."

"It wasn't. I think I offended him."

"How?"

"I told him he was wrong to arrest Kim."

She heard the water turn off and, soon, the smack of a toilet lid as it hit the tank. "Yeah, guys don't take too well to being told they're wrong," Stephanie mused. "But I'm sure you can smooth things over on your date this weekend."

"*What* date?" At her car, she turned and leaned her back against the driver's side door.

"Oh no."

She swallowed. Blinked fast. Swallowed again. "Oh yes."

A sound she chose not to try and identify was followed, soon after, by the distinct sound of a flush. "Wow. I'm sorry, Emma."

"Me, too."

Another stint at the sink led to a door being opened and Stephanie's voice growing closer. "All that aside, I'd be lying if I didn't say I'm looking forward to another case."

"Another case . . ." Slowly, Emma turned back to the car, fished her key ring out of her duffel bag, and inserted the right one into the door's lock. "You do realize you sound like Dottie when you call it that, right?"

"I guess. But we're looking into stuff, right?"

She tossed her duffel bag onto the passenger seat and slid in place behind the steering wheel. "I'm going to see what I can find out about the girlfriend, sure. But—"

"And Dottie is going to see if she can get you access to talk to Kim . . ."

"True, but—"

"And to the police report."

"But—"

"Accept facts, Emma. We're working the case."

Movement out of the corner of her eye had her turning in time to see Jack emerge, wet with sweat, into the lot from the gym's back door. He moved with his usual purpose down the steps and over to the sensible sedan he drove, but still, there was something missing. "Jack thinks I'm questioning his ability to do his job."

"Because you are."

She recoiled at Stephanie's words. "No, I'm not! I'm simply questioning his choice of suspect."

"Which is the same as questioning his ability to do his job." The return of the squeaky bed coil let Emma know Stephanie was likely sitting on the edge of her bed. "At least in his eyes."

"So what are you saying? If I listen to my heart and my gut where Kim is concerned, Jack and I are over before we even start?"

"I can't answer that. But if you're right and Kim is truly innocent and we're able to prove that, things might turn around where he's concerned."

She watched Jack climb into his car, start the engine, and carefully back out of his parking space. "And if they don't?"

"Then you'll know that he's the kind of person who would rather *be* right than *do* right."

She considered Stephanie's words, weighed them against everything she valued in a person, and gave the only response that fit. "You're right."

"I know."

"Then I guess I'd best get started, huh?"

"On . . ." Stephanie prodded.

"On our investigation."

She could hear Stephanie's smile in her ear. "Dottie would be so proud of you right now, Emma."

"At the risk of sounding like your own personal parrot, *I know.*"

Chapter Ten

⟐

If she could have only one word to describe Kim in that moment, it would be *defeated*. It was there in the dark shadows under her eyes, the restless wringing of her hands, and the slump of her very being.

But what Emma could do to fix it wasn't quite so easy to see, especially when, after nearly ten minutes, the only thing Kim had shared was her worry for her children and the fact that they were not only mourning the death of their father but also having to grapple with the fact their mother was awaiting arraignment for his murder.

Shifting forward on the less-than-comfortable metal chair within sight of an armed deputy, Emma looked down at the empty page in her hastily purchased notebook and tried to recall the random questions Dottie had insisted they needed to answer.

"You found out about Roger's death from your son, right?" Emma asked, readying her pen to record her client's answers.

Kim closed her eyes. Nodded.

"What did you do after you and I met at the park in town on Wednesday?"

"I went to the grocery store. Got some gas, I think. Called my daughter to see if she wanted to meet for coffee." Kim exhaled slowly, her eyes still closed. "But she didn't."

"Anything else?"

"Not really, no. I eventually just went home, had something to eat, added those things to our bucket list I already told you about, and eventually fell asleep on the couch."

"Did Roger have any enemies during your marriage?" Emma asked, stilling her pen. "Anyone who might want to see harm come to him?"

Kim separated her hands long enough to wipe them down the sides of her shirt and then bring them back together again for another round of wringing. "No. Roger was devoted to me, to the kids, to his job. He didn't hang out in bars; he didn't have some secret life."

A sound that was part laugh, part sob found its way between Kim's lips. "Until he did. With . . . Brittney."

"Right. Brittney." Emma wrote down the name. "And what was her last name?"

"Anderson."

"And she was his secretary, correct?" At Kim's nod, Emma added that information to the page. "For how long?"

Kim closed her eyes, drew in a breath, and then opened them onto a spot just above Emma's head. "A little over four years."

"Four years," she repeated as she wrote. "What kind of business was Roger in, exactly?"

"He owned a PR firm."

"A lot of employees?"

"No. It was just Roger, Brittney, and Reece—" Kim's face crumpled. "Oh, Reece . . . I wonder if anyone has told her about Roger yet. She'll be so upset."

"Reece?"

"Reece Newman. A lovely young woman from a not-so-great home life who got herself through college with nothing but sheer determination and grit and came to work for us about three years ago."

"*Us*?" Emma echoed. "Were you part of the business?"

Kim brushed her hand at the question. "If by 'part of it' you mean helping to create the name, and to get it off the ground, and to take care of the children so Roger could turn it into the success it became, sure. But really, I just said 'us' out of habit. Because, for a long time, I saw it as part of us—like our home, and our children, and our life."

Emma took it all in, made a few notes, jotted a few questions in the margins. "What was everyone's role in the business?" she asked.

"Roger was the face of the firm. He found the clients, handled the campaigns. Reece came to us with a PR degree, so she actually worked with clients, among other things. She is a Type A dynamo. And Brittney"—Kim lowered her gaze to first Emma and then the table—"she was the secretary I insisted he needed so he didn't have to waste his time updating the website, maintaining a social media presence, and scheduling appointments."

"Hiring her was *your* idea?"

Kim's nod was so slight Emma might have missed it if she hadn't been locked onto the woman's every expression.

"Oh."

"There's more . . ." Kim drew in another breath, held it a beat, and then blew it out with such force the deputy standing at the door looked over. "I'm actually the one who pulled her résumé out of the applicant pile and told Roger she was the one he needed to hire."

Unable to think of a response, Emma stayed silent, waiting.

"And at first, it seemed like a good decision. Brittney was competent enough, thereby lessening Roger's load and enabling him to get home in time for dinner on a more regular basis. It was"—Kim wiped her hands down the sides of her shirt again—"wonderful. Roger was less stressed because he wasn't pulled in so many directions at work, I had someone to cook for with Caleb being out of the house and Natalie being away at school at that time, and, because he wasn't so bogged down, he heard me more when I made suggestions for the business."

Emma looked up from the page that was starting to look a little less empty. "What kind of suggestions?"

"Clients he should seek out, positive PR he could get for himself by donating to charities or speaking to local high school students, et cetera. Nothing earth-changing per se, but all things that—when he did them—showed positive returns for both the business and his image. Sometimes even in ways neither of us anticipated."

She let Kim's words simmer for a moment and then waded back into uncomfortable territory. "You said Brittney worked with him for how long?"

"A little over four years."

"Do you think they were involved the whole time?" Emma asked, making a note of the time in which Brittney was in Roger's employ.

Another audible inhale, another, louder exhale. "No. Brittney was a newlywed when she started with Roger."

Emma stopped writing. "Brittney was married?"

Relaxing her hands, Kim raked them through her already disheveled hair. "She was."

"Do you know anything about her husband?"

"He was . . . *fine*." Kim lowered her hands back to the table and fidgeted them along the table's many scratches. "Nothing to write home about, that's for sure. In fact, Roger and I both thought she could've done so much better."

Kim's laugh drew the attention of the deputy once again, but if she noticed, it didn't show. Instead, she leaned back against her chair and sighed. "And, somewhere between two and three years later, she *did* do better. With *my* better."

"It was his loss, Kim."

For a moment, Kim said nothing, her expression so blank Emma wondered if the woman had even heard her. But just as she was getting ready to say it again, a tear slipped down Kim's cheek. "I know I should've seen it that way, but I never did. Roger was my first and only real love. I mean, sure, I dated in high school, but those were the kind of relationships that burned bright and hot and then died out as quickly as they began. But me and Roger? It was different . . . It was all-encompassing . . . It was building something lasting together . . . It was creating a family together . . . a life neither of us had ever had before . . . My world literally revolved around Roger and the kids. Although, when I begged him for a reason as to why he could give up on us the way he was, his answer was that Brittney put him first. That Brittney *saw* him in a way I had stopped doing once the kids came along.

"I told him he was wrong. That my heart still quickened when he walked in the room, that I still thought of him and what he'd like when I got dressed every morning. And that's when he told me that was no longer the case for him with me."

Emma wanted nothing more than to stand up, make her way around the square table, and pull Kim in for a hug, but she couldn't. Dottie's contact at the sheriff's department who made it so Emma could be there had warned her off physical contact of any kind. And right now, more than a hug, Kim needed Emma's help. "I repeat: his loss. Truly."

A second, fatter tear escaped down Kim's other cheek before disappearing behind shaking hands. "I loved him so much, Emma. I-I can't believe he's . . ." She choked back a sob. "*Gone.*"

Emma waited through a round of quiet crying and then, when it seemed Kim was ready to continue, moved on, the questions she wanted to ask tiptoeing around the edges of insensitivity. "Do you know if they had talked marriage at all?"

"I don't know. I never asked. That's not something I was prepared to hear. I wanted to pretend he'd simply taken leave of his senses." Kim wiped away the last of her tears as she creaked forward a smidge on her chair. "So, to that end, I holed up in the house unless I was spending time with Caleb or Natalie. And even then, I wouldn't ask them about their father's relationship, either. I told myself it was because I didn't want them in the middle of an already difficult situation. But I think, even more than that, it was me not wanting to hear how happy Roger was with her."

"I'm sorry, Kim." And it was true. She was. She was also angry at Roger for being such a pathetic, middle-aged cliché.

Returning her pen to the page, she waited for Kim to catch her breath. "What was her husband's reaction to being walked out on?"

"I don't know."

"You don't know if he was angry or upset?"

"I never asked." Kim's eyes, still wet with tears, fixed on the ceiling for a moment, maybe two. "I-I was too consumed with my own hurt and, then, my own anger to even consider the fact I wasn't the only one who'd been put out to pasture."

"Understandable."

Kim looked at Emma again. "Is it? Really? Because now that I'm thinking about it, it sounds kind of selfish of me. I mean, maybe he might've needed someone to talk to—someone who got it because he, too, was going through the same thing."

"I didn't ask you that to make you feel bad. I was just curious if you knew—"

"I could've brought him dinner, or made him cookies, or sent him your way so you could help him like you're helping me."

Emma pulled a face. "I only wish that was the case."

"I don't understand."

"I'm the reason there was a warrant in the first place, Kim. If I hadn't assumed the police knew about your notebook, you wouldn't be here now."

Kim leaned forward, her gaze finding and holding Emma's. "You were trying to help me."

"Some help."

"Are you kidding me?" Kim asked. "You being here? You're a godsend, I tell you."

She rested her pen on the notebook and held Kim's gaze with her own. "Just so you know, I'm here because I know you didn't do this."

"You and no one else, apparently."

"That's not true."

Kim's smile was joyless. "I'm sitting here, aren't I?"

"Unfortunately, yes. You are." Emma tapped the page. "But that's why I'm going to do everything I can to find the person who *should* be sitting here instead of you."

"You don't need to be wasting your time on me!"

She was shaking her head before Kim had finished her sentence. "You being here? For the reason you are? *That's* the waste, Kim."

"I-I don't know what to say," Kim said, wiping away the tears building in her eyes again.

"And I'm not sure what questions to ask, so I guess we match in a way." Emma looked down at her notes, read through them twice, and then looked back up at Kim. "Question. Why did you say you and Roger thought Brittney could do better than her husband? Was there something wrong with him?"

"Wrong with Trevor? No, not really. He just didn't have much of a personality in contrast with Brittney, who was always so gregarious, so fun, so interesting, so . . ."

Emma waited for Kim to continue, but she didn't. Instead, the woman merely wiped her eyes again, her lips trembling.

"I'm sorry, Kim. I'm not trying to make all of this harder

on you than it already is. I'm just trying to find a direction in which to start."

Their attention was hijacked by the opening click of the room's lone door and the uniformed deputy now stepping to the side to afford access to another, taller, infinitely more familiar deputy. The nod and smile Jack had for his brother in blue—or brown, as was the case with Sweet Falls' deputies—froze in place as his visual sweep of the room yielded a clearly unexpected face.

"Emma?"

Instinctively, she pulled her pen and notebook close to her body. "Hey, Jack."

"What"—his blue eyes shifted to Kim and then back to Emma—"are you doing here?"

"Speaking with my friend."

"Your . . ." He snapped his focus back to his fellow deputy. "What is this, Chuck? Lawyer only, remember? Until after she sees the judge."

The deputy shrugged. "Just following orders, Jack."

"*Orders*? Orders from whom?"

"Our acting sheriff. By way of Rhonda. She said he approved a thirty-minute supervised visit between the suspect and Miss Westlake."

"Rhonda," Jack repeated as, once again, he pinned Emma with a disbelieving stare.

"That's right. And"—Deputy Chuck looked up at the clock on the wall—"they've got just under five minutes left. After that, I'm thinking about calling in a lunch order at Giuseppe's. You want in?"

"Emma?"

She willed her attention back to Kim. "Yes?"

"Do you really think you can get me out of here?"

Emma didn't need to look back at the door to know Kim's question had been heard by more than just her own ears. The room-filling silence that ensued told that story just fine all on its own. But it didn't matter. If she believed in Kim's innocence the way she said she did, her answer was her answer no matter who was or wasn't listening.

"I do, and I will," Emma said, closing her notebook and rising. "You have my word on that."

Chapter Eleven

S he'd just backed out of her parking space behind the sheriff's department when an incoming call had her pushing Accept underneath Dottie's name on the dashboard screen.

"Hey, Dottie."

"How did it go?" Dottie asked. "What did you get?"

Emma shifted into drive and headed toward the lot's exit. "You must be psychic. I literally just got back in the car."

"I had a hunch, dear."

Emma grinned at her friend's failed attempt at playing innocent, took one last look at the brick building in her rearview mirror, and turned left onto Main Street. "What you really mean is Rhonda called you the second I walked out of the building."

Dottie's sniff of indignation echoed in Emma's ear. "Maybe."

"More like *yes*."

"You got to see Kim, didn't you?"

At the stop sign, Emma changed her screen back to the

map feature and turned right. "I did. Thank you. It's probably best I don't know how you pulled that off, but I'm glad you did. Kim needed that."

"So, what did you get us?"

"I'm not sure I got anything, Dottie."

"Did you take notes like I suggested?"

She glanced over at her notebook and pen sitting atop the passenger seat and then back at the expected arrival time on her screen. "I did."

"Then bring them by. I've always been fairly good at deciphering your chicken scratch."

"I can read my own notes, Dottie."

"Yet you're not sure you got anything. And this after spending thirty minutes alone in a room with no interruptions until the very end."

Momentary surprise had her letting up on the gas pedal. Irritation had her pressing back down on it. "What? Was your source watching the whole thing from some closed-captioned television I wasn't aware of or something?"

"Don't be silly, dear. It's called positioning. And, by George, the new receptionist desk I outfitted the department with earlier this year has it. In spades."

Given that she was driving, Emma refrained from closing her eyes and went straight for the sigh. "You might have pushed your luck a bit too far today, Dottie."

"Oh?"

"No one is supposed to see Kim other than her attorney."

"And your point?"

"It was against protocol, from what I gathered."

"Ben Watkins, our illustrious acting sheriff, doesn't stand on protocol. Instead, he's guided by his good sense."

At the four-way stop sign, Emma again consulted the map and turned right. "*And* your history of generous contributions to the department, of course."

"He's guided by his good sense," Dottie repeated, undaunted.

Her answering laugh was short lived as her thoughts circled back around. "As I said, you might have pushed it a bit too far. I suspect Rhonda might be getting a talking-to as we speak."

"From your young man?"

"He's not my young man, Dottie."

"Uh-oh."

At the next stop sign, she did close her eyes. And sigh. "There's no uh-oh."

"Oh, there's an uh-oh. I can hear it plain as day."

"Fine. There's an uh-oh. But I don't—*I can't*—deal with that right now." A honk had her opening her eyes, glancing at the screen, and turning onto the final street. "I just need to make this one stop for Kim and then hightail it back home before Scout thinks he's been abandoned."

"A stop for Kim?" Dottie parroted. "Where? Why? To do what?"

"She's afraid that—"

"Wait! You're not wired!"

Emma pulled alongside the curb outside her intended destination and cut the engine. "Excuse me?"

"You're not wearing the body wire!"

"You can't be serious."

"I can and I am. I ordered the whole apparatus after our last case."

She waited for any sort of sign the octogenarian was kidding, but there was nothing. Instead, Emma tilted her head against the headrest and sent up a silent *Why me?* in the direction of the ceiling.

"Dear? Are you still there?"

"Can I say no?"

"No."

"Fine. I'll play. I don't *need* a wire, Dottie. Not now. Not ever. I'm Emma Westlake. I live with the smartest and sweetest dog known to mankind. I'm working on getting a new business off the ground. You're Dottie Adler. You're in your mid-eighties. And you're more than a little pushy. We're not cops. We're not private detectives."

"The term is *amateur sleuths*. And it's our job to keep criminals from running amuck in our town."

"We really need to get you out more, my friend. This obsession with your cozy mysteries is getting a little out there." She stopped, weighed the fallout of continuing, and then did so anyway. "They are fiction, you know."

Dottie's answering silence was deafening.

It also continued so long that any satisfaction Emma may have earned from saying her piece was wiped from existence by guilt—the hand-wringing, heart-thudding, face-flaming kind. "A-a wire is a *wonderful* idea, Dottie," she finally said by way of a series of tail-between-the-leg squeaks. "I can stop by sometime tomorrow, and you can show me how it works."

"And you will bring back the last cozy I loaned you."

Emma sat up tall. "I haven't finished reading it yet!"

"I don't care."

"Dottie, c'mon! I'm only three chapters in!"

"That's three chapters too many as far as I'm concerned."

"But—"

"I have nothing left to say to you at this time, Emma. Other than the spine had better not be broken."

She searched her memory of her most recent reading session and tried to remember if the sound she'd heard when she opened the book wide that one time had been from the book itself, or something she'd been chewing at the time. Wiping her hands down the outer seams of her jeans, Emma willed her voice to sound as upbeat as her nagging uncertainty would allow. "It—it's not. I swear."

"Good."

"I'm sorry, Dottie. It's just been a really long day on top of an even longer yesterday."

"Be here, with my book, at 9 a.m. *Sharp*. And wear a loose-fitting top."

She pulled a face at the name on the screen. "A loose-fitting top?"

There was no mistaking Dottie's exasperated sigh, nor the glare Emma knew accompanied it. "To hide the wire, Emma."

If not for the tasteful white sign in the center of the front lawn and the number that matched the one listed on the Internet, Emma never would've known Felder PR was a business from the outside. In fact, if you removed those two factors from the equation entirely, the house in front of her embodied the proverbial American dream.

Both snippets of side yard were edged by a white picket fence . . .

The fieldstone walkway leading to the front steps was bordered by perfectly manicured flowers . . .

The window shutters were robin's egg blue against a sea of white . . .

And the cushioned swing, powered by the faintest of afternoon breezes, swayed oh-so-subtly on the wide front porch . . .

Yet instead of drawing her in as she suspected had been the intent, the whole scene niggled at her sense of fairness and decency. It was clear Kim had helped create this space as the business owner's behind-the-scenes right hand. Emma knew it because the same welcoming sense that oozed from every square inch of the structure in front of her mirrored that of the home Kim had created for the business owner's personal life, as well.

"You were an idiot, Roger Felder," she murmured as she made her way up the flower-flanked walkway. "A true idiot."

At the base of the porch steps, Emma took one last Dottie-clearing breath and followed it with a silent reminder of her reason for being there. No matter what she thought of

Kim's husband, the woman on the other side of the door had a different history with the man—a history that entailed daily interaction and shared goals and successes. Potentially hearing news of his death for the first time would likely be painful, and she needed to be sensitive to that as a human being.

A flash of movement behind a frontward-facing window drew first her attention and then her feet onto the porch in anticipation of a greeting—and a door opening—that didn't come. Confused, Emma looked back at the window, noted the desk and the smattering of picture frames she could pick out on the other side of the parted curtain, and a lone lamp her clearly overactive imagination could've sworn had been on when she first pulled up. Then again, with her current frame of mind, lack of sleep, and the *Please come in* sign hanging below the door handle, the likelihood her mind was making a mountain out of a molehill was by no means out of the realm of possibility.

She read the sign again—just to be sure—and entered, the quick yet distinctive jingle triggered by the opening door preceding her into what was clearly a waiting area equipped with cozy seating, a plethora of magazines to peruse, and a stack of cups next to a pitcher of what looked to be flavored water of some sort. Closer to the window was the desk she'd spied from outside. Tucked between the picture frames and the computer monitor it housed was a coffee mug with a hint of lipstick below the rim, and a rectangular pen holder beside a stack of lime-green sticky notes. The quiet yet steady tick-tock of a gold-trimmed clock on the interior wall was the only sign of life in the otherwise silent room.

"Hello?" she called, shifting her attention to her left and the hallway that boasted three doors—all closed. "Is anyone here?"

The sudden creak of a chair was quickly followed by the click-clack of low heels on an uncarpeted floor and, seconds later, a voice accompanied by a flood of sunlight. "Oh,

I'm so sorry. You missed me by about ten seconds, it seems."

A woman in her late twenties to early thirties stepped into the hallway, closed tight her office door, and made haste toward Emma with an outstretched hand. "Welcome to Felder PR. I'm Reece Newman."

"Hi, Reece. I'm Emma—Emma Westlake."

Reece's grip was warm yet firm, her smile welcoming yet professional. Dressed in a stylish pale pink dress topped with a simple silver pendant necklace, the young woman released Emma's hand and ushered her toward the first of two comfy chairs in the waiting room while taking the second for herself and the business-speak she clearly anticipated. "What can I do for you this afternoon, Emma?"

"Kim asked me to come."

Reece's smile faltered, disappeared. "How—how is she? Is she . . ." Reece stopped. Looked at her lap. Returned her gaze to Emma's. "I drove by her house yesterday, but when I didn't see her car, I figured she was with one or both of the kids."

"So you know, then?" Emma asked. "About Roger."

"I'm the one who found him. In his condominium." Reece stood, wandered over to the window, and stared, unseeingly, out at the road. "I'm not sure that's something I'll ever be able to forget. The scarf knotted around his neck . . . his eyes . . . the color of his skin . . ."

Reece shook her head. "I keep trying to tell myself it's not real, that he's going to stroll into my office at any moment with a question about the books or one of our clients. But he hasn't, and he's not going to ever again. It's just so—so surreal. So impossible to wrap my head around."

"Oh, wow. I'm so sorry. I didn't realize you're the one who found him. I take it you were close?"

Reece turned, studied Emma studying her, and finally offered a single, slight nod. "I struggled with what he did to Kim and the way he turned his back on what they had for"—Reece swept her manicured hand toward the desk in the corner, her jaw tightening—"someone like *Brittney*, but he's not the first man to be blinded by a pretty face, and I'm quite sure he won't be the last. Sadly.

"That said, I've found a career I love through Roger and I can't just forget that, either. I love what I do. I love my clients. I love knowing that actions I've taken, and decisions I've made, have helped grow this place into something more than just a little PR firm in some small Tennessee town. It's exciting. It's validating. It's—"

Reece returned to her seat and sighed. "It's why I'm here. Today, of all days. Because this place has always balanced me. It's where I have control—where I can see the fruits from things I've planted since being here. I can't bring Roger back. I can't push a button and undo the mistakes he made in regard to his marriage or the lapse in common sense he had with Brittney. But I can and will nurture the seed this place has planted in my life. It's all I can do, you know?"

"I do," Emma said. And she did. Work was her true north, as well. When things got dicey, financially, she turned to work. When loneliness reared its head, she turned to work. When a problem arose she wasn't sure how to solve, she turned to work. When life felt unsettled, she turned to work. Of course, in her home-based travel agency days, the very nature of her work provided opportunities to escape both mentally and, at times, physically. But even now, with A Friend for Hire, Emma often found herself wandering into her office at all hours of the night to create a new flyer or post a new ad. It was her version of warm milk or a soothing bath when sleep proved elusive.

Well, that and Scout.

Glancing toward the mantel clock, Emma mentally calculated the time Scout had been on his own in the house. Another twenty minutes, tops, and she'd have to leave to—

"I can't imagine how Kim has been doing any of this: the separation, Natalie moving out on her own, Caleb moving in

with a girl, and now Roger's death. She doesn't have something like this to lose herself in. She's just"—Reece threaded
her fingers together, only to pull them apart and run them
along the armrests of her chair—"*in* it. All the time. With
nothing to lose herself in or distract herself with. It's . . . *sad*,
you know?"

And, once again, Emma *did* know. Because she felt the
same way.

"Kim is why I'm here," Emma said, scooting forward on
her chair. "She was worried you might not know about
Roger, and she didn't want you to hear about it from anyone
but her if you didn't."

Reece's brow furrowed in confusion. "So she sent *you*?"

"Until she sees the judge and he makes his ruling as to
whether she can go home, there really was no one else."

"The judge? Why?" Reece asked. "Roger is dead. It's
over."

Suddenly, the worry over how best to deliver the news of
a death to a woman she didn't know became how best to
deliver the news of a bogus arrest to a woman already grap-
pling with the aforementioned death and—

"Emma?"

Shifting her focus from the spot just over Reece's head
she wasn't really seeing anyway, Emma reached across the
space between them and covered Reece's hand with her
own. "Kim has been arrested."

"Arrested?" Reece echoed, lurching her hand away. "For
what?"

Emma closed her eyes, gathered her courage, and slowly
parted her lashes to find Reece staring at her, waiting.

"What was she arrested for, Emma?" Reece repeated.

"Roger's murder."

The staring continued. Only this time, instead of con-
veying impatience, it was as if Reece's face was an old-
fashioned movie moving from reel to reel.

Shock.

Disbelief.

Back to shock.

Horror.

Back to shock once again.

And, finally . . . *amusement*?

"Oh, please . . . *Kim*? Yeah, I don't think so."

Emma bobbed her head a hairsbreadth until Reece's eyes were back on hers. "It's true. She's being held down at the sheriff's department."

The shock was back. Followed, seconds later, by a rapid swallow and a flurry of hand movements that had Reece picking a piece of lint off her chair, pressing at her cheeks, and, finally, pushing herself up off the chair once again. "I don't understand. Are they nuts? Kim's whole world was Roger and their kids. And I mean that quite literally. Her. Whole. World. She did everything for them, all the time. And by everything, I mean everything. Especially the kids. They sneezed—she was there with a tissue. They had difficulty figuring something out—she figured it out for them. They accomplished some trivial thing—she practically ordered up a marching band to celebrate. They had a bad day—she was there with cookies to make it better. Why on earth would they think she . . ."

Reece stopped, took a step, and then sank back onto her chair. "No, no, no . . . She . . . I . . . She . . ." Pitching forward, the woman raked her fingers through her hair. "I-I thought she was kidding . . . That she was just blowing off steam . . . I didn't think she was—no, she wasn't! There's no way!"

Dropping her hands in conjunction with a cheek-puffing exhale, Reece shook her head. "Kim was hurt, sure. Angry, sure. Who wouldn't be in that situation? But to actually do it? To actually . . .

"No. I'm sorry. I don't buy it," Reece said, standing yet again. "This woman makes cookies morning, noon, and night. Chocolate chip, butterscotch, peanut butter, oatmeal raisin, you name it. She doesn't kill people. Especially not someone she gave thirty years of her life to. Why would she?"

"I imagine *that's* the why," Emma said. "*Revenge*. Her husband left her. For his secretary."

"That doesn't mean she killed him," Reece hissed.

Emma held up her hands. "I know that. But she said some things and wrote some things and—"

"They were just words. Frustrations. A way for someone like Kim to strike out. That's all. She's a creative person. Creative people imagine; they fantasize. It's how they work through things."

"So she said that stuff to you, too?" Emma asked, scrubbing her hand across her face. "About wanting to kill Roger?"

Reece nibbled her lip inward, nodded.

"Where?" Emma pulled her bag onto the chair, foraged inside for the notebook Dottie had insisted she get, and opened it across her lap, pen at the ready. "Here?"

"No. She didn't come here after Roger left her—not that you could blame her."

"Then when would she say this stuff to you?"

"On the phone when I'd call to check on her . . . When I'd pop over to make sure she was eating . . . She was upset. Hurt. Destroyed. Saying that stuff was the only thing she *could* do, really."

It was Emma's turn to nod. To consider. To release a sigh of frustration. "The problem is, she wrote it down. On paper. In multiple places. Which means the cops think they have real, concrete evidence she killed Roger."

"Thanks to me," Reece said on the heels of a loud moan.

"*You?*"

"I'm the one who encouraged her to write her thoughts and feelings down, like in a journal or a random notebook or whatever. It's something a therapist encouraged me to do back in college as a way to work through a less-than-stellar childhood. She said that getting it out was always better

than internalizing. And paper was a good place to do that."
Reece ran her fingertip along the desk, the pen holder, the
edge of the computer screen, and then sank down onto the
desk's rounded edge. "But now, because of me and that
stupid suggestion to *write stuff down*, Kim is sitting in a jail
cell for a murder she didn't commit? Wow. Great friend I
am . . ."

"You had no way of knowing any of this would happen,
Reece. And trust me, you suggesting she write out her frustrations and her anger wasn't the stupid part. Telling one of
the deputies about it was."

Reece returned to her feet, propelled, no doubt, by the
horror now splayed across every facet of her face. "I didn't
tell a deputy about the stuff Kim was writing!"

"I know," Emma murmured. "That lovely honor and act
of compelling friendship belongs to no one but me."

"You?"

"Yup."

A half dozen or so emotions ranging from disbelief to
confusion gave way to one: disgust. "Why would you do
that?"

"Because I thought he already knew about it, and I just
wanted him to see it for what it was—innocent venting and
nothing more." Emma stabbed the still-closed pen into the
notebook. "But he didn't know."

"Wow."

"He used the information I gave him to obtain a search
warrant for Kim's house. And that's when she got arrested,"
Emma said, looking up. "So, yeah, Kim being in that jail
cell waiting to see the judge on murder charges? That's one
hundred percent *my* fault, not yours."

"I don't know what to say."

"No worries. I do. And it's been on a continuous loop in
my brain since the moment he showed up at her door with
that warrant. I'm an idiot. Plain and simple. But I'm going
to fix this. I promise you that."

"Fix it? Fix it how?"

"By figuring out who really killed your boss." She led Reece's gaze down to the notebook and then flipped back through the notes she'd made prior to getting there. "A friend of mine pulled a few strings and got me some time with Kim today—just before I came here, in fact. I asked her some questions, and made some notes, and . . . well, it's nothing just yet, but I'll get there. I *have* to. I owe Kim that."

For what seemed like an eternity, the only sound in the otherwise silent room was that of the clock, its relentless ticking a reminder of all the things Emma needed to be doing, but wasn't. But just when she thought she was going to go mad, the ticking bowed to Reece's strained voice.

"I think there might have been some trouble brewing."

Emma snapped her gaze back to the statuesque blonde. "Trouble? What kind of trouble?"

"Between Roger and Brittney." Pressing her hands to her face, Reece squeezed her eyes closed for a moment, a breath. "I-I don't know what it was. I didn't ask, and he—knowing how I felt about that whole thing—didn't include me in any of it. But it was something—something big. I'm sure of it."

Chapter Twelve

———

"Hey, boy, I don't know if you're hearing my voice right now, but if you are, I'm on my way home, I promise. I just want to do a quick drive-by on an address." Emma noted the next direction change on the top section of the dashboard screen, made it, and then glanced back at the name displayed in the center. "I won't be stopping, and I won't be lingering. I just want to know where it is and see if it's an area that'll give us a place to snoop around under the guise of a walk, okay?"

She paused long enough to allow Scout the inevitable head cock that always accompanied mention of a walk and turned left at the next stop sign. "So just hang tough for another five—maybe ten—minutes and then I'll be home to . . ."

The rest of her plan faded into nothing as her gaze, which had begun moving from mailbox to mailbox in search of the house number she'd procured from Reece, came to rest on a realtor's sign. A separate sign below the main one bore the words OPEN HOUSE.

"Well, well, well. Isn't this interesting?" Emma looked from the sign to the realtor's shiny SUV in the driveway and, finally, to the house itself, a small ranch-style structure lacking in anything resembling character. The front door, a basic wood-grain flat-panel affair, stood open to the late afternoon air, inviting potential buyers and nosy neighbors to come in and give the place a thorough once-over from the inside out.

Shifting the car into park, Emma looked back at her dashboard screen. "Scout? I'm going to hang up for a few minutes so I can check something out real quick, but I will be home to you right after that, okay? And when I am, I'm going to give you two of your favorite doggy biscuits as a reward for being such a good boy."

Reaching forward, she pressed the red button to end the call, glanced back at the house on the opposite side of the street, and shut off the car. Maybe the fact that Brittney's home was for sale was about nothing more than the woman's own impending divorce and a need to liquidate assets so they could be divided between her and her husband. But maybe, just maybe, it wasn't. Maybe it was about getting out of Dodge.

Her mind made up, Emma tucked her key ring into the small zippered compartment on the outside of her bag and stepped out onto the road, her mind's eye quickly cataloguing details she'd overlooked at first glance.

Brittney's home, like its counterparts to the left and right, was small—a two-bedroom at best. The concrete walkway leading to its front door was riddled with cracks and holes capable of turning an ankle. And the railing that ran the length of the porch was in desperate need of a paint job or, better yet, a total gut job.

"Hello! Welcome!" A man dressed in a pair of freshly pressed khakis and a pale-blue collared shirt stepped onto the porch and extended his hand. "I'm Brad Forrester of Forrester Realty, and you are?"

She shook his hand. "I'm Emma."

"Welcome, Emma. Come on in." Stepping back to let her pass, Brad waved her in, his lips seemingly frozen in full smile mode. "How did you come across this listing?"

"I was just driving by and noticed the Open House sign."

"I'm glad you did." He reached around her to a small table just inside the doorway and liberated a flyer from a neatly stacked pile. "This gives you an overview of the neighborhood and the town that you can keep for reference. It also has my name and number on the bottom, should you find that you have any additional questions once you leave. Are you working with a local agent for your house search?"

She took the flyer and shook her head, deepening his smile in the process.

"That's perfectly fine. I'm happy to assist you in your search," he said, motioning her to follow him down the small interior hallway. "This particular home is your typical bungalow-style build. It's a one-bedroom as is, but there are options on that front, as you will soon see."

Halfway down the hall, he stopped and turned back to Emma. "This study can easily be converted into a second bedroom."

She followed the sweep of his hand to a closet-sized area on her left. Centered on the back wall was a window that could double as a porthole. *"This* could be a *bedroom!"*

"With a few minor and relatively inexpensive modifications, yes."

"How big is this?"

"It's eight by five."

"Eight by five? That's"—she pulled out her phone, opened her web browser, and did a quick search—"barely big enough for a twin-size bed."

"But it would fit."

"With less than two feet to maneuver in and out of the room," she protested.

The man's smile dimmed momentarily before reclaiming its full wattage for the next stop on the tour. "And this is the living room."

She stepped forward, onto the only scrap of flooring that wasn't covered by the poorly cut carpet remnant being held in place by a sofa with three wooden feet and a pile of coasters serving as the fourth. The lone end table held a lamp, a book she'd bet good money sat open for staging purposes, and a pair of folded glasses. In front of the couch, taking up the bulk of the room's remaining footprint, was a coffee table topped with a bowl of fruit. A closer peek revealed a set of tooth marks on one of the apples.

In a perfect world, the shudder invoked by her surroundings would have been an in-thought-only sort of thing. But, based on the realtor's answering slump, it hadn't been.

"I know. Trust me, I know." Brad leaned into the doorway and sighed. "But there's only so much I can do. That said, a fresh coat of paint, a pretty valance"—Brad pointed to the room's one window—"and maybe some new flooring could really transform this room into something special."

Passable? Maybe.

But *special*? No, that required a level of imagination she simply didn't—

A trifold picture frame centered atop the mantel of the room's one saving grace propelled her around the coffee table and over to the fireplace.

"This is Brittney?" Emma asked, pointing to the blushing, starry-eyed bride in the center photograph. "The owner?"

Brad's nod was quick, terse. "We always ask our clients to remove personal photographs from around the home prior to an open house so potential buyers can visualize the space as their own. Most oblige, but there are always a few who . . . mmm . . . *resist*."

She took a moment to really take in the woman who inserted herself into Kim's marriage—the bottle-blonde hair that needed a serious touch-up, the simple off-white summer dress more suited to a summer barbecue than a wedding, the soda can pop-top gracing her left hand's ring finger, and the all-in smile with which she looked at her groom in the presence of . . .

"*Elvis Presley*?" she asked.

"Guy looks pretty good, doesn't he?" Brad stepped in beside her, ran his finger along the mantel, and flared his nostrils at the dust it accrued. "Seriously?"

Murmuring something about it not being a problem, Emma's gaze moved to the groom. No more than an inch taller than his bride, Trevor Anderson was nothing to write home about. His hair, which fell below his shoulders, shared the color and consistency of wet mud. His nose had clearly been broken a time or two in his life. And the puffiness below his heavy-lidded eyes suggested the beer bottle in his hand was a staple. Yet, despite the countless reasons he'd likely go unnoticed by the vast majority of women, there was no denying the way he looked at Brittney.

"They look so in love."

"And it's been like that every time I've seen them."

She snapped her focus onto the man now dusting the far side of the mantel with the end of his tie. "Excuse me?"

"Those two." Brad paused his futile cleaning efforts and nudged his chin and Emma's eyes back to the frame. "Removing this place from the equation, they've got it all. Looks. Money. Love. The whole nine yards."

"Wait." She stepped back to allow Brad room to dust the area in front of her and then pointed at the wedding picture. "You're talking about *them*?"

He inspected the end of his tie, pulled a face, and untied it from around his neck. "Let's just say that being married clearly agrees with him."

"You've seen them together?" she asked.

"Of course. They own the home."

She knew she was staring, but she couldn't stop. It was as if he was speaking a language she didn't know and she was desperately hoping for him to say something—anything—

she might recognize. When nothing came, she scanned the flyer in her hand for something that would make sense of what she was hearing.

"How long has this place been on the market?" she asked, looking back at Brad.

"Officially? About four weeks. But we didn't open for showings until last weekend."

His answer pushed her back a step. "So when you said you've seen them together, you're talking recently . . ."

"As recently as this morning, in fact." Brad rolled the tie into a tight ball and stuffed it into the front pocket of his khakis.

"And by together you mean just to sign papers regarding the house, or more like *together* together?"

"As in I should've announced my presence, yet again, before I stepped inside what I assumed was their vacated bedroom." Impulsively, he reached out, moved the trifold frame to the left a quarter of an inch, and then hooked his thumb toward the hallway. "So, shall we move on to the kitchen?"

She assumed she must have nodded or, at the very least, grunted something resembling a yes on account of the fact Brad started walking, but outside of the whooshing sound gaining ground in her ears, she wasn't entirely sure about anything.

Brittney and Trevor were together again?

Had that been the source of the tension Reece had picked up in Roger in the days leading up to his death?

And if so, why didn't he say something to—

"It's small, certainly, but there are things that can be done to make it more user friendly," Brad said, his words lassoing her thoughts back to the latest stop on the tour. "For instance, you could gut this peninsula and replace it with one of those movable islands that allows you extra work space when you need it, and floor space when you don't."

She saw his lips moving, even heard bits and pieces of what he was saying, but every time she tried to focus, she found her thoughts scurrying back to Brittney and Trevor's picture . . . to her visit with Reece . . . to Kim's assertion she'd done nothing wrong . . . and, finally, back to the picture and—

"Are they leaving Sweet Falls?" she asked.

Brad circled the café-style table positioned near the kitchen's lone window and stopped in front of the single basin sink. "The homeowners?"

"Yes."

"Actually, no." The smile with which he'd greeted her at the door made its way across his face, once again. "They bought a home in the Walden Brook Community. On the lake. Which is why I didn't expect to find them the way I did this morning. But apparently they returned for a forgotten box and . . . yeah. More than I wanted to see, I'll tell you that."

"Wait. Did you say Walden Brook?" she asked.

His smile brightened. "I did."

"Isn't that place expensive?"

Crossing his arms in front of his chest, Brad leaned back against the edge of the counter. "Homes in there are tapping at a half mil in some cases. But when you take into account the size and style of the homes, as well as the lake and everything it brings in terms of amenities for the homeowners, it's really not a surprise."

"But from *this*"—she looked around the room, finally seeing the peeling linoleum, the chipped Formica countertops, the missing cabinet pulls, and the lopsided peninsula that not only could but should be gutted—"to a place in Walden Brook? How does that happen?"

"It's unusual, I admit, but it's not for me to ask. My job is simply to help them find what they want and do what I can do to help them get it." Brad parted company with the counter's edge and guided Emma's attention toward an exterior door at the back of the room. "Would you like to see the backyard? It's completely fenced should you have a dog or a cat or—"

"Scout!"

Brad stopped mid-step, his brow furrowed. "Is something wrong, Emma?"

Swiveling her bag forward on her arm, Emma reached inside, fished out her phone, and checked the time. "Oh no . . . I have to go."

"But you haven't seen the backyard yet," Brad protested. "It's a real selling point for the property and—"

"I'm sorry. I can't. I really, *really* have to get home. I didn't intend to be here this long."

"Maybe it's speaking to you," Brad suggested, his tone hopeful. "Houses have a way of doing that to people. I've seen it many, many times."

She didn't mean to laugh, she really didn't. Yet the answering slump of his shoulders had her rushing to reign in the sound. "Thank you for showing me the place, Brad. I really appreciate it."

At the door, he liberated another flyer from the stack and thrust it in her direction. "I put together a flyer with information on the area—the school district, area hiking trails, driving time to the closest airport, and drive time to places like Chattanooga, Nashville, Atlanta, and Knoxville."

"You already gave me one," she said, lifting the first flyer into view in lieu of taking another. "So thank you for that."

He followed her onto the front stoop. "My number is on the bottom in case you have any questions about the house, or if you'd like to schedule a time to come back and see the rest."

"Thank you."

"And if you find that this place isn't speaking to you, call and I'll pull together some other listings I'd be happy to take you to see."

She inched her way off the stoop and down onto the walkway. "I'll keep that in mind, thank you."

"In fact before you go, what's a good way for my assistant, Gwen, to follow up with you on today's tour?" He patted his front shirt pocket, moved on to his trouser pants, and, when his search proved futile, took a step back toward the door. "If you can just give me a minute, I've got a pen inside and—"

"No worries. I've got your number."

Chapter Thirteen

If she'd ever questioned her importance in someone else's life, Scout had laid it to rest the moment they'd walked out of the Sweet Falls Animal Shelter together seven months earlier. From that point on, she only had to walk in her front door, open her eyes in the morning, or step out of the shower to know she was his whole world.

He said it with his eyes, he said it with his tail, and he most definitely said it with his tongue. Even when she knew it wasn't deserved.

Burying her head in his fur, she breathed in his lingering joy at her presence and willed it to dispel the last of her guilt. "I am the luckiest dog mom on the face of the earth, you know that, boy?"

Scout's lolling tongue disappeared with a quick swallow and then returned for yet another lickathon of her chin and cheek.

"Okay, okay, yes . . . yes. I know you're happy I'm home. I'm happy to be home every bit as much." She mopped her face with the leftover napkin from their outdoor dinner and then set it down on the empty plate to her right. "So? What do you want to do now? Sit here a little longer? Play ball? Go for a walk? What? It's your choice for being such a very good boy while I was gone."

Scout looked from Emma, to her plate, to the front yard and its lack of squirrel traffic, and back to Emma, his tail's ceaseless wagging offering no clue to his preference.

"Could you be any cooler?" she asked as his tongue took yet another chin-to-forehead pass on her face. Grinning, she grabbed her plate, stuck it on the floor just inside the front door at her back, and stood. "Let's take a walk, okay? Stretch our legs a little bit? See the sights? Terrorize a few squirrels? Score some pets and a little adoration along the way?"

At the increase in wag-speed earned by each new suggestion, Emma stood, closed the door, and snapped Scout's leash into place on his collar. "Lead the way, sweet boy. This walk is all yours."

The words were barely out of her mouth when she started laughing. After all, Scout always took point, determining whether they went left, right, or straight based on whichever distant sound intrigued him most.

Sometimes, it was the bounce of a basketball . . . When it was, they went left toward Pete's house. The teenager always stopped his one-person game to come out to the road and scratch Scout on the belly.

Sometimes, it was the sound of children playing hide-and-seek or riding their tricycles on their driveway . . . When it was, they went right toward the Elliotts' house, where Scout was guaranteed to earn a few happy squeals and, if he was really lucky, get to chase some bubbles.

And lately, on account of her own encouragement, they went straight, and then right, and then left, and then straight again until they got to Jack's street. It was a long walk, but on the days when the deputy's eight-year-old son, Tommy, was there, Scout couldn't wag hard enough.

At the base of their yard, Scout stopped, cocked his head as he always did, and, after a few seconds of indecisiveness, tugged forward on his leash. "Whoa, whoa. Are you sure?" she asked, pulling back ever so gently while simultaneously nudging Scout's over-the-shoulder glance to the right. "There could be bubbles . . ."

Scout stopped. Considered. Tugged forward, once again.

"Petey might be out . . ." she tried, tugging backward. "Basketball? You want to play basketball, Scout?"

Again, Scout stopped. Considered. Continued forward.

Drawing in a breath, she leapfrogged her thoughts in the direction Scout led, her mind's eye delivering up alternatives to what she knew was the intended destination. Maybe if they went left instead of right at the stop sign . . . or left instead of right at the big tree . . . , surely, they'd come across a sound Scout couldn't resist.

All it would take was one kid blowing bubbles along the way, or one teenager jumping curbs on a skateboard, or one elderly man who seemed to know the best places to scratch, or just one house emitting the aroma of chicken from its open windows for Scout to forget where he was going. She knew this. She'd lived it firsthand dozens of times. So why, then, was her hand growing clammy around the leash? Why was her heart rate picking up speed? Why were her feet growing heavier and heavier with each passing step? Why—

She looked up at the evening's summer sky, puffed her cheeks, and deflated them with a knowing exhale.

Nothing could distract Scout from Tommy.

Something about Jack's son spoke to Scout so completely that when they were together a parade of rotisserie chickens could pass by and he wouldn't notice. Likewise for Tommy with Scout. It was a beautiful thing to watch from the top step of Jack's porch with Jack seated beside her.

But now, after questioning Kim's arrest, she wasn't sure

she'd be welcome on that step anymore, wasn't sure Scout would be welcome, either.

"So, Scout? I know where you're taking us, and I still think it's sweet and all, but we can't go there." Her eyes were waiting when he looked over his shoulder at her. "Remember your new friend, Kim? From the park yesterday?"

At the mention of his fifth-favorite word behind *food*, *out*, *walk*, and *squirrel*, Scout's pace slowed ever so slightly, only to resume its previous speed just as quickly. "She's in trouble for something I know in my heart she didn't do, and Jack isn't happy with me for that. So I'm pretty sure he's not going to be all that excited to see us."

Scout kept walking.

"And I know it's Friday and all, but considering the fact Jack and I were going to have our first official date this weekend, I'm pretty sure Tommy must be with his mom."

At the mention of the youngster, Scout's pace quickened.

"Meaning, he's not going to be there, boy," she said, pulling back on the leash.

Scout, in turn, stopped, cocked his head at Emma, and whimpered ever so softly.

"Awww, c'mon, boy. Don't do that to me. I know you were alone the better part of the day. And I know I said I was on my way home when I called you and didn't actually walk in the door until an hour later, but . . ." Sighing, she loosened her grip on the leash. "Okay, fine. If you want to walk past Jack's, we will. But it's a fly-by, only. No stopping, no turning up the driveway, no front porch. Got it?"

Scout continued forward, his pace quickening—and her stomach tightening—as his intended destination drew closer. At the end of the street, he turned them left, his gaze racing hers to the third house on the right.

Sure enough, the sight of the gray bungalow with the black shutters and maroon-colored door earned an increase in Scout's tail velocity. The black midsize sedan parked in front of the single-car garage did the same for Emma's heart rate.

Pulling in a breath, Emma held it for a moment and then released it slowly, summoning Scout's full attention in response. "Okay, see? They're not outside. Sorry, boy."

She shortened the excess leash inside her hand and began to turn them toward home. But Scout was having none of it. Instead, he looked from Emma . . . to the house . . . and back again, inserting an encore of the whimper that had gotten them there in the first place.

"Knock it off, Scout. I think three biscuits, an hour of playing fetch, and letting you captain our walk to this point has more than made up for today, don't you?" She tugged him to turn. "C'mon. Let's go. It's time to call it a night and—"

The opening click of a door sent first Scout's and then Emma's full attention back to Jack's house in time to see the deputy's mini-me in everything from the dark blond hair and overall body shape, to the smile and left-cheeked dimple it spawned, race onto the front porch and down the stairs in their direction. Scout, in turn, gave his leash such a quick yet strong tug that he was off and running toward the eight-year-old before Emma could fully process what was happening.

"Scout! Get back here right . . ." The reprimand died on her lips as the pure joy that was Tommy and Scout's reunion played itself out on the grassy stage in front of her via a blur of paws and sneakers, fur and—

"Thomas Matthew Riordan!" The voice, coupled with the tone, yanked her attention back to the house and the man now standing at the top of the steps. Unlike his son, he was not smiling. "You know better than to run out of this house like that!"

"But look, Dad! *It's Scout*!" The little boy rolled his way back onto his feet, his dimple on full display as his gaze turned in her direction. "*And Emma*! Hi, Emma!"

"Hi, Tommy! How—"

"Tommy, I'm speaking to you."

The child's smile faltered, only to resume its full strength as Scout bounded up the steps to Jack. Seconds later, after a few hard tail wags and a lick-fest that included Jack's hands and wrists, the tension-diffuser that was her golden retriever won.

"Fine." Jack detached the leash from Scout's collar, patted him on top of the head, and then motioned him back down onto the yard. "You two have ten minutes. That's it. Make them count."

"Thanks, Dad!"

And, just like that, Tommy's total focus became Scout, Scout's became Tommy, and Jack's became hers.

Aware of the weight of his stare, she drew in a quiet breath, held it to a silent count of five, and then let it out in conjunction with a few tentative steps toward the house. "I'm sorry about this. I really am. I know I'm probably the last person you want to see right now. But Scout was pretty determined with his route this evening and now"—she swept her hand toward Tommy and Scout—"I see why. Clearly, he knew something I didn't."

At his answering silence, she looked back at Scout and Tommy and swallowed. "Anyway, I don't want to take your time with Tommy, so we'll head out now."

"I told them ten minutes. It's only been two," Jack said, his tone clipped.

"I know, but you're clearly angry at me."

"Do you blame me?"

She shrugged. "No. I get it. You think I'm second-guessing you."

"Aren't you?"

"No." Slowly, she made her way in the direction of the porch steps, her heart a steady beat inside her ears. "That's not what this is at all. At least for me it's not."

His laugh held no shred of lightness. "So, you telling me I've arrested the wrong person for murder and then going over my head to arrange a visit with her isn't second-guessing me? Really? Wow. I don't know what to say."

Fisting her hands at her side, she met his steely stare head-on. "This isn't about you at all, quite frankly. It's about Kim Felder."

"A woman you've known how long now? *A day or two?*"

"I know how it looks, Jack. Trust me, I do. But have you ever had a gut feeling about someone right from the start? When you just feel like you know them—*really* know them—in a way that usually takes a lot longer? Whether it's a strong connection or an instant distrust?"

In lieu of answering, he coughed. Swallowed. Looked out at his son.

"Because I have. Many times. Several in just the last month or so, in fact."

He abandoned his view in favor of Emma but, still, said nothing.

"Kim was—*is*—one of those for me," she rushed to explain. "It's like her warmth and her generosity was this tangible thing . . . It's behind some clouds right now, but it's still there. And I just know in my gut she didn't kill her husband."

"You mean the guy who dumped her for his secretary," Jack corrected. "That's a key component here."

"She still loved him."

"She plotted ways to kill him, Emma."

"Fantasized, maybe. As a way to deal with her pain. But to say she plotted to kill him sounds like she had actual intent to do so." Emma inched her way closer to the bottom step but remained standing. "That's the part that isn't meshing with the woman I met the other day, or the one I sat with in the police station this morning."

"Divorce changes people. It just does."

She considered his words, pondered his shift in tone, noted the dullness in his otherwise brilliant blue eyes. "Did it change you?"

For a moment, she didn't think he was going to answer. In fact, if it hadn't been for the subtle way he worked his jaw, she might've thought he hadn't heard her question. Eventually though, he lowered himself to the top step, his back flush with the railing. "More than I care to admit some days."

"In what ways?"

"I'm more wary. A little less open. And, when I think about the stuff I'm missing with my son, sometimes a little bitter, too."

She followed his gaze back to the front yard and the little boy who'd stolen her dog's heart. "He's crazy about you, Jack. Tell me you know that."

"I do. And I'm grateful for that. But it's the little stuff I'm missing that gets to me sometimes. Seeing him off to school in the mornings . . . Playing ball with him after dinner in the evenings . . . Telling him to turn down the TV or clean up his stuff . . . Saying good night as I close his bedroom door on another day . . ."

Lifting his chin, he looked up at the sky and blew out a long breath. "When she first told me she was leaving, I was hurt, I was angry, I was"—he waved his hand—"*lost*, quite frankly. And then, during the whole legal process, I became pretty bitter. My life with my son was being altered because of *her* choices. I resented that. Still do, on occasion."

"You do a good job of hiding it."

"I have to. For Tommy. I mean, I didn't ask for the divorce, but looking back, I can see why we didn't work. We had different priorities, different life goals. But none of that is—or should be—Tommy's issue. So I keep my interactions with his mother as polite yet infrequent as possible and keep my focus where it needs to be—on raising Tommy to be a good person."

Again, she looked out at the pair playing hide-and-seek behind a tree, and smiled. "For what it's worth, Scout and I think you're doing a great job."

"Thanks, I'll take it," he said, his soft laugh easing the tension between them.

Slowly, she lowered herself onto the bottom step, her fingers instantly fidgeting the leash he handed back to her. "I'm sorry about today, Jack. I wasn't trying to go over your head; I really wasn't. Dottie knew I was worried about Kim, and she arranged for me to see her. I-I didn't know there was a protocol on stuff like that. This"—she opened her palms across her lap—"whole talk-to-a-murder-suspect thing isn't something I'm all that familiar with, you know?"

"Your friend is a royal piece of work."

"Who? *Dottie?*" Jack's nod spawned a harder one of her own. "Oh, trust me, I know. But I also know she'd do anything for me or for Scout if we needed her to."

"How did you meet her?"

Setting the leash down, Emma rested her cheek on her bent knees, her words serving as a time portal for her thoughts. "From the time I was a little girl, I've always loved flowers. Daisies, tulips, tiger lilies, roses, black-eyed Susans, you name it. If I had a choice between a shirt with a cartoon character or a flower on it, I chose the flower. When I was a kid and in a Scout troop, the first patches I earned at each level were tied to plants and flowers. They made me happy.

"So it was only natural, I guess, that when I finally got to putting my own stamp on my place, I wanted to fill the yard with flowering trees and plants and bushes. Only I quickly discovered I wasn't all that good at it."

"No green thumb?" he asked, grinning.

She closed her eyes. Nodded. Opened them again. "Let's put it this way. I was to plants what mention of the word *broccoli* is in a discussion about dessert."

His laugh echoed in the summer air. "Ouch."

"I know." Emma shook her head at the memory of her earliest efforts. "But then I met Alfred."

"Alfred?"

She nodded. "Dottie's husband. Apparently, they walked past my house every evening after dinner, and they'd watched me destroy every plant I put in the ground. One day, when I was actually outside bemoaning my latest victim as they were walking by, Alfred stopped and struck up a conversation with me. He pointed at the plant I'd most recently killed and told me how it would do better on a different side of the house.

"So I tried it. And a few months later, when I happened to catch them walking by my house again, I went out and thanked him for the tip and asked him about another plant. Soon, we were talking plants a few evenings a week."

"And Dottie?"

"She was there, in her chair, but she didn't like me all that much."

"Why?" he asked. "How could anyone not like you?"

Her face warmed at the earnestness of his question. "She thought I was dense."

He laughed again.

"Anyway, Alfred and I struck up a real friendship and Dottie tolerated it, more or less. He even invited me over to see his yard and"—she breathed in the memory—"it was stunning. Absolutely stunning.

"Little by little, I started making progress in my own yard. Not like Alfred's, of course, but things were living and thriving and my neighbors were noticing and saying things. And then . . ."

She stopped, shrugged. "Alfred got sick. Real sick. He was dying, and I wanted to do something for this man who had been so sweet and encouraging and wonderful to me. At first, he said there wasn't anything I could do. But then, right before he passed, he called me and asked if I would continue his Tuesday afternoon teas with Dottie. I said yes, he gave me a manifesto on how to do it all exactly the way he had, and the rest is history."

"When did he die?"

"Nineteen months ago."

"And you're still doing the tea thing?"

"Every week."

"Wow." He leaned forward on his legs, his fingers threaded together. "I take it she no longer thinks you're dense?"

It was Emma's turn to laugh. "Uhhh, I wouldn't go that far."

"Wait. Seriously?"

"It's okay. Beneath all of her posturing, I know she cares about me." Emma nudged her chin toward the pair racing around the yard. "In fact, if it wasn't for Dottie, I wouldn't have gone to the shelter and found Scout. And that? I can't even imagine."

"He's a good dog."

"He's a *great* dog," she corrected. "And an even better friend."

"And that was Dottie who made that happen?"

"It was Dottie who gave me the nudge to go. It was Scout who said, *Pick me, pick me.* And, oh, how glad I am that I did." She waited for her voice to steady again, and when she was ready, she turned back to Jack. "It was also Dottie who . . . um . . . *encouraged* me to try my hand at the whole A Friend for Hire thing."

"You mean *pushed*?"

Her answering laugh mingled with Jack's. "I do. But honestly? I'm glad she did. So far it's been the perfect fit for me. With the lone exception of my first official client dropping dead in front of me, of course.

"Oh, and my newest one sitting in a jail cell waiting to face a judge on murder charges." She dropped her head into her hands, groaned, and sat back up. "Aside from that, I've met some pretty amazing people—some of whom are quickly becoming actual friends."

"Like Stephanie from the gym?"

"Like Stephanie, sure. But also Big Max . . . and John

Walden . . . and John's son, Andy . . ." She stretched her legs out in front of her and wiggled her toes inside her flip-flops. "I've had a few other clients over the past month, too, but those four, in particular, have claimed a piece of my heart for themselves."

"Tell me."

And so she did. She told him about the many ways in which Stephanie made her laugh. She told him about Big Max's innocence and how being around him made her look at things differently. She told him about Andy Walden and how his devotion to his aging father touched her heart. And she told him about John Walden, himself, and how his stories about his life always left her wishing for more time with him.

"These people hired *me* to keep from being alone. And yet"—she spread her hands wide—"I can't help but feel as if *I'm* the one who truly won."

"That's pretty cool."

"It is. And Jack? I felt that connection with all four of them right from the start. Just like I did the other day."

Jack held her gaze for a moment, maybe two, and then broke it in favor of a long, slow exhale. "You mean when you met my suspect, Kim Felder."

"Yes."

"There's more than just the notebook, Emma."

She stared at him.

"There's the murder weapon." A whooshing sound filled her ears as Jack continued. "It belonged to Kim."

"Reece said there was a scarf around his neck."

"And there was. Kim's."

"How do you know it was hers?" Emma challenged.

"She was wearing it in a picture we came across during our search."

Her stomach tightened, swirled. "Unless it was custom-made, you can't be sure it was hers," Emma argued.

Jack's eyebrow arched.

"Let me ask her where hers is and I'll bring it to you."

Jack folded his arms across his chest. "She doesn't know where it is."

"You asked her?"

"Of course we did. She claims she lost it."

"Then there you go! The real killer planted it there to make it *look* like Kim did it!"

"That's a mighty big supposition, Emma."

"Maybe. But Kim is not a killer. I'm sorry, she's just not."

"I don't know what you want me to say, Emma."

"I don't either," she said. "But maybe you could try to realize that my feeling the way that I do doesn't mean I'm second-guessing you or your ability to do your job."

"Doesn't it, though?"

"No. It doesn't. I mean, I didn't like knowing that you used what I told you in your office yesterday to get a search warrant on Kim's house. But when I stepped back—with Stephanie's help—and saw it from your perspective as a member of law enforcement, I understood it." Again, she spread her hands. "I didn't like it, but I understood it. So maybe you could try to do the same for me—as Kim's friend?"

"But you just met her two days ago and . . ." He stopped, raked his fingers through his dark blond crop of hair, and shook his head. "I know. I know. I don't entirely get it, but I can respect it."

"Thank you."

"You're welcome." He looked from her, to his clasped hands, and back again, his expression difficult to read. "I hope they realize how lucky they are."

"They?" she echoed.

"Dottie . . . Stephanie . . . the elderly man and his son . . . and Big Max."

She smiled at the images borne on the mention of each one and then stood. "No, *I'm* the lucky one, Jack. Just like I am right now."

He, too, stood. "I don't understand."

"Being here. With you. And with Tommy." Retrieving the leash from the step, she smiled at Scout and his companion, and then turned her full attention back on Jack. "That sense I had about the others? It was there for me with you, too."

"You mean when I was trying to figure out what your connection to my first murder victim was?"

She laughed. "Okay, so maybe it was a wee bit delayed. But only because I was afraid you were going to throw me in jail for a crime I didn't commit."

"Like you think I'm doing with Kim Felder?"

"You have to do what you have to do, Jack. I get that."

She left him to weigh her words and headed out into the yard. "Okay, Scout, it's time to head home. It's been a long day, and I need to get some sleep."

Scout stopped. Eyed Tommy. Wagged his tail. And, after a full chin-to-hairline lick of the little boy's face, meandered his way over to Emma. "Good boy," she said, clicking his leash into place before directing her attention to the rosy-cheeked eight-year-old watching her every move. "He really loves you, you know that?"

Tommy's answering grin gave way to an emphatic nod.

"Good." She looked back down at Scout and patted his side. "Take us home, boy."

"Whoa . . . Whoa . . . Hold up a minute." Jack fell into step beside them as they made their way across the rest of the yard to the street. "I'm glad you came, Emma."

She felt her heart flutter just a little and allowed herself a moment to savor it, as well as the relief she felt clear down to her toes. "So am I."

"Kim's a lucky girl, having you in her corner."

"I don't know about that."

"I do." He bent down, scratched Scout behind the ear, and then traveled his gaze back to hers. "And just so you know, I'm feeling pretty lucky myself, too."

Chapter Fourteen

⟨⟨⟨⟩⟩⟩

It was exactly nine o'clock when Emma and Scout exited the car in favor of the flagstone walkway that meandered around the side of Dottie's house. She knew, from the aromas wafting through the wrought iron fence, fresh-from-the-oven scones were on the breakfast menu. She also knew, from the presence of Stephanie's car in the driveway, those same scones were already being eaten—inhaled, actually.

"We're here. We're here," Emma said as she pulled closed the gate in their wake and made their way around the flowering hedges and bushes that were Alfred's legacy. Along the way she stopped to caress a four-o'clock, sniff a confederate jasmine, and to make occasional mental notes on placement in relation to her own yard.

Maybe, if she transplanted her own confederate jasmine to the back of the house, she could put something entirely different in the flower bed beneath her living room window . . .

It could work, she mused, especially if—

"You're late, dear."

Startled, Emma looked up to find Dottie drumming her fingers atop the armrest of her wheelchair. Seated opposite the octogenarian, Stephanie stared into her coffee cup as if waiting for something.

"You said nine," Emma protested. "And it's nine."

"Actually, it's 9:07."

Lowering her tote bag to the ground beside the lone vacant chair, she stared at the woman. "I shut off the car at exactly nine, Dottie. I looked at the clock."

"It doesn't take seven minutes to get here from the driveway."

"Maybe your clock is fast," she countered.

Dottie's chin lifted. "Maybe you dillydallied."

"I didn't dillydally. I just . . ." She glanced back at the walkway and then claimed her seat with a heavy sigh. "Fine. I got sidetracked, as per usual, by Alfred's gardening prowess. But I'm here now, right?"

"You are."

"Okay, then let's move on, shall we?" She turned to Stephanie, and when there was still no movement, no acknowledgment of Emma's presence, she clapped her hands. "Earth to Stephanie, come in, Stephanie."

"She's not a morning person, dear. But at least she's here—and on time, I might add."

Rolling her eyes, Emma helped herself to a scone, two pieces of bacon, and a spoonful of scrambled eggs. "So, I came across two things yesterday. One of which could be of interest."

Dottie lowered her teacup to the table and exchanged it for her notebook and pen. "Go on. We're listening."

"I don't think Roger and his secretary were still involved at the time of his death."

Stephanie stirred to life beside her. "Oooh, do tell."

"Welcome to the party," Emma said, laughing.

"Parties don't start at ungodly hours on a Saturday morning."

"Touché." She watched Stephanie take a sip of her coffee, a bite of scone, and did the same. "When I saw Kim yesterday, she asked me to stop by Roger's office to make sure his employee, Reece, knew about his death."

"Did she?" Dottie asked, readying her pen.

"Considering she's the one who found his body? Yes, she knew."

"Wow," Stephanie said, leaning forward. "You see that stuff on TV all the time, but to actually walk in and see one? I can't imagine."

"Reece didn't know about Kim's arrest, though," Emma added.

Dottie looked up from whatever she was writing. "How did she take the latter?"

"She was upset. Even more so when I admitted it was my fault Kim had been arrested. But when I explained how it happened and that I was going to do everything I could do to prove it wasn't Kim, she—"

"We."

"Excuse me?"

"*We* are going to do everything we can to prove it wasn't Kim," Dottie said on the heels of an indignant sniff.

"Of course." Emma motioned to the table, the food, Dottie's notebook, and Stephanie. "How could I possibly forget?"

"That's better. Go on."

She took a bite of eggs and an even bigger bite of her scone. "Anyway, it was when I said I was going to help Kim that she mentioned some trouble between Roger and Brittney. She didn't know what it was, but she said it was something big."

"Do you mean like a lovers' quarrel or something?" Stephanie asked across the piece of bacon she hijacked from Emma's plate.

"I thought that, at first. But I think it was more than that. Like maybe they broke things off."

Dottie stopped writing and looked up at Emma, waiting.

"Brittney and her husband are selling their house," Emma said.

"Because of their divorce?"

Emma turned back to Stephanie. "No, because they're buying a new place in Walden Brook. Together. As a couple."

"Then why does Kim think Brittney and Roger were still involved?" Dottie asked.

"That's a good question. I'd think it was a recent thing since she didn't know, but from what I was able to gather from the realtor selling Brittney's house, she and her husband have already secured and closed on their new home."

"Walden Brook," Stephanie repeated. "I've heard of that place, but I'm not sure why. Is that one of the places you've dragged me to in my house search?"

Emma laughed. "Uh, no. We're talking big bucks to live in that place. *Big* bucks."

"What does Brittney's husband do that he can afford that?" Dottie asked, trading her pen for her teacup.

"That's the thing. According to Kim, Trevor—Brittney's husband—was a struggling musician."

Stephanie finished off Emma's bacon and moved on to another scone. "So maybe he got picked up by a label? Or maybe Roger gave her a raise when things were good between them, and then couldn't take it away when they broke things off?"

"It would've had to be one heckuva raise to be able to afford a place in Walden Brook." Emma thought back to the open house, the memory spawning a furious shake of her head. "And we're not talking about simply moving up to the next level of house. The difference between the place they're selling and the kind of house you find in Walden Brook is substantial."

Stephanie turned an inquiring eye on Emma. "Are we talking tens of thousands or hundreds of thousands?"

"Oh, the latter. Without question." She reached into her tote, pulled out the flyer the realtor had handed her during the open house, and held it out for first Stephanie and then Dottie to see. "This is the house they're selling."

Dottie took the paper, scanned down to the price at the bottom, and then swapped it for her pen, once again. "Good work, Emma. Very, very good work."

"*If* it means something."

"Oh, it means something, dear."

"But what?" she asked, as she retrieved the flyer and set it down next to her plate.

"That's what we're going to have to figure out."

"We can't ask Roger." Emma pushed her chair out from under the umbrella and lifted her face to the morning sun. "And from what I've been able to gather from Kim, she tried to turn a blind eye to what Roger was doing as a coping mechanism. So that leaves us with Brittney."

"Very good, dear."

She lowered her chin until Dottie was back in view. "So what? We're going to walk up to her and ask her about her affair with Roger Felder? And why it ended? Because really, who wouldn't answer questions like that from total strangers . . ."

"Sarcasm doesn't become you, Emma."

"Sorry. But I'm serious, too. She doesn't know us from Adam."

Stephanie grabbed one last piece of bacon, nibbled her way around the outer rim, and then finished it off in a single bite. "Which is why we need to be extra clever."

"How so?"

"For starters, we find out if she goes to the gym," Stephanie said. "If she does and we can find out when, we make a point of being there at the same time."

Emma's laugh brought Scout running from whatever corner of the yard he'd been sniffing. "You can't even be there at *our* time, let alone someone else's time."

"Semantics."

"No, not semantics. Fact."

Stephanie patted Scout's front paws onto her lap and rewarded him with a kiss on his head. "Fine. Then we employ this gorgeous canine creature to be of assistance when I'm not working. Like later today or, even better, tomorrow."

"Um, how?"

"Scout likes walks, doesn't he?" Stephanie asked between continued kisses. "So let's take him for a walk in this fancy-schmancy neighborhood you keep talking about. See if Brittney is outside."

"And what? Strike up a conversation that has her sharing her innermost secrets with us? Yeah, I don't think so."

Stephanie pulled a face at Scout. "Is your momma always this much of a wet blanket?"

"Yes."

Emma swung her attention back to Dottie. "That's not nice!"

"Stephanie's idea is a good one, dear. So, too, is wearing a wire."

"I'm not wearing a wire."

Rolling her eyes, Dottie huffed out a breath. "And why not?"

"Because if I'm with Stephanie, we have two sets of ears. That's more than enough to—wait." Emma narrowed her eyes on Stephanie once again. "Hold up a minute. We had a deal, remember? You're going with me out to Andy and John's place tomorrow afternoon so you can pick Andy's brain about house ideas while I visit with John."

Stephanie groaned. "Ugh. I forgot about that."

"Well, I didn't. Which is why I'm picking you up at two o'clock." Sensing Stephanie's incoming protest, she held up her hand. "By that time, you will surely be awake and dressed, and it'll make it so I can still have you home in time to do work stuff you might need to do before morning."

"Can I fire her?" Stephanie asked, glancing at Dottie.

"Of course."

Emma shot a glare at Dottie. "Wow. Such loyalty, such support . . ."

"She asked if she could fire you, dear. I answered the question."

"Great."

"But if her question had been *should* she fire you, I would have said no." Dottie pointed her pen at Emma. "You said you came across something else yesterday?"

She felt her body drain of some of its pep. "Oh. Right."

"We're waiting, dear."

"The murder weapon . . ."

Dottie and Stephanie leaned forward, in unison.

"Jack says it belongs to Kim."

Dottie's inhale was drowned out by Stephanie's "Uh-oh."

"But evidence can be planted, right?" Emma asked.

Dottie's nod was slow, thoughtful. "Indeed. Happens all the time in my books."

"And in my crime shows, too," Stephanie added.

"But why?" Emma looked at Scout. "Why would someone do that?"

"To get away with murder." Dottie returned her focus to her notebook, scanned the notes she'd made, and then flipped back a page to a series of questions written in red ink. "While Brittney is certainly on my suspect list, we can't ignore her husband, either."

"You mean Trevor?"

"Trevor . . ." Dottie wrote the name in the margin of her second question. "I would imagine he was no more pleased about his wife getting involved with Roger than Kim was. Which gives us another viable suspect to explore."

"True. But from what the realtor said yesterday, he's forgiven her enough to not only take her back, but also buy another—and much more expensive—house with her." Again, Emma retrieved the house flyer, took in the details, and let her thoughts wander the home's tiny, rundown rooms once again. "That seems really off to me."

The clap of Dottie's hands broke through Emma's wool-gathering. "Good! Good! Follow that!"

"Huh?"

"What you just said? That's your gut talking to you, dear. So listen to it. See where it takes you."

"Where it takes me?" she echoed.

"When something seems off, it usually is. Now all you need to do is figure out why."

"Whoa. Whoa. Whoa." She looked from Dottie to a nodding Stephanie and back again. "*Me?* I'm not the one hell-bent on playing detective. You two are."

"So you're content sitting back and losing another client?"

"No. Of course not. But this thing with Kim isn't about losing a client, Dottie. It's about my gut telling me she didn't do it."

"Okay. Then if your gut is telling you something is off, follow it," Dottie mused. "See if you're right."

"How?"

"Find out what Brittney was making. Find out if she has a second job. Find out what Trevor does for an income. If his music isn't the source, what is? And, most importantly, find out his level of hatred toward Roger."

"And how am I supposed to do that?" Emma asked. "I've never met either of them."

The legs of Stephanie's chair grated against the patio as she stood. "We take Scout for a walk. Like I already said."

"And? If they're not outside when we walk by?"

"We walk by a second time, and a third time . . . We talk to neighbors who may know things . . . We invent a problem that necessitates the use of a phone . . . We knock on their door because we love the color of their house so much we must know what it's called . . . I don't know, Emma; we'll figure it out."

She followed Stephanie into the yard with her eyes, watched Scout trot behind her in the hopes a belly scratch was on the horizon, and, when it was, looked back at Dottie and sighed. "I can't believe I've let you talk me into this whole amateur sleuth thing yet again. Once was more than enough, you know?"

"So then you'll take the walk?"

Grabbing hold of the flyer, Emma stuffed it into her tote, and stood. "I'll take the walk."

Chapter Fifteen

───•─•───

W ow. You weren't kidding, were you?" Stephanie asked, stepping onto the sidewalk next to Emma, her mouth gaping. "I mean, *look* at these places. They're huge."

"Told you."

"I know you did, but . . ." Stephanie spread wide her hands and turned in a slow circle.

Nodding, Emma snapped Scout's leash onto his collar and nudged him in the direction they needed to go. "The size is especially jarring when you compare it to the place I just drove us by, right?"

"No kidding." Stephanie fell into step next to Emma, only to stop in front of the next house and stare. "From that to this? How does that even happen?"

"I have no idea."

"If only they could bottle whatever they did and sell it. Think of the money they'd have then."

Emma shrugged. "I guess . . . if they need more money . . . But one thing I know for sure is they don't have Scout, *do they, boy?*"

Scout's tail picked up speed.

"You really have the whole dog-mom voice going on."

"Dog-mom voice?" Emma echoed.

Stephanie took one last look at the house in front of them, and then nudged Emma back in the direction they'd been walking. "It's a thing. Everyone I know who has a dog has one. Cat owners, too. But"—Stephanie yawned, once, twice—"it's . . . *cute*. Fun."

"Have you given any more thought to going to the shelter and getting a cat?" Emma asked as they passed another house.

"I have. But I've gotta figure out what kind of place I want to build first and I haven't had a whole lot of time to think about it lately. Work has been crazier than ever—something I didn't think was possible, but . . . there you go. I'm going to live with my mother until I'm old and decrepit."

Emma checked the numbers on the next two mailboxes they passed and kept walking. "No, you're not. You're going to figure out what you want in a house, have it built, get yourself a cat, and live your best life as the smart, hardworking woman that you are."

"Ha!"

"It's true. And it starts this afternoon. With Andy. You'll see." Emma traveled her gaze three mailboxes ahead and immediately slowed her steps. "That's it," she whispered, pointing her chin and Stephanie's attention toward a large, Mediterranean-style home. "That's the house number I found on the Internet last night."

Stephanie stopped. "Whoa."

"'Whoa' is right," Emma murmured as she took in the circular driveway, the stone steps, the chandelier and curved staircase she could see through the front window, the—"

"Don't look now," Stephanie said, grabbing hold of Emma's arm and squeezing. "The front door is opening."

Sure enough, the door swung open and, seconds later,

deposited a young woman onto the stone stoop. Dressed in the kind of athletic wear that was more about being seen than actually sweating, she bent down, retied her left sneaker, and bounded down the trio of steps, her bottle-blonde ponytail swishing against her shoulders.

"Is that her?" Stephanie whispered. "Because she looks . . . *young*. Like you."

Emma thought back on the woman she'd seen in the picture frame at the open house and mentally compared her with the one making her way down the driveway.

Beach-blonde hair: check.

Washboard abs: check.

Long, shapely legs: check.

High cheekbones: check.

And, last but not least, huge—

"How does she *run* with those things?" Stephanie asked on the heels of an audible inhale. "I mean, all that bouncing? Wouldn't it hurt?"

Emma pursed her lips against the instinct to laugh and, instead, shrugged. "I wouldn't know."

"Wow. Just wow."

Nodding, Emma shortened the gap between herself and Stephanie to mere inches. "As for your other question?" she said. "Yeah, that's most definitely Brittney Anderson."

With a gentle shake of her head, Stephanie bent down, cupped her hand underneath Scout's chin, and lifted his eyes to hers. "Okay, this is all you, boy. All. You. So, work it, okay?"

"What's all him?"

Rolling her eyes, Stephanie snatched the leash from Emma and began walking, the gap between them and Brittney rapidly decreasing.

"Hey . . . hey . . . slow down," Emma hissed. "What are you doing?"

"*We* are doing what we came here for."

Before Emma could process, let alone protest, Stephanie

lifted her non-leash-holding hand in a wave as Brittney reached the end of the driveway. "Hello! Welcome to the neighborhood! I love your outfit!"

"Thank you." Brittney stepped onto the sidewalk and immediately squatted down next to Scout. "Who is this handsome boy?"

"This is Scout. He's Emma's dog," Stephanie said, sweeping her hand toward Emma. "And I'm Stephanie—Stephanie Porter."

Brittney paused in her petting of Scout to flash her full-wattage smile, first at Emma and then Stephanie. "I'm Brittney. Brittney Anderson."

"When did you officially move in?" Stephanie asked.

"We moved in on Thursday."

"Thursday?" Emma echoed. "But that's the day—"

"That's the day Emma and I meet up for cappuccinos. Which is why we missed your moving van, I guess."

"No, that was the day—*owww*!" Emma met Stephanie's steely eyes with a glare of her own. "What was that—"

"We didn't really have a moving van." Brittney gave Scout one more pet and one more scratch behind the ears and then straightened. "My husband Trevor and I decided to start from scratch. New house, new furnishings, new start. Which means the search history on my computer the past few days is filled with almost nothing but furniture and home décor sites. Fun, sure, but also worthy of more than a little nail biting."

Brittney held out her hand, inspected her sunshine yellow nails, and laughed. "Thank God for fake nails, right?"

"Whoa. Your ring!" Emma leaned in for a closer look at the soda pop top turned enormous diamond. "It's . . . gorgeous."

"Fresh new start. Fresh new house," Brittney said, turning her hand this way and that.

"So, so true." Stephanie glanced at Emma, shook her head so subtly Emma wasn't entirely sure she actually had, and then made a show of breathing in the picture-perfect June day. "It's perfect out today, isn't it?"

"Beautiful," Brittney agreed. "Makes me want to sit outside on the back patio and listen to my husband play his music."

Stephanie's brow arched. "Oh? What kind of music does he like to listen to?"

"He plays his own. He's a musician."

"Might we know his work?" Stephanie prodded.

Brittney beamed. "Not yet. But you will soon. Everyone will."

"So he's really talented, then?"

"So, so talented." Brittney's smile dissolved into a proud sigh.

Stephanie took in the house again. "What does he do in the meantime? For a living, I mean?"

"He's focused on his music. With a talent like his, he has to be."

Emma didn't need to meet Stephanie's eye to know the amusement she would find there. Instead, she took a turn at the helm while her friend regained her composure. "Where did you move here from?"

A flash of something Emma likened to surprise weakened Brittney's smile ever so slightly. The discomfort that clearly followed had the woman's hands twisting around each other. "We're from here."

"Do you mean here as in Tennessee?" Stephanie slipped another glance at Emma. "Or here as in Sweet Falls?"

Brittney separated her hands, wiped them down the sides of her petal-pink running pants. "Sweet Falls, actually."

"Oh, how lovely. What neighborhood?"

The last of the woman's smile drained away. "Jennings Road, actually. But only until we . . . um . . . had a better feel for the town and . . . um . . . where we wanted to end up."

"Smart. How long were you there? Just a few months?"

Brittney shifted from foot to foot, clearly uncomfortable. "No, we, um . . . Too long; we were there too long."

"Wait." Stephanie made a show of drawing back, taking in the totality of the house, and then leaning forward. "Is this a David thing?"

Confused, Emma took the bait and asked the question she saw reflected on Brittney's face. "*David* thing?"

"The guy that helps lottery winners find their homes on that one show." Stephanie pulled a face at Emma's continued confusion. "Seriously? You've never watched that show? Are you nuts? He's this super-fun guy, with a completely adorable smile, who—"

Stephanie stopped. Laughed. Led Emma and Brittney's attention back to the house in question. "He must've loved your price point." She scrunched her nose. "Because so, *so* many of these lottery home winners give him this paltry budget to work with and it absolutely kills him. Every single time.

"Makes me laugh, though. My mom, too." Stephanie met and held Emma's gaze for a beat. "You really should watch it, Emma. Makes you wish you could win the lottery just so you could hang out with him for a few days and—"

"I'm so sorry, ladies. But it sounds as if I've got a phone call I need to take." Brittney looked over her shoulder, waved in the general direction of her house, and then shrugged a forced smile at Emma and Stephanie. "So much for getting to know my new neighbors, right?"

"But what about your run?" Stephanie asked.

Another shrug. Another forced smile. "There'll be other times for that." Brittney stepped backward onto her driveway. "Anyway, I better go. It was very nice meeting both of you. Scout, too."

Stephanie bent down, rubbed her head against Scout's. "It was nice meeting you, too, Britt—"

"Save it, Steph." Nudging her chin toward the now-empty driveway, Emma liberated Scout's leash from Stephanie's hand and wrapped it around her own. "I guess she got her run in after all, huh?"

Well, she seemed fairly normal to me," Stephanie said as Emma took her place behind the steering wheel. "A little high maintenance, maybe, but normal."

"Hmmm."

"I feel bad she didn't get her full run in on account of us waylaying her, but I've never really understood the concept of running for the sake of running, anyway. So maybe we did her a favor?"

Emma ran her finger around the steering wheel and then dropped her hand into her lap.

"Hello? Earth to Emma, come in, Emma."

She looked across at the woman in her passenger seat and waited, her mind working. "I'm sorry, what?"

"Did you not hear anything I've said since we got in this car?"

"No, I heard you," Emma murmured. "I think."

Stephanie turned in her seat to address Scout. "Is it just me, boy, or is your momma completely checked out here?"

Scout temporarily pulled his tongue into his mouth, stuck his head between the seats, licked Emma's face, and then continued looking out the back windows.

"I'm pretty sure that was a yes." Stephanie said, repositioning herself in her seat. "So what's with you? Are you upset we didn't get anything just now? Because while that would've been awesome, you need to remember we just started. I mean, the pieces all fall into place quickly on cop shows, but we're not cops, and TV suspects don't usually get whisked away by phone calls, you know?"

"There was no phone call," Emma said, looking back down the sidewalk to the edge of Brittney's driveway she could just barely see from where they were parked. "She made that up—I'd bet the farm on that."

"You have a farm?"

Yanking her attention back into the car, Emma stared at Stephanie. "It's an expression. It means I'm—"

"I know what it means. I was just being a pill. It's my specialty, according to my mother." Turning so her back was flush with the passenger door, Stephanie folded her arms across her chest. "Talk to me. Why do you think there wasn't a phone call?"

"Because she looked back at the house *after* she said she had a call to take. And I didn't hear a phone ringing, did you?"

"No. But I assumed, since she waved up at the house, that her husband must've called out."

"Did you hear him call out?" Emma asked.

"No, but I was talking about David from the lottery house show and—"

"No one called out."

Stephanie cocked her eyebrow. "You sure?"

"One hundred and fifty percent." She followed Stephanie's gaze out the front window and then met it with a raised eyebrow of her own when it returned. "Which begs the question of why, don't you think?"

"Theory?"

Emma blew out a long-held breath. "She wanted out from under your questions about the other house, specifically the vast differences between it and"—she motioned down the street—"this one."

"Maybe she didn't want us to look down on her? Or think our expensive neighborhood was going to hell in a handbasket because she moved in?"

"As if . . ."

"Hey, one of us could win the lottery, too, one day," Stephanie reminded. "And then we really would be walking Scout in our neighborhood."

Emma was shaking her head before Stephanie had even finished her sentence. "No. This was more than that. I'm sure of it. And it's more than just the pretend-phone-call thing."

"Okay . . ." Stephanie accepted the lick that was Scout's way of letting them know he was still there and then rolled her finger for Emma to keep going. "I'm listening."

"First up, did you note the day she said they closed on this place?"

Stephanie, again, looked out the window. "Not particularly. Why?"

"They closed on Thursday." Emma held up her finger. "Quick sidebar. *Cappuccinos?*"

"Look at where we are. It fit."

"Whatever."

"So catch me up on the significance of Thursday."

"Thursday, Stephanie. *Thursday.*" At Stephanie's continued blank stare, Emma dropped her head back against the seat rest. "That's the day after Roger—Brittney's boss and former lover—was found dead. Which, by the way, was just three days ago."

"Oh. Right." Stephanie ran her fingers through her graying hair. "Yeah, I wouldn't have guessed she just lost someone she worked with, let alone someone she'd been involved with."

"Exactly."

"Interesting."

"Isn't it?" Emma nudged Stephanie's eyes back toward Brittney's place. "Next, we've got confirmation that Trevor is still hanging his hat on making it as a musician. Aka, not currently working a job with a paycheck."

"Good point," Stephanie said, nodding. "This whole rags-to-riches thing smells pretty bad, doesn't it?"

"It does indeed."

"So what now?"

It was a good question, and one she was at a loss to answer in that moment. But maybe, with a little time and space, she could . . .

"Buckle up," Emma said, clicking her own seat belt into place. "We've got places to go and people to see. Everything else will fall into place in its time."

Chapter Sixteen

There was something innately calming about the rural roads between Sweet Falls and Cloverton. The wide-open horse pastures, the occasional meadow of wildflowers, the five-mile stretch of pavement canopied by trees, and the occasional trailhead that had her longing to stop and explore was exactly what the doctor ordered, if the decreasing knot of tension in Emma's neck and shoulders was any indication. A glance at the sleeping occupant of her passenger seat told her she wasn't alone.

"Hey . . . Steph? It's time to start waking up," Emma said as they approached the turn for Old Hawley Road. "We're almost there."

Stephanie's eyelashes fluttered open in time with a quick stretch and a yawn. "Already? I thought this place was in Cloverton."

"It is." She glanced at Scout in the rearview mirror as the telltale ping of loose gravel greeted their departure from the main road. Sure enough, Scout crossed to the other side of the back seat, stuck his nose out the window, and wagged his tail in anticipation of what he clearly knew was their destination.

"Wow. That was fast."

She laughed. "Not really. You just slept the whole way."

A second yawn was followed by a sheepish shrug. "Sorry about that."

"Don't be. I needed exactly what this drive gave me." Slowing their pace to accommodate the side road's many ruts and haphazard graveling, Emma made one final turn onto Sunnybrook Lane.

At the mailbox bearing the number 11, she stopped, cut the engine, and allowed herself the same joy responsible for Scout's sudden and enthusiastic squeal-like whimper. "You know where we are, don't you, boy?"

"At least one of us does," Stephanie managed past yet another yawn.

"We're *here*." She pointed Stephanie's attention up the driveway to the grove of sugar maples and the fairytale cabin nestled among them and waited.

She waited through the stunned silence.

She waited through the hushed inhale.

She waited through the mouth gaping.

And she was ready with a knowing smile when Stephanie temporarily abandoned her view of their hosts' home in favor of Emma.

"How could you not tell me about this place?" Stephanie asked. "It's . . . it's . . . I don't even know where to begin."

"I don't, either. And that's why I didn't tell you."

Stephanie led Emma's attention back to the cabin with its shingled walls, flowering window boxes beneath long, dual, six-pane windows, and its arched opening leading to the front door.

"I-I feel like I stepped into a book," Stephanie mused. "Something from my childhood—something warm, and magical, and . . . *welcoming*."

"A perfect description. Now wait until you see the inside."

Stephanie glanced back at Emma. "You mean it's like this inside, too?"

"In more ways than one."

"Meaning?"

"I want you to see for yourself." Emma looked in the rearview mirror and readied her hand on the door handle. "Ready, boy?"

Her answer came via a snap of Scout's head to the right, a high-pitched whimper of pure joy, and a hard tail thump against the back of Stephanie's seat. Leaning forward, Emma gazed back up the driveway to the elderly man caning his way through the now-open front door.

"That's John. He's seventy-three, and—as you can see—utterly beloved by Scout, not to mention me."

"I can see . . ." Stephanie's words traded places with a quiet gasp and, seconds later, a sigh of pure awe. "Who is *that*?"

Emma looked past her elderly friend to the thirty-six-year-old keeping pace just past the older man's shoulder. Roughly six feet, three inches tall, Andy Walden was good-looking. His warm chocolate-brown hair, dimpled cheek, sparkling eyes, and physically fit body told that part of the story. But it was his gentle spirit and kind heart that pushed him into one-of-a-kind status.

"That's Andy. John's son."

"He's . . ." Stephanie stopped. Swallowed. Tried again. "He's *beautiful*."

Emma nibbled back her answering grin lest she give away her true intentions for their visit. "In more ways than one, as you're about to see. So c'mon. Let's go. Before Scout literally breaks through a window opening the size of his nose to see his special friends."

With a quick tug of the door handle, Emma stepped onto the gravel road and waited as Scout pushed his way between the two front seats and bounded out of the car. After yet another *C'mon*, Stephanie joined them for the trek up the driveway.

"I thought that was you, Emma," John said, stepping closer to the edge of the stone step. "And you brought a friend, I see."

"I did."

Scout barked once, twice, and wagged his tail, hard.

"Now, now, Scout. I see you. But a gentleman always addresses the women first. Always." Grinning, John bent forward with the help of his son and patted his thigh with his free hand. "Now come get your pets and your scratches, Scout. And when we're done, I have a little something special for you inside."

Instinctively, Emma stepped forward. "Scout," she cautioned. "Be gentle, okay?" But even as the words left her mouth, she knew they weren't truly necessary. Scout really knew no other way to be, and it was one of the many reasons she loved him. And if he suddenly forgot his manners, Andy was right there, beside his dad, to make sure all was well.

But Scout didn't forget. Instead, despite the speed of his tail, he slowly made his way up the trio of stone steps to his special friend and returned every pat, every scratch with a heartfelt all-paws-on-the-ground lick. And when Andy looked across the top of his father's head to smile at Emma, she was waiting with one of her own.

"Hi, Andy."

"Hey, Emma." With his father steady and in place, Andy made his way down the steps to the driveway, the yellow flecks in his brown eyes seeming to dance in the sunlight as he brushed a kiss across Emma's cheek and extended his hand to an eerily silent Stephanie. "Welcome. I'm Andy Walden."

Stephanie's cheeks tinged pink as her hand disappeared inside Andy's. Yet still, she said nothing.

"This is Stephanie—Stephanie Porter. She's toying with the idea of building a home and I thought maybe you two could talk about that a little, seeing as how you're an architect and all."

It was the truth, of course.

It just wasn't the whole truth.

The rest was up to fate. Fate and maybe the fingers Emma was crossing behind her back.

"What's your vision?" Andy asked as he released Stephanie's hand.

Stephanie looked down at her hand, swallowed. "I-I don't have one. Not really, anyway. I don't know where—*or how*—to even start."

"I have some books inside that we can look at."

"Sure. That would be"—Stephanie's shoulders lifted with an inhale—"that would be great. Thank you."

Holding back a victory grin, Emma stepped aside as Andy led a still pink-cheeked Stephanie up the stairs. At the top, he glanced back over his shoulder at Emma.

"You okay out here with Pop?" he asked.

"Of course."

Andy nodded, pulled open the front door, and followed Stephanie inside, her immediate *oohs* and *aahs* over her surroundings only deepening Emma's smile.

"You wouldn't make a very good poker player, young lady."

Emma looked up at John and her still tail-wagging dog. "Oh? Why do you say that?"

"For starters, your back was to me."

"Meaning?"

"Your fingers were behind your back . . ."

She laughed. "Oops."

"Next, your heels literally came up off the ground when my son took the bait."

"Bait?" she echoed, grinning. "What bait?"

John's laugh mingled with hers as he gave Scout one last

rub and then readied his cane for use. "Nice try. Now, shall we go inside? I picked up a little something special for Scout, and Andy and I made a batch of my mother's famous anisette cookies in preparation for your visit today."

"You had me at *cookies*."

"I had myself at *anisette*." John motioned her up the steps, and when she was in position at his elbow, he led the way to the door as Scout brought up the rear. "We'll settle down in the sunroom so as not to interfere with your . . . *efforts*."

"In the interest of getting to those cookies sooner, I'm just going to bypass the whole denial thing, okay?"

John's laugh ushered them inside. "That's okay by me, young lady."

The sound of murmured voices punctuated by soft laughter had the trio making haste past the kitchen's arched entryway to the living room beyond. Together, they wound their way past the floor-to-ceiling stone fireplace, the built-in shelves filled with books, framed photographs, and memory-laden knickknacks Emma never tired of exploring, and through yet another arched opening.

Here, as in the living room, *cozy* found a rightful home alongside *stunning* in everything from the wall of windows with its mountaintop view, to the glorious sunlight that streamed through them and onto the cushioned settee John was caning his way toward with a speed that defied his limited mobility. Next to the chair and topped with a bow was a bone-shaped treat John retrieved with his free hand.

Turning around, he settled his gaze on Scout even as he directed his words at Emma. "You remember me telling you about the dog my brother and I had growing up, right? And how he was the spitting image of Scout here?"

"His name was Rocket," she said by way of agreement. "He died in the fire along with your parents."

"Rocket was smart. Like Scout. He just seemed to have a sense about people and their needs. With me, he'd be rambunctious. With my mother and father, he'd use his best manners. And just as Scout is gentle with me"—he wiggled his hand atop his cane—"Rocket was the same with my brother. He just . . . *knew*."

Slowly, she made her way over to the chair opposite the settee and sat down. "Did your brother have a disability?"

For a moment, she wasn't sure he'd heard the question, but just as she was getting ready to ask it again, he looked down at the treat. "Everyone said he did."

"You didn't agree?"

He lifted his eyes to Emma, but it was clear he wasn't really seeing her at all. "It didn't matter. I was just a kid, and he was my big brother."

She opened her mouth to speak but closed it as he shook himself back into the room. "Would you listen to me, talking about the past when this handsome fella here is waiting to sink his teeth into this special treat?"

Holding the bone-shaped treat in front of his cane-holding hand, he pulled off the bow and held the dog biscuit out to Scout. "Here you go, boy. Let's see if you love this as much as ol' Rocket used to."

Scout took the treat between his teeth, wagged his tail in thanks, and then carried it over to the window while John settled onto his settee. Seconds turned to minutes while they watched Scout slowly, yet surely, devour the treat and then lick the surrounding area with continued gusto.

"It appears Rocket was a very good judge of treats," Emma said, shifting her attention back to John in time to find the elderly man rushing to wipe his eyes with the back of his hand. Before she could inquire or even weigh the decision *to* inquire, he liberated a plate of cookies from the end table to his right and held it in her direction, his smile returning. "If these aren't the best cookies you've ever had, I'll eat my hat."

"You're not wearing a hat."

"I've got one hanging on the bedpost in my room."

She leaned forward and helped herself to a cookie. "I've had some mighty good cookies in my life . . ."

"You haven't had my mother's anisette cookies."

"You sound mighty sure of yourself," she teased him.

"That's because *I've* had them."

Lifting the cookie in a mock toast, she grinned, nodded, and took a—

"Whoa." She looked down at the now-bitten cookie and then closed her eyes in full-on taste-bud euphoria. "What *are* these? And why am I just now having one?"

"I only make them once a year. On my mother's birthday—which was yesterday."

She took another bite, and another, and another until her empty hand sagged her back against her chair. "Wow. Just . . . wow."

John held the plate out again, his smile widening over the renewal of hers. "I was hoping they'd help ease your worry a little."

"My *worry*?" she asked, looking up from her second cookie.

Returning the plate to the table, he nestled back against his own chair and tented his fingers beneath his chin. "I heard it in your voice last night when you called. You're worried about something."

Oh, how she wanted to argue, to tell him everything was fine, but she couldn't. And while being there, with him, had enabled her to push reality into the background for a little while, the truth in his words and the knowing look in his eyes brought it to the forefront once again.

"I'm a good listener, Emma."

"I know you are," she said, looking down at the cookie.

"Then let me listen. At worst, it gives you a chance to vent. At best, I'm able to offer you a counterpoint or maybe even a little wisdom earned over seventy-plus years."

And so she told him. About Kim. About Roger. About

her hand in Kim's arrest. About the tenuous truce between her and Jack. About her promise to Kim. And about her fear of not being able to live up to that promise. When she was done, she dropped her head into her hands and groaned.

"Sounds like your new friend is in a heckuva pickle."

"A pickle of my making," Emma murmured. "A pickle I want to get her out of, but I'm not sure how . . . or even if I can."

"You can."

Emma peeked at John across her fingertips. "You sound so sure."

"Because I am." John snapped for Scout, and when the dog happily obliged, he patted him up and onto the settee. "You've shown me those before-and-after pictures of your yard. You figured *that* out."

"With the help of my dear friend Alfred, God rest his soul."

"Did Alfred plant all of that stuff?"

"He had some of the same stuff in his yard, too. Sure."

John stilled his hand midway down Scout's exposed side and shook his head at Emma. "No, I mean, did he do the actual planting in your yard?"

"No. No, of course not."

"Did he water and nourish your plants?"

"No."

"So you may have taken his ideas and suggestions, but you're the one who actually implemented them."

"Right."

"And it all worked beautifully from the start?" John asked, transitioning his pets into the kind of perfectly positioned scratching that made Scout's eyes practically roll back in his head. "No hiccups?"

Emma lowered her hands back to her lap and laughed. "Uh, no. I rebought more than a few plants before I figured out the right location and the right techniques."

"So a lot of trial and error . . ."

"*A lot*, a lot. And, a few times, I tried something completely different and found that it worked better for my yard."

"Then do the same here. With your quest. Make a plan, work through it, and don't be afraid to abandon one idea—or one way of doing things—in favor of another if it makes more sense." John returned his hand to the spot between Scout's ears and slowly rubbed in a circle. "Like your yard, it'll fall into place."

"But this is serious stuff, John," she protested. "Kim's freedom and the ability to finally move on with her life are so much more important than how my yard looks."

"I'm not saying it's not. I'm just saying you can do whatever you put your mind to. Including clearing this woman's name."

She sat with his words for a moment and then took another bite of her cookie. "But I'm not an investigator."

"And you weren't a gardener, either."

"Touché."

He smiled down at his sleeping seatmate. "One last question. Did you get your whole yard to what it is now all at one time?"

"Good heavens, no. My wallet can't afford that." She took another bite. "No, it's one small section at a time. Which is why you've only seen pictures of the front and one side. I've not even started the north or back side of my house."

"So a little at a time . . ."

"As funds allow."

"So employ the same technique with helping your friend."

She paused the remaining cookie just shy of her lips. "It's taken me nearly two years to get the little bit I've gotten done, *done*. Kim's alone in that jail *now*. Her kids need her *now*. She needs to find her way *now*. Not two years from now."

"You're being too literal, Emma. Just focus on one aspect of your investigation at a time. Learn everything you can about this young female employee Roger was involved with. Her husband, too. See where that leads. If it leads somewhere else, let *that* be your focus for a while.

"It's like I've told Andy since he was no bigger than my knee: one step at a time gets you to the same place."

It was good advice. The key was embracing it well enough to actually live it. "I'm a doer. I don't like to fail."

"I know you are, and I know you don't. So don't fail."

She let loose a low, whistling sigh. "No pressure there."

"It's not meant to be, Emma. I just want you to believe in yourself the way I do. To attack this problem like you would a plant that isn't growing, or a lull in your business, or whatever it is you're trying to do out there with my son and your friend."

Her face flushed with the truth of his words. "Andy is great—*special*. Stephanie is, too."

"You can do this, Emma."

"You say that with such certainty, yet we haven't even known each other for two whole months yet," she protested.

"We spent a lot of time together when Andy hired you to look in on me. Far more time than you put on your invoice, that's for certain."

"I liked coming here. I liked spending time with you."

"And I treasured every minute you did." He settled his hand on Scout's side and mingled his gaze with Emma's. "You're a special one, Emma Westlake. A smart one, too. You'll figure this out."

They sat in silence for a few moments as she digested his words, a wry smile finding its way across her lips. "If you'd told me six months ago that I'd be playing detective for the second time in as many months, I'd have thought you were nuts. Yet now, here I am . . . playing the reluctant sleuth once again."

"Maybe when you're done with this one, you'll be a little less reluctant the third time."

Scout lifted his head at her laugh. "*Third* time? Yeah,

no. I'm hanging up my magnifying glass just as soon as this stuff with Kim is over."

Something that looked a lot like disappointment skittered across the elderly man's face, only to disappear alongside a labored shrug.

"Wait," she said, studying him closely. "What was that expression just now?"

John looked down at Scout. "No expression. Just remembering as I always do around their birthdays. But I get through it."

"I wish you could find out what happened to your brother after your parents passed . . . where he went . . . what became of him . . ."

"You and me both, Emma. But Andy has tried. Many times. Clearly, he got lost in the system."

"But how?"

"People care more about people with special needs these days than they did back then. And I was too young to ask the right questions at the time. Sadly."

She looked down at her cookie and then back up at her elderly friend. "Maybe I could try. I'm pretty good with the computer."

"But that would mean another sleuthing job. And you said there wouldn't be a third time."

"I'd be willing to make an exception for you," she said, smiling.

"One step at a time, Emma. One step at a time . . ."

Chapter Seventeen

There was no sign of Sleepy Stephanie as they made their way back to Sweet Falls. Instead, the silence that had been Emma's on the way to Andy and John's just two hours earlier bowed to nonstop chatter from the passenger seat.

The horse pastures they passed were not only noticed but used as a springboard for a childhood story involving a horse and Stephanie's mother running for the hills.

The meadow of wildflowers they passed were *oohed* and *aahed* over in a way Stephanie never *oohed* and *aahed* over anything.

The five-mile stretch of road canopied by magnolia trees tickled another memory of Stephanie's childhood, this one involving Stephanie, a pair of scissors, and an irate neighbor.

No matter what story Stephanie shared, though, she always found her way back to the same single word: Andy.

"Have you seen Andy's photo album? The one with pictures of some of the homes and businesses he's designed?"

Stephanie asked without pausing for an answer. "He's so incredibly talented! And that house he and John designed together for themselves? I don't know how he keeps from pinching himself on a daily basis just to be sure it's all real."

"It's pretty amazing," Emma agreed.

"And that view? Those woods? That utter peace and quiet? What I wouldn't give to be able to live in a place like that." Sighing, Stephanie looked out the passenger-side window. "Such a nice, *nice* guy.

"Oh, and the way he talks about his dad? He so clearly idolizes that man."

"John is pretty incredible, no doubt."

"And Andy not only asked about my job, but he listened, too. I mean he really, *really* listened, Emma." Stephanie's smile was audible. "He told me how his life had been pretty much all work until his mom died. And when she did, he decided to strike out on his own—work-wise—so he and his dad could move here, to land that had been in his mother's family for generations."

She knew Stephanie was still talking, even picked out occasional words that let her know her attempt at playing matchmaker may have actually been somewhat successful, but try as she did to focus, she couldn't keep her thoughts from finding their way back to her own conversation with John.

No, she wasn't a detective.

No, she didn't have a fascination with TV crime shows the way Stephanie did.

No, she didn't read paperback mysteries out of some desire to be an armchair sleuth, as Dottie did. She read them for entertainment, period.

But she knew right from wrong, and she was smart. Even Dottie, who was hard-pressed to compliment Emma about anything, often pointed to Emma's resourcefulness when it came to figuring—

"Emma?"

Startled back into the moment, she shifted her attention back onto Stephanie. "Huh?"

"Have you heard *anything* I've said the past few minutes?"

"Of course. Andy's land . . . been in his family for generations . . ."

Stephanie pulled a face. "The song? The deer? The zing I felt when he helped me over that fallen log? What about that stuff?"

"*Zing?*" Emma echoed. "What zing?"

Another sigh—this one of the irritation variety—accompanied Stephanie's glance at Scout in the back seat. "You were listening to me, right, Scout?"

Scout temporarily left his post beside the rear passenger-side window to lick Stephanie's face, wag his tail, and meet Emma's eyes in the rearview mirror.

"What gives, Emma?" Stephanie asked. "Where were you just now?"

"I think I need to talk to Kim again. See if she'd be okay with me reaching out to her kids. I mean, maybe they know something about their father's relationship with Brittney that Kim didn't." Emma slowed their speed as they approached Sweet Falls' city limits and, soon, the area surrounding Camden Park. "I'm also curious as to where Roger was living at the time of his death. Did he go straight to the condo he was found in after leaving Kim? Did Brittney live there with him at some point?"

"Well, would you look at you . . . thinking about our case all on your own . . . Dottie would be so proud."

"I think I was just overwhelmed by it all at first, you know?"

"And now?" Stephanie prodded.

"Let's just say that ability you mentioned earlier—the one Andy has—that makes you really think . . . and see things in a different way . . ." She returned Stephanie's answering smile with one of her own. "Let's just say he got that from his pop."

Resting her head against the seat back, Stephanie drew in a breath, held it for a beat or two, and then let it out along with a barely restrained squeal. "He told me that he hoped I come with you the next time you visit."

"Ooohhh. That sounds—"

"Watch out for that guy," Stephanie said, pointing Emma's full attention back to the road and the lone figure exiting the park entrance on foot. "And, side note, what on earth is he *wearing*?"

Slowing still further, she took in the tall, lanky man . . . the long-sleeved sweater in June . . . the plaid knickers . . . the navy socks . . . the—

"Look, Scout! Look who it is!" The words were barely out of her mouth when Scout's head lurched forward across the center console, his tail thumped against the back seat, and the squeal of joy that followed echoed throughout the cabin.

"Wait." Stephanie looked from the spectacle that was Big Max to Emma and Scout and back again. "Wait. You're telling me you actually *know* that guy?"

"Know him and love him, yes." Emma pulled onto the side of the road, shifted the car into park, and, after checking her side-view mirror, looked back at Scout. "Stay in here with Stephanie, okay? And make room for Big Max."

"Big Max?" Stephanie echoed. "That's Big Max—your client?"

"It is."

"And we're giving him a ride?" Stephanie asked.

"If he'll take one, yes."

"But—"

Wrapping her fingers around her door handle, she met and held Stephanie's eyes. "Prepare to fall in love, my friend."

"*In love?*" Stephanie echoed as, once again, her focus strayed back to the road and the man now turning to look at them.

"*Totally* in love. You'll see." Quickly, she stepped out of the car and hurried along the edge of the road. "Big Max! Big Max!"

At the sound of his name, Maxwell Grayben broke out in a grin that lifted his bushy white eyebrows nearly to the lid of his cap. "Hi, Emma!"

She closed the gap between them to give her friend a hug and then pointed back at the car. "Can I give you a lift to wherever you're going?"

"Is Scout in there?"

"He sure is. And so is my friend, Stephanie."

Big Max looked down at his outfit and back up at Emma. "It's a beautiful day for a little golf."

"It sure is," she said, hooking her thumb toward the park entrance. "I didn't realize there was a course in there."

"There isn't."

She reached out, squeezed his hand. "It's good to see you, Big Max."

"I thought you were the cookie lady." Big Max's brown eyes led hers to the empty road ahead. "But it's not Wednesday, is it?"

"Nope, it's Sunday."

"That means I'll see her in three more days."

"Big Max, I don't think . . ." She took in his sweet smile, his proud posture, and let the rest of her words go. Wednesday was, in fact, still three days away. With any luck, maybe Kim would be back home and making cookies by then. "C'mon. There's a spot in the back seat for you, and it's right next to Scout."

Together, they made their way back to the car, Scout's renewed yelps of excitement at the sight of his friend impossible to miss. "See? Scout is excited to see you."

Big Max stopped, patted the pockets of his knickers, and slumped. "I didn't bring him any of his special treats."

"That's okay. Scout had a treat at a friend's house just a little while ago, and he really needs to rest his tummy."

"I will have them next time."

"I know you will." She opened the back door, motioned for Scout and his overzealous tail to move into the spot behind her seat, and helped her friend into the car. When he was settled, she ran around to her door and settled herself behind the steering wheel. "Stephanie Porter, meet Big Max. Big Max, meet Stephanie."

Shifting around in her seat, Stephanie extended her hand to Big Max. "Hi, Big Max."

Big Max's cheeks tinged red as he took her hand, held it, and then looked across at Emma. "Your friend sure is a real looker, Emma."

"I agree."

"Wait. *Friend*?" Stephanie echoed, her own face pinking. "He's talking about . . . *me*?"

"Last I checked, you're the only other person in the car," Emma said, grinning.

Clearly dumbfounded, Stephanie returned her hand to her lap. "Wow. Okay. Thank you, Big Max."

"Today is a beautiful day for golf."

"I see that," Stephanie said as, once again, she inventoried his ensemble. "Where did you play?"

"I didn't. It's just a beautiful day for it."

Emma met Stephanie's silent question with a subtle shake of her head and then returned her attention to the rearview mirror and the lovefest going on in the back seat between her passenger and Scout.

"I'm sorry I don't have a treat for you today, Scout," Big Max said, resting his head against Scout's. "But I will next time."

Scout wagged his tail, licked Big Max's cheek, and wagged some more.

"As you can see, Big Max, seeing you is treat enough. Isn't it, boy?"

Scout wagged his tail harder.

"So?" Emma shifted the car into drive, checked her side-view mirror, and, when it was clear, pulled back onto the road. "Should I drop you off at home? Or are you going into town?"

"I'd like to go to the center."

"The senior center?" she asked.

"Yes."

"But it's Sunday, Big Max. Isn't it closed?"

He nodded in the rearview mirror. "I need to get my ukulele."

"I'm pretty sure you won't be able to get inside."

"I left it in back. Under the bush with the fluffy white flowers."

She felt Stephanie's questioning eyes but didn't turn to meet them. Instead, she stopped at the four-way stop and turned left toward the senior center. "Okay, that's fine. You can get it, and then I'll bring you home."

"I ain't going home."

"Oh?"

"I'm going to play some ukulele music for Ethel."

"That's your friend from the center?" Emma asked. "The one you say is nice but not much of a looker, right?"

Stephanie laughed.

"Maybe my music will make Ethel smile again." Big Max pressed his face to his window and took in the passing houses and businesses.

"Is Ethel okay?"

"She didn't smile at bingo on Thursday."

"I see." Emma slowed as they approached the brick building that was the Sweet Falls Senior Center. "So can I drop you off there? After you get your ukulele, of course?"

"No, thank you."

"Are you sure?"

"It's a beautiful day for golf."

"You're right. It is." Emma pulled into a parking spot in front of the center and shifted the car into park. "So where do you walk to on Mondays again? Because maybe Scout and I could meet you for a little while."

"I walk to the town square on Mondays."

"That's right," she said, meeting his gaze in the mirror. "You like to wave at the little ones on the swing sets, right?"

"I miss her," Big Max said, his voice void of its usual pep.

"Who? Ethel?"

"No. The cookie lady." Big Max grabbed hold of the door handle but stopped short of actually opening it. "She said she was going to make them for me this week. But she can't make them if she don't ever come home again."

"She'll be able to come home again soon, Big Max. I'm going to see to that." She tilted her chin toward the woman sitting next to her. "Actually, *Stephanie* and I are going to see to that, isn't that right, Stephanie?"

Startled back into a conversation she was clearly checking in and out of, Stephanie narrowed her eyes on Emma. "Isn't what right?"

"You're going to bring the cookie lady back home." Big Max opened the car door and then leaned forward between the seats for a better view of Stephanie. "She's my friend, you know. Like Emma and Scout. And, now, like you, too."

Big Max pointed their collective attention to the small covered plate visible through the opening in Emma's tote bag. "Maybe, if she made *you* the special cookies, she's okay."

"Those?" Shaking her head, Emma hoisted the bag onto the center console and liberated the plate of cookies from its resting place atop her wallet and phone. "Actually, I got these from a different friend just a little while ago, but you can have them if you'd like."

"You have a cookie lady, too, Emma?" Big Max asked.

"Nope. These were made by a cookie *man* and his son."

Big Max took the plate from her hand and held his nose to the plastic covering. "Mmmm. Perfect-o."

"*Perfect-o*, eh?" she said, trading a quick grin with Stephanie. "Just wait 'til you actually *try them*, Big Max. They're . . . they're . . ."

"*Perfect-o*?" Stephanie supplied.

Emma laughed. "Yeah . . . that . . ."

Satisfied, Big Max tucked the plate under his arm, stepped onto the sidewalk, and pushed the door closed, prompting Emma to roll down Stephanie's window. "Hey, Big Max . . . It was good to see you."

With little more than a nod and a smile, Maxwell Grayben turned and headed toward the brick walkway that meandered around the back of the senior center. When they could no longer see him, Stephanie turned back to Emma as she shifted into drive and steered them away from the curb.

"He's adorable."

"Right?" Emma piloted them toward the stop sign at the end of the block. "I told you that you'd love him."

"Who's this cookie lady he's so enamored with?"

"Kim."

Stephanie's eyebrow lifted, first with surprise and then intrigue. "You mean, *jailhouse* Kim?"

"I prefer to call her Kim or Kim Felder, but yes, that Kim." Emma turned at the next road. "Apparently, she stops and gives Big Max a homemade cookie every Wednesday morning."

Stephanie turned her attention onto the passing landscape for a block, maybe two, and then looked back at Emma. "So what kind of things does Big Max hire you for?"

"I was his plus-one for a dance at the senior center, that garden club party I went to a month or so ago, and a few bingo games here and there."

"You have to have a plus-one for stuff when you're that age, too?" Stephanie dropped her head back against the seat rest and groaned. "Ugh. I thought there'd be light at the end of the tunnel at some point before I die, you know?"

"First, Big Max hires me to be his plus-one for that stuff because he's using me as bait."

"Bait?"

"He thinks it'll impress the ladies and make them more apt to see him as a good catch."

Stephanie laughed. "Seriously?"

"Yep. And as for the rest of what you said? About the light at the end of the tunnel? Andy gave you his number, yes?"

At the mention of Andy's name, Stephanie's eyes took on a dreamy glint. "He did. So I can ask him house stuff if I want."

"Right. So you can ask house stuff . . ."

Stephanie sat up tall, pinning Emma with a stare. "What are you saying?"

"I'm not saying anything. Just repeating what *you* said."

At the next stop sign, Emma turned left and then right at the end of the next block, her thoughts taking her back to a different neighborhood, a different labyrinth of streets. "Hey, can I ask you something?"

"Shoot."

"My idea about maybe reaching out to Kim's daughter? Would that be insensitive?"

"Why would that be insensitive?"

"Because her father just died?"

"Right." Stephanie grew silent for a moment as she considered Emma's question. "I don't know, Emma. It's been what? Four days? Maybe give it a little more time. Let's just focus on Brittney for now."

"I know you're right. It's just . . ." She pulled into Stephanie's driveway. "I feel like I need to get a better handle on Roger—who he was, what made him tick, how the affair with Brittney came to be, and why it ended."

"Can't Kim tell you that stuff?"

"Some, I suppose. But I don't want to keep throwing salt in her wounds, you know? She loved the guy."

Stephanie released her seat belt, angled her cheek for a farewell lick from Scout, and then opened her door. "Look, Emma, I'm the first to admit that I'm not an expert on relationships. I'm forty. I still live with my mother. But I've watched a few of my patients go through hell and back because of a relationship gone wrong, and their emotions are all over the place. Sometimes they're sad, sometimes they're out of it, sometimes they're angry, and sometimes they're all of the above. It's human nature. Emotions run the gamut about all sorts of things. And each person's reaction to the same basic circumstance can vary just as much."

"Why are you telling me all this?" Emma asked.

"Kim was rejected by her husband, humiliated in front of their friends and family."

"Okay . . ."

"I want to believe she's innocent, especially since you're so sure she is. But I've got to admit, I'm struggling with the whole scarf thing."

"Don't. There's got to be a reasonable explanation."

"I'm trying, Emma. I really am. But sometimes I can't help but wonder, you know?"

"No. I don't. You haven't met her," Emma protested. "*I* have."

"Five days ago, maybe."

She opened her mouth to argue but closed it as the truth in her friend's words took her back to the park and the woman who'd sat down beside her on the bench.

The joyless eyes . . .

The restless hands . . .

The voice that rasped more times than not . . .

And the transforming smile that had accompanied talk of murdering Roger . . .

Emma squeezed her eyes closed. Was Stephanie right?

Was she tying her insides into knots for no reason? Was Kim playing her like a—

No. No. No.

Parting her lashes, she turned to find Stephanie watching her through the open passenger-side window. Waiting, she suspected, for some sort of nod or verbal concession. But she couldn't. Wouldn't.

Kim was innocent. She could feel it in her bones. And, come hell or high water, she was going to prove it.

Chapter Eighteen

Emma was more than ready for the day to be over when she finally slipped between the sheets she'd intended to launder but hadn't. Normally, she despised having unchecked items on her daily to-do lists, but, in that moment, she was simply too tired to care.

Rolling onto her left side, she slid her hand under the pillow and nestled her face in its softness while Scout turned and turned in pursuit of his own sleepy-time sweet spot on the bottom half of the bed. "It was a busy one, wasn't it, boy?" she said between yawns. "Filled with all sorts of friends. Andy and John . . . Big Max . . . Stephanie . . ."

She yawned again. "And a big thinking-walk this evening."

Scout stretched his face across his front paws and looked at her with such love and trust that she couldn't help but invite him closer—an invitation he accepted with two quick skootches. "That's better." She ran a gentle hand across Scout's front paws and reveled in the feel of his fur. "You really are the best listener around, you know that?"

She kissed her finger, touched it to Scout's nose, and

then tucked her sheet up around her shoulder. "Let's get some sleep, okay? Five a.m. will be here before we—"

With a quick shove of her sheet, Emma sat up, felt her hand across the top of her nightstand, and closed it around her phone as Scout's head popped back up. "No, no, it's still sleep-time. I forgot to set my alarm and . . ."

The rest of her sentence faded from her lips at the sight of the voicemail indicator on the now-illuminated screen. She pressed her way into the menu, noted Stephanie's name and the time stamp beside it, and held the phone to her ear.

"I'm sorry for calling so late, Emma. I'm guessing you're probably asleep and, therefore, won't see this until morning, which makes me feel even worse than I already do. But Mr. Evil wants me in his office before the start of our workday. Not sure what that's about, but I expect nothing less from him these days. Of course, I'd love to tell him to shove it, but that would probably be bad form seeing as how I'm still a good twenty years away from being financially able to retire. So, once again, I won't be able to meet you at the gym in the morning. Wednesday should be fine—no, *will* be fine. But tomorrow is out. I'll still pay you, as usual, but . . ." Stephanie grew silent for a moment but picked up again before the phone could decide she was done. "I hope you're not mad at me for what I said about Kim earlier. It's just that . . . well, I'm worried about you and the stress you're putting on yourself trying to prove something that might not be the case."

Another beat of silence was followed, seconds later, by an audible inhale and an even louder exhale. "Anyway, thanks for today. Everything we do together is fun. Good night, Emma. If we don't talk sooner, I'll see you at our usual meeting spot outside the gym at five thirty Wednesday morning. And I *will* be there."

"I'll have to see it to believe it," Emma murmured as she returned the still glowing phone to the nightstand. "But at least she told us before I set the alarm, right, boy?"

She wiggled herself back under the sheets, turned onto her side, and, once again, sandwiched the corner of the pillow between her hand and her cheek. "Okay, Scout, let's get some—"

This time, the glow of the incoming call guided her fingers straight to her phone, while a check of the screen and the unknown local number it revealed had her fumbling for her bedside lamp.

"Hello?"

"Emma, it's Kim."

She tightened her grip on the phone. "Are—are you okay?"

"I'm still in jail, if that's what you're asking. Still waiting to see the judge. But the deputy you know? The one who came to the house and arrested me? He's letting me make this call, even though he probably shouldn't."

"Okay, I'm listening."

"I was wondering if you could maybe go by the house for me and water my plants? And bring in my mail, too? I'll either pay you myself for your time when I get home, or, if I'm unable to, I'll have Reece write you a check for me. I'd ask her or one of the kids to do this stuff, but considering everything going on right now, I just can't."

"Of course I can. But how will I get in?"

"Go in through the garage. The code for the keypad is 0514. Then, once you're inside, you'll have sixty seconds to disarm the security system, which is denoted by beeping. When the beeps start coming together really quickly, you're down to fifteen seconds. The code for that is 1028. I have plants in the living room and in the kitchen. The watering can I use is under the sink."

"Hold on, I'm writing those codes down." Emma yanked open her nightstand drawer, pulled out a pad of paper and a pen, and jotted the two numbers down. "And the mail? Is there someplace special you'd like me to put that?"

"On the desk in the kitchen is fine. But if you see something that is for the company, maybe you could run it over to Reece so she doesn't have to come looking for it? I'd just feel better knowing she's got an eye on everything right now. For the kids' sake."

"I'll go over after breakfast in the morning," Emma said, setting the paper and pen on the nightstand. "Once I've walked Scout."

"You can bring Scout. His box of treats is on the top shelf in the pantry. Right-hand side. Next to the cereal."

She leaned back against the headboard and watched, with amusement, as Scout scooted closer. "*His* box of treats?"

"I picked them up on the way home from the park the day we met. I figured I'd be seeing the two of you a lot and so it just made sense to have treats on hand for him."

"Are you serious?"

"I had them the other day when you came by. But you said he was fine."

"I didn't know you got something especially for him!"

Kim shrugged. "It just made sense."

"Thank you for that. Scout will be thrilled." She ran her hand down Scout's head and felt the answering thump of his tail against the mattress. "Won't you, boy?"

"Thank you, Emma. For doing all this. I really appreciate it."

"You're very welcome," she said, her smile fading. "It's the least I can do, considering I'm the reason you're there in the first place."

"I wish you'd stop saying that."

"Why? It's true."

The answering silence in her ear didn't last long. "He's a nice guy, by the way."

"Who?"

"Your deputy friend," Kim said, her voice quieting. "Anyway, I should go. Don't want to take advantage of a kindness."

"You deserve kindness, Kim. Remember that."

"I'll try. Good night, Emma."

"Good night, Kim." Slowly, she lowered the phone to her lap, her labored exhale prompting Scout to pick his head up off his paws with sleepy curiosity. "No, it's still sleepy time, boy."

He waited a moment, shifted his gaze between Emma and the bedroom door, and then slowly lowered his head to the sheets with a faint yet happy whimper. Casting her attention back to her phone, she noted the time and, after some silent deliberation, scrolled her way down her contact list to Jack's name.

Pressing the message icon, she began to type, her thumbs fairly flying across the tiny keypad.

About that phone call just now . . . It was—

She stopped, deleted the two last words, and continued typing.

I know that wasn't something you had to—or probably even should've—done. But it clearly meant a lot to her.

She stopped again, deleted the period, replaced it with a comma, and then, after a muted groan lest she disturb Scout, deleted the comma and inserted the period again.

It meant a lot to me, too. Thank you.

Pausing her thumbs above the keypad, she reread the text, considered deleting it completely, and then hit Send.

Less than a minute later, the phone vibrated with his response.

My pleasure. She's a very thoughtful person.

She typed again.

I agree. Anyway, have a safe rest of your shift, Jack. Good night.

Before she could hit send, he sent another.

Any chance you're free for dinner on Tuesday? Maybe a raincheck on that picnic I blew?

Smiling, she deleted her way through her unsent response and began again.

I'd love that, Jack.

His response came quickly.

I would, too. We'll talk between now and then to finalize. In the meantime, I should probably get back to work and let you get your sleep. Good night, Emma.

She pulled the phone to her chest and then quickly lowered it in favor of one final text.

Good night, Jack. Have a safe rest of your shift.

Chapter Nineteen

Emma punched the four-digit code into the keypad on the laundry room wall and listened as the rapid beeping Kim had warned her about came to an abrupt end. Sighing, she collapsed against the closed door and looked down at Scout.

"That was a close one, huh?"

Pulling his tongue into his mouth just long enough to swallow, Scout looked from Emma to the kitchen and back again, his anticipation over being somewhere he remembered seemingly muted by the fact something was different.

"Yup, feels weird to me, too." She parted company with the door, and together they wandered into the kitchen, stopping just inside the doorway.

The walls were still the same pale yellow . . .

The cabinets were still blue . . .

On the countertop next to the six-burner stove stood the same baking canisters boasting the same duck wearing the same chef's hat and holding the same rolling pin in his webbed hands . . .

The refrigerator still held the same duck magnet . . .

The lower cabinets had the same duck-stamped knobs . . .

The table still hosted the same duck-themed placemats . . .

And—

Emma looked back at the center island and the glass-topped cake case that adorned it, and felt her whole being slump in response. Visually, Kim's home was as she remembered it, right down to Scout's presence at her side. Yet without Kim being there to greet them, to talk to them, to fuss over them, it was as if everything was different.

"I hate this," she murmured.

A glance at Scout's subdued tail had her drawing in a breath, noting the various plants she could see from where she stood, and making haste toward the sink's cabinet and the watering can Kim had mentioned. When the can had been filled, she set about the task of fulfilling Kim's request. Plant by plant, she made her way through the kitchen while Scout looked out at the backyard from his spot by the bay window.

When she'd watered every one she could find, she headed for the open doorway on the far side of the room. She knew, from what Kim had said, that the living room hosted plants in need of some water, but as it was a room she hadn't been in before, it took a moment to locate them.

The first one she spotted was on the mantel, next to a series of framed photographs she couldn't help but stop and study.

There was college-age Kim sitting on a set of steps, looking up at the young man on the next step with such joy Emma couldn't help but smile, too. A textbook lay open on Kim's lap, a notebook atop the young man's. But the only thing either of them clearly saw was each other.

There was another of an early twenties Kim, clad in a wedding dress, finger-feeding cake to the young man from the first picture. This time, though, instead of a rugby shirt, the young man wore a suit and tie, his mouth closing around the cake, mid-laugh.

There was a slightly older Kim, cradling her newborn son in her hospital bed with the same young man from the wedding looking at both of them with utter awe.

Then there was another baby-in-the-hospital picture, but Kim was holding an infant daughter while the now-knocking-at-thirty male balanced a toddler on his arm.

The next framed picture highlighted a vacation on the beach for the family of four. Like the pictures before it, Kim and her husband wore the kind of joy and happiness that made people stop and stare. And the kids—probably six and eight at the time—clearly embraced their parents' positivity.

Next came the graduation pictures: one each for the son's high school and college ceremonies, and one each for the daughter's.

Stepping back, Emma took in the totality of the visual timeline, her gaze moving down the mantel one face at a time.

Kim . . .

Roger . . .

Caleb . . .

And Natalie . . .

In the time span of nine photographs, she could see the aging process. For the kids, it was everything—their limbs, their height, their facial structure. For Kim and Roger, though, it was more about softening and maturing and, in Roger's case, a gradual receding of his hairline. Yet despite all the outward changes from one frame to the next, one thing stayed the same: Kim and Roger looked as happy and in love with one another in the ninth picture as they had in the first.

"I don't get it," she murmured. "I just don't get it."

She scanned the pictures one more time and then made herself move on to the window and the potted tree laced with a string of miniature bulbs. Setting the watering can on the windowsill, she quickly located the plug, inserted it into the outlet, and stepped back as two dozen tiny white lights twinkled to life. To the right of the tree and the window it flanked stood a ladder shelf. The top shelf held a lavender-colored candle. The second shelf contained a smattering of seashells and sand dollars arranged around a sprinkling of sand. The third, fourth, and fifth shelves held an assortment of family games, their misshapen boxes a clear nod to the hours of fun spent playing them.

The click of Scout's nails as he abandoned his squirrel-watching post cut short Emma's self-guided tour of Kim's life and sent her scurrying back to the twinkling tree and the watering can she'd left behind. With quick fingers, she unplugged the lights, watered the tree, and took one last look around the room. No more plants, no more flowers.

"Watering is done." She lowered the can to her side, patted Scout's head with her free hand, and motioned him to follow her back into the kitchen. "Now all we have left is to sort the mail, see if we need to drop any of it off with Reece, and then get you home and fed."

Scout's tail thumped against the kitchen cabinet as he looked up at Emma.

"I know, boy. But we've got to sort first." She made her way toward the kitchen desk and the pile of mail she'd deposited onto it upon their arrival, but stopped as Scout let off his best high-pitched squeal. "This isn't our house, Scout. I can't just go rooting through cabinets looking for . . . Wait!"

She captured Scout's face between her hands and planted a kiss on the center of his nose. "Ooooh, wait right here. This is your lucky day, sweet boy. Just you wait and see."

With quick steps, Emma crossed to the pantry, Kim's instructions guiding her way. Top shelf . . . right-hand side . . . next to the—

Her fingers were barely around the familiar red box when Scout's tail started knocking soup cans and loose cookie sleeves off the bottom shelf and onto the floor. "Whoa . . .

whoa . . . I know, Scout. I know. But really? The tail?" She waved the box at the mounting carnage. "Could you *not* just this once?"

His answer came via a can of tomato soup she quickly swooped down and returned to its proper shelf. When everything was as it should be, she opened the box, handed him a treat, and pocketed a second one for later while he was too busy to notice. "You'll get a real meal when we get home."

With Scout satisfied, she turned her attention to Kim's mail. A few ads . . . what looked to be a greeting card from someone in New York . . . a letter from a children's charity addressed to—

"Okay, *this* needs to go to Reece." She set the envelope off to the side and continued sifting through the mail, adding two more envelopes bearing charity names to the pile before declaring the task done. "Well, Scout, we're done here. Now all we have to do is make one quick stop, hand over these three envelopes, and head home. Sound good?"

The ears that perked at the mention of home quickly turned in the direction of the laundry room and the creak of an opening—

"Hello?" Emma called. "Who's there?"

The only sound she heard, save for the thumping of her own heart, was a low growl from Scout.

"Hello?" she said again, her voice beginning to shake. "Who's there?"

Slowly, quietly, a face peeked around the corner, revealing the same wide-eyed fear she felt coursing through her own body. "What are you doing in my mother's house?"

"Your mother's . . ." Emma slumped back against the desk, relieved. "You must be Natalie. Thank God. I was . . ." She stopped, swallowed, and then held out her hand. "I'm Emma. Emma Westlake. I—"

"The hired friend person."

She lowered her hand down to Scout's back. "Yes."

"What are you doing here? In my mother's house while she . . ." Natalie shook her head, pressed her fisted hand to her mouth.

"Your mom asked me to water her plants and bring in her mail."

Clutching a folder to her chest, Natalie stepped all the way into the kitchen. "Why didn't she ask me?"

"Because of what you're going through," Emma said. "With the loss of your father and her being in . . ." Unsure of what to say, she grew silent.

"With her being in jail," Natalie finished for Emma while simultaneously wiping at eyes that were beginning to grow misty.

"She didn't want to bother you with something so trivial as plants and mail."

Natalie's answering laugh held no sign of humor. "That's mom for you. Always putting us ahead of herself."

"Your mom is a special lady."

"She—she . . . d-didn't . . . h-h-hurt m-m-my dad," Natalie managed past the tears now freely flowing down her round cheeks. "I-I know she didn't."

Scout, sensing his least favorite emotion, trotted over to the mid-twenty-something and licked her forearm.

"Scout and I know it, too," Emma said, closing the gap between them with slow, even steps. "And somehow, someway, I'm going to prove it."

"H-how?"

Emma fought against her answering slump. "I'm not sure, exactly. Finding stuff out? Tracking things down? Whatever it takes. I have friends who want to help, too. I know, between the three of us, we'll get this mess figured out and corrected."

Silence blanketed the room for a few moments as Natalie feverishly worked to juggle the folder in her hand while trying to stem the stream of tears still making their way down her cheeks. "I-I c-can't stop thinking . . . about . . .

how fast things changed, you know? One—one minute my p-parents were h-happy and . . . then it was over and he was different . . . and now he's d-dead . . . and—and they think . . . they think Mom d-did it."

"They're wrong."

Natalie sucked in a breath, steadied her hitching shoulders. "They are."

"You know it, and I know it. And sometime soon, everyone else will know it, too." Emma pointed to the table and backed up a step or two. "Why don't you sit down for a little bit, and I'll get you something to drink while you catch your breath."

Emma followed the young woman's watery gaze to the table and then glanced back at her just in time to catch the slow, hesitant nod. "Come on . . . Scout would love a few more minutes to look out at the squirrels while we talk."

"I don't know what to say."

"Then we'll just sit. Together. Until you're okay."

"Thank you," Natalie whispered. "I-I'd like that."

When they were both settled, with glasses of ice water in front of them, Emma mustered the smile she knew Natalie needed. "I understand that you're the one who put me on your mom's radar. Thank you for that."

"I didn't know she'd actually done anything with the information. I-I figured she just stuffed it in a drawer, never to be looked at again."

"Nope, she emailed, and we met up in the park the very next day."

"Was she receptive to you?"

Emma spread wide her hands. "I'm here, aren't I?"

A faint tug on the left side of Natalie's mouth hinted at a smile. "True."

"We started a list, in fact," Emma said.

Natalie took a sip of water. "What kind of list?"

"A bucket list of sorts—things we could do together that would get her living again."

"I like that idea." Setting her glass back on the table, Natalie leaned forward on the folder. "What kind of things does"—she stopped, sucked in a breath, and released it with a heavy sigh—"*did* she want to do?"

"A baking class. A road trip up to Ohio to order something from an ambulance-turned-food-truck with emergency-themed desserts. And to start a book club with a few other ladies."

Natalie drew back. "Mom wanted to do that kind of stuff?"

"She did. Does. Will. Just as soon as this whole mess is behind her." As soon as the words were out, she knew they sounded callous. "I mean the part about her being the one who killed your dad. Not about him being gone. That's not a mess. It's just awful and sad and"—Emma reached across the table and patted the young woman's hand atop the folder—"I'm so sorry for your loss. I really am."

"Thank you. He made some mistakes, he really did. Big ones. Hurtful ones. But . . ." Natalie trailed off as she pulled her hand from under Emma's. "I don't know. Maybe I was just seeing what I wanted to see. Maybe he really didn't want things to go back to the way they were with Mom."

Emma sat up straight. "You think your father wanted your mom back?"

Natalie's gaze traveled out the window, her thoughts clearly somewhere far beyond the yard she'd played in as a child. "I know he lamented being impulsive and stupid. I heard him say those very words in reference to himself when he stopped by my place last Tuesday evening. I mean, maybe he wanted me to tell him he was fine, to tell him not to say those things about himself, but I didn't. Because he was.

"No one could hold a candle to mom on any level. She was—*is*—the complete package. For everyone else, that is. Not as much for herself, though, for some strange reason— something I didn't notice until just recently."

"And that's why you sent her in my direction, yes?"

Natalie's nod was slow, steady. "Mom was always our biggest champions—mine, Caleb's, and Dad's. So much so, all of her time and effort went into us. Making sure we had fun birthdays, experienced new things, took memory-making vacations, tried new activities, nurtured our friend-ships, soaked up our extended family, and reached for our dreams. She did that for me, she did that for Caleb, and she did that for Dad. I took it for granted, Caleb took it for granted, and Dad? He threw it away like it was meaning-less. Like he didn't already have the greatest woman by his side."

At a loss for what to say, Emma said nothing. Instead, she waited and watched as the young woman wiped a few new tears from her cheeks and then tapped the top of the folder. "I thought maybe something in here might help Mom once she's back home. Because she's blamed herself for his actions long enough. It wasn't her; it was *never* her. It was Dad. And it was a mistake."

"What is that?" Emma asked, looking from Natalie to the folder and back again.

Natalie lowered her own gaze to the folder and shrugged. "Stuff that made him and his company stand out . . . be-cause of Mom. I didn't spend too much time going through it because when I started to, I got really angry at him. And right now it feels really bad to be angry at him. But of the millions and millions of things Mom taught me along the way, the one about things happening for a reason might very well apply here. With *this*."

"I don't understand," Emma said.

"Stuff happens for a reason, you know? Like that theater house office job I was so crushed I didn't get earlier this year, only to end up getting an even better one two months ago. Or like that street I made a wrong turn on and ended up spotting a For Lease sign outside the apartment I'm now living in." Natalie pulled back the folder's cover, ran her hand down the gold-and-purple letterhead topping the stack inside, and then let it drift closed again. "Maybe my dad was *meant* to leave this on my kitchen table when he left that last evening . . . So I could give it to Mom now that he's gone . . . So she can know that he *did* get it. That he did get back to knowing what he should've known all along. Even if it was too late to fix it before . . . before he . . . *died.*"

Again, Emma patted her hand. "Maybe you should leave it right here, on the table. So she can see it when she gets home."

Natalie's lips trembled as she fixed her watery gaze on Emma. "I want her to come home."

"And she will. Sooner, rather than later."

"I'm dreading the wake tomorrow," Natalie rasped. "I don't want to see . . . *her.* I just don't."

"You're talking about Brittney, right?"

"Mom told you."

Emma nodded.

"We all thought she was so nice when she started working for Dad," Natalie said, her voice growing wooden. "I guess because she was on the younger side, I identified with her a little more. I could talk movies and music with her and Trevor in a way I couldn't with other people Mom and Dad would have over for barbecues and other stuff. You could tell Trevor didn't have a whole lot going on, as Mom would say, but Brittney never seemed to notice or care.

"When I'd stop by the office to see Dad, Brittney always talked to me while I was waiting for him to finish up a client call or whatever."

Emma pulled her drinking glass close, looked down at the water she'd barely touched, and forced herself to take a sip. "Did you . . . I don't know . . . notice when things started to, um . . ."

"To change?" Natalie asked. At Emma's slow nod, the young woman shrugged. "I guess. A little. I mean, it seemed like maybe she was back in his office instead of at her own desk more often than not in the weeks leading up to Dad dumping Mom. But the firm was doing really well. They were finding new clients, making more money. And Dad was still doing good things with it."

Wanting Natalie's version of things, Emma leaned forward. "Good things with what?"

"The money. I mean, granted it benefited him, too, when it came to taxes and stuff, but instead of finding ways to hide it, he filtered it into organizations that could use it to make a difference in people's lives." Natalie looked down at the closed folder, ran her fingers across the cover, and squeezed her eyes closed. "Kind of ironic that the suggestion Mom made to help him is the same one that came back and hurt her so much."

Emma was waiting when Natalie's lashes finally parted again. "How so?"

"Dad donated a lot of money to a lot of charities because of Mom. She saw it as a way for him to give back, and for him to stand out to prospective clients. And she was right. The press he got for some of the charitable events he sponsored and groups he donated to put him on the radar of companies and businesses that might not have known about Dad's company otherwise."

"Makes sense," Emma said.

"Mom is smart. And kind to the core. That's why her encouraging Dad to do that instead of buying a bigger house or newer cars made so much sense. It went with everything she'd ever taught us: To whom much is given, much is required, she'd say. And it made sense. It was the right thing to do."

Emma felt Scout's nose on her elbow but kept her attention steady on Natalie. "I imagine it was. So then how, in your opinion, did your mom end up getting hurt by it?"

"It was Dad's donations, and the attention he got for doing it, that seemed to be the thing that brought Dad and Brittney together."

Intrigued, Emma leaned forward even more.

"That's when Brittney started looking at Dad like he walked on water. She laughed the hardest in the room at his jokes . . . She commented on his clothes . . . She gushed about him on the phone to prospective clients . . . Followed him around the room with her eyes and had a ready smile waiting when he noticed . . . That sort of stuff.

"I missed it at first. But even when I started to see it, I thought I was crazy. I mean, it was my dad, you know?" Natalie's laugh dripped with sarcasm. "And Mom? She was always so busy looking in on my brother and me and trying to do stuff for us that she was completely blindsided when he said he was leaving her for his way-too-young-for-him secretary."

"So what happened then? Where did he go?"

"He rented one of those townhouses on the southern edge of town. Furnished it with the kind of furniture you'd equate with someone going through a midlife crisis."

"Did Brittney move in with him?"

Natalie pulled a face. "Surprisingly, no. She didn't want to be—get this—a cliché."

"Because the secretary-boss thing wasn't one already?" Emma retorted, only to hold up her hands in surrender. "I'm sorry. I shouldn't have said that. That was out of line."

"No, it wasn't. It's what anyone would say, hearing this. My dad having been the boss in this equation doesn't change that."

"Still . . ."

"Instead, she—or more likely my dad, *for* her—rented some sort of garage apartment on the opposite side of town."

"And Trevor?" Emma prodded. "How'd he take his wife leaving him for her boss?"

"He didn't come after my dad the way Caleb and I thought he would. In fact, from what Dad said, he took it surprisingly well. Which says something to me."

Feeling her thoughts starting to wander, Emma willed them back to Natalie. "Tell me."

"Tell you what?"

"What it says to you."

Natalie pushed back from the table and stood. "It says she wasn't anyone worth losing sleep over."

Was Kim's daughter right? Was the lack of fight in Trevor over the betrayal of his marriage really a reflection on Brittney? Or—

"I need to get going. I'm supposed to meet my brother at the funeral home to go over a few final details before the wake tomorrow." Natalie looked out at the backyard, shook her head, and then pushed her now-empty chair into place at the table. "It was nice meeting you, Emma. I really hope Mom gets to do those things on that list with you."

Just like that, the young woman's tears were back. "I-I've been so—so short with her lately. So—so dismissive of her. I know it hurt her. I saw it in her eyes. But I . . . I hated seeing her so lost and knowing that I couldn't fix it. Dad was the only one who could and he . . . he didn't get to."

Pushing back her own chair, Emma rose. "We're going to get your mom back home, Natalie. We truly are. I promise you that."

Chapter Twenty

⋘·⋙

I promise you that . . ." Emma glanced up at the rearview mirror and the furry occupant in her back seat. "*I promise you that*? Seriously? Why don't you stop me before I say inane stuff like that?"

Scout's tongue disappeared with a swallow, only to reappear with his usual steady, peaceful pant.

"You could hit me with your tail . . . give me your infamous my-bowl-is-empty look . . . bark . . . anything to get me to shut up before I put my foot in my mouth." She slowed as her turn drew closer, her gaze bouncing between the road, Scout, and the trio of envelopes on her passenger seat. "It could be your way of earning your keep, you know?"

Blowing out a breath, she glanced again at the envelopes and then behind the passenger seat to the manila folder sticking out from beneath her bag. Why she'd taken it rather than leaving it on the table in the wake of Natalie's exit was the part she couldn't wrap her head around. Because, really, the notion of bringing it to Kim was great in theory but completely ludicrous in reality.

"But there you go," she murmured, looking back at the road. "What's better than one dumb move? A *second* dumb move. Always."

Once again, she made eye contact with Scout. "You probably should've held out for someone smarter, sweet boy."

Scout stuck his head between the seats, licked her cheek, and went right back to panting and checking out every yard they passed.

"I love you, too, Scout."

She made the final turn and immediately slowed to a crawl as her attention skipped ahead to the now-familiar white house with its robin's-egg-blue shutters and the FELDER PR sign in the yard. This time, unlike on her previous visit, the front door stood open to the warm June day and the breeze that surely made its way inside via the outer screen.

When they reached the same stretch of curb where they parked the first time, Emma shifted into park and cut the engine. "This will be a quick stop, buddy. Just long enough to drop these envelopes off, be polite, and then we're out of there. I promise."

Slowly, she gathered up the envelopes and stepped out onto the road. "C'mon, boy. Let's go see Reece."

Together, they made their way around the car and up the flagstone walkway to the base of the porch steps. A glance at the front window revealed a still-empty desk chair and a lack of anything resembling movement to its left or right. A similar inventory of the driveway netted the same nondescript four-door sedan from her first visit.

"I need you to wait here on the front porch, okay?" she said as they reached the top step. "Because this is a business, not a home. And Reece might not be terribly excited about having a dog inside."

Scout stepped back, let off a tiny yelp, and wagged his tail.

"I know, I know. The injustice, right?" She pulled a face

at the dog. "I'm sorry, Scout. But the good news is that you *will* survive this unfair treatment."

This time, instead of backing up, he dropped onto the porch and rested his head atop his paws.

"That's my boy." Crossing to the screen, she pulled it open and stepped inside. "Hello? Reece? It's Emma—from the other day. Kim asked me to—"

"I'll be right with you."

She nodded down the hallway from which the voice had come and then slowly made her way into the cozy sitting area. She took in the magazine covers splayed across the coffee table . . . the coffee machine housed on a narrow table on the wall to her left . . . the desk with the picture frames and computer monitor . . . And—

Curious, she crossed to the far wall and the array of certificates and framed letters that graced the wall over the copy machine. The letters, like the certificates beside them, spoke to Roger's history of giving to those less fortunate in health and opportunities.

There was the letter from the Sweet Falls' Women's Shelter thanking Roger for the two new computers that would enable residents to look for jobs . . .

There was the handwritten note from the parents of a terminally ill child letting him know that his donation made it so they could live near the hospital and thus be closer to their son for the last two months of his life . . .

There was the letter with a purple and gold logo praising him for his continued generosity to a familiar group home for children who'd aged out of the—

The telltale click of heeled shoes stole Emma's attention from the framed letter in front of her and sent it racing toward the hallway in time to see Reece Newman step around the corner. As at their first meeting, Roger's employee wore a stylish summer suit, the teal blue of today's ensemble a perfect pairing with the woman's eyes.

"I'm so sorry I had to keep you waiting, Emma."

"And I'm sorry if I interrupted something important." Emma waved her letter-holding hand at the wall. "Roger really did a lot for a lot of people, didn't he?"

"He did."

Again, she turned back to the frames, her gaze skipping across the letters and certificates she'd yet to read. "Did he have a reason for picking the groups he chose to help, or was it more of a random thing?"

"Some of them were because of Kim. Like the women's shelter. Kim saw an article in the paper about a single mom who'd lost everything in a fire the same evening she was let go from her minimum-wage job. Until the fire, she'd managed to support herself and her two kids without any assistance and no high school diploma."

"How?" Emma asked.

"She bagged groceries while they were at school, and cobbled together other moneymaking ideas to do when they weren't. But the store where she worked let her go as a cost-saving measure. The computer she'd salvaged from someone's trash the previous week in an effort to teach herself how to type was what started the fire. And the shelter where she was staying with her kids didn't have a computer, either.

"This woman was so determined to learn how to type, and therefore open more doors for herself, she found a picture of a computer keyboard and drew one on which to practice."

"Wow."

Reece leaned her shoulder against the wall. "I remember Kim marching in here with the newspaper story in her hand. Roger had just signed two new clients and was celebrating the money that was poised to come with them. Kim listened, congratulated him, and when he started questioning what they could do with it, she told him he was buying two computers. One for this women's shelter and one for the single mom herself."

Pointing Emma's attention toward a handwritten note

framed beside the shelter's typewritten one, Reece continued, "That kindness changed her life so much she's actually working to earn her high school diploma and is entertaining the notion of going to college one day, as you can see."

Emma read the letter from start to finish and then looked back at Reece. "I can see why *that* grew into *this*," she said, gesturing toward the myriad of framed thank-you letters around it. "That kind of feedback? Knowing you made that kind of difference? It has to be rather contagious."

"It was. So, too, were the fringe benefits that came with it."

"You mean the good-guy publicity and the tax benefits, right?" Emma asked.

"Indeed." Reece motioned for Emma to follow her to the same chairs they'd sat in the previous week and immediately pulled off her heels. "I don't know why I torture myself with these things," she said, rubbing the balls of her feet. "And they're not even all that high."

Emma grinned. "Yeah, not something I have to worry about when my job has me doing things like going to the gym, and the bingo hall, and to someone's home for tea."

"Sounds glorious. And so much less painful." Reece moved on to her other foot, pressing her fingers into her skin and kneading. "So, any word on Kim?"

Emma felt her smile falter and then disappear completely. "I spoke with her last night. Briefly. She asked me to stop by her house and do a few things for her. Like getting you this mail."

Reece took the letters from Emma's outstretched hand, thumbed through them quickly, and then tucked them next to her on the chair. "Thanks."

"My pleasure."

"The wake is tomorrow," Reece said.

"I know. Natalie told me."

Reece's eyes dropped from the clock to Emma. "You talked to Natalie?"

"I did. She stopped by the house while I was there."

"How is she holding up?"

"She's struggling, of course," Emma conceded. "With all of it. Her father's untimely death, her mother's arrest, all of it."

"I understand. Having no one to rely on for every little thing is brand-new territory for her, and for Caleb." Reece pushed at the air as if it was closing in around her. "All of it is so surreal, you know? I keep thinking I'm going to hear his key in the back lock or his footsteps in the hallway. But like it was for Kim when he walked out on their marriage, what was normal and everyday here just stopped, too."

"Meaning?"

"Meaning, Kim came by here every day before Roger walked out on her." Reece slipped her feet back into her shoes and stood, the steps that followed proving aimless. "Before that, she'd bring some sort of homemade breakfast bread in the mornings, and then pop back in later in the afternoon with a plate of cookies to keep us going until it was time to call it quits. A lot of the time, she'd set up at the desk in the back room and quietly do the various jobs she'd been doing since Roger opened the firm. She was always cheerful, always supportive, and always ready to pitch in wherever he needed her.

"Then Kim's parents started to decline in health, and I took on some extra tasks around here as a way to help lighten her load."

"Makes sense."

"In theory, yes. But Kim is one of those women who gives her all to her kids and her husband. I never had that, myself, so it was a little hard to watch at times, but it was what it was and I just lived vicariously through them whenever I could.

"Anyway, because of that, I think she felt a little displaced. She never said anything, but it was there. Of course, when her parents passed and Natalie graduated and moved out on her own, Kim wanted back in, but by then, we had it all under control and Roger encouraged her to take some time for herself.

"And that's when Brittney moved in for the kill. With Kim coming in less and less, Brittney started popping in to ask Roger questions at random times throughout the day. At first, he seemed bothered by the distractions—Kim, like me, had always handled things so quietly, so efficiently. But with Kim not being around all the time, it was Brittney who was there—in the moment—when he signed a new client. Brittney who whooped and hollered. Brittney who appealed to his ego by telling him how brilliant he was, how impressed she was, and on and on. Looking back, I should've seen where it was heading, recognized it for what it was, and found a way to head it off at the pass. Instead, I just shut my door and tuned them out."

Reece stopped in front of the window and sighed. "Next thing I knew, Roger was leaving Kim, Kim stopped coming in, and Brittney—of all people—was given the task of managing the company's finances. It was insane. I wanted to reach out to Kim, to tell her he was a fool, but considering I was Roger's employee, I didn't think that was wise. So I said nothing. Did nothing. Except throw myself into work so that, one day, I could do what I'd always wanted and strike out on my own, away from women like Brittney."

"You want your own agency one day?" Emma asked.

"Actually, I signed a lease—a week ago this evening—on what will be my very own boutique PR agency," Reece corrected, turning back to Emma. "And, boy, does that feel both wonderful and horrible to finally say out loud to somebody."

Emma stared at Reece. "I'm the first one you've told?"

"That wasn't the plan, of course, but yes."

"Wow. Congratulations."

A smile stirred at the corners of Reece's mouth. "Thank you." Then, as quickly as the smile appeared, it fell away. "I took Tuesday morning off to get a few things done, met a client for lunch, and then headed for the office, fully intending to tell Roger I'd be leaving. But when I arrived, he was in his office with the door closed, and I could tell he was on a call. I couldn't hear what he was saying, but I knew he was clearly upset. And later, when his call was over, he still didn't come out."

"Did you knock on his door?" Emma asked. "Tell him you wanted to talk to him?"

"I should've, but I didn't. You see, unlike Brittney, I understood a closed door to mean a need for privacy. And frankly, with as many personal days as she seemed to get and take, I was spending a lot of my time fielding calls and doing the stuff she should've been doing, in addition to all of my own work. So time got away from me, I guess."

"I see."

"When he finally emerged an hour or so later, his office looked like a bomb had gone off. There were papers and files all over his desk, the floor, his keyboard, you name it. When I asked him if he was okay, he said he'd been a fool—*a world-class fool*, in fact. Since I figured it was something to do with Brittney, I didn't argue with him. How could I? He was a fool to have left Kim. Before I could think of something I could say, though, he raced out the back door with a client folder in one hand and his phone in the other."

Reece turned back to the window, her body sagging. "And that was the last time I saw him. Alive, anyway."

"He didn't come in Wednesday?" Emma asked, silently running through the timeline in her head.

"No."

"So how did you come to find him the way that you did? In his townhouse?"

"I needed to tell him I was leaving so that the end of my two weeks' notice would fall where I needed it to fall. So I called and asked if I could stop by. He sounded distracted, maybe even a little intoxicated, but I had to tell him. So I drove over and . . ." Reece closed her eyes. Shook her head.

"And Brittney?"

Reece's long lashes parted. "What about her?"

"Did she come into work that day?"

"No. She took yet another personal day, I imagine. Because, after all, sleeping with the boss has its perks."

Emma surveyed the magazine-topped tables, the empty coatrack in the corner, the view of the street through the window, the wall-mounted camera pointed toward the front door, and, finally, the Felder PR name engraved on the sign above the clock. "I'm not sure Brittney ever truly left her husband."

Reece whirled around, wide-eyed. "Excuse me?"

"I'm wondering if it was just a clandestine thing."

"Roger got her an apartment."

"Right. Natalie mentioned something about that." She stopped and regrouped. "Maybe Trevor didn't care all that much, then?"

"Of course he cared! I have the pictures to prove it!"

"Pictures?" Emma echoed.

"Of what he did to this place in retaliation." Reece held up her finger, disappeared down the hallway, and returned a moment later with her phone. "Here. Look."

Emma took the phone and looked down at the screen and its depiction of the very room in which she now sat. The chairs were turned over, the desk computer was smashed on the floor, and the Felder sign had obscenities written across its bold lettering. "Whoa."

"I know, right?" Reece took back her phone, looked at the same picture, and then shook her head in disgust. "The only saving grace that day was that both Roger and I had locked our office doors for some strange reason. If we hadn't, it all would've been a much, much bigger deal."

"And you think *Trevor* did this?"

"We *know* Trevor did this. We have him on camera."

Emma watched Reece return to the window and then move on to the desk . . . the coffeemaker . . . and, finally, the chair she'd vacated. "Was he arrested?"

"He should've been. He would've been if I'd had any say in the matter. But Brittney pleaded his case, begged Roger to be understanding. And, for her, he was."

"Wow."

"Tell me about it." Reece rested her forearms atop her legs and cradled her chin in her hands. "But as Roger said himself, just last week, he was a fool."

"And when did Trevor do this?"

"When the flirting moved on to the next level," Reece said.

"And nothing like that happened again?"

"No. I think even Trevor knew that wouldn't be wise."

Emma heard what Reece was saying, had seen the picture of the damage with her own two eyes, saw the camera that would've recorded it all, yet it didn't fit. Not the timing. Not the anger. Not Brittney's big huge house in Walden Brook that she now lived in with a clearly forgiving Trevor.

"What did Brittney do here, again?"

"You mean beyond her affair with our boss?" At Emma's slow nod, Reece fixed her eyes on the ceiling. "Not a whole lot at first. Scheduling, fielding phone calls, sending thank-you notes to prospective clients after a meeting with me or Roger, social media, and website stuff. But then, as I said earlier, when Roger left Kim and Kim stopped coming in, he turned the books over to Brittney, as well."

"Did she get paid a lot?"

"A buck or two over minimum wage." Reece lifted her head off her hands, looked up at the clock, and sighed. "I probably should get back to work. I have a few more clients still to call about my leaving."

"I imagine, with Roger's death, a lot of the clients you had here will go with you to your new agency?"

"That would be nice." Reece grabbed the envelopes off

the cushion and stood. "Though hearing myself say that sounds so wrong."

Emma, too, stood. "I'm not judging."

"I appreciate that, Emma. Thank you. Now, if I can only refrain from judging *myself*, I'll be good to go."

"You will. Anyway, good luck with everything."

"Thank you." Reece took a few steps toward the hallway and then stopped, her hand flicking Emma's attention toward the open door. "Your dog is really well-behaved."

"My . . ." Quick-stepping to the door, Emma found Scout exactly where she'd left him—still sitting, still waiting. "Oh. Wow. Talk about judging yourself . . . Who forgets their dog is waiting outside?"

She pushed her way onto the porch and, at Scout's answering and joyous wag, knelt down beside the golden retriever. "I'm so sorry, Scout. Do you forgive me?"

Scout's answer came via a flurry of licks across her hand, her wrist, her chin.

"Enjoy your day, you two."

Emma glanced through the screen at Reece's receding back, called out a goodbye, and returned her full attention to Scout. Closing her fingers around the small, bone-shaped treat inside her pocket, she readied her nose for its incoming lick. "Want a treat?"

Chapter Twenty-One

Emma sank down onto her back stoop and lifted her face to the afternoon sun. So many times over the past hour, she'd wanted to sit in that exact spot and breathe in the aromatic fruits of her ongoing gardening efforts, but she'd resisted.

Work first, play later. It was the mantra that had been her guiding force for as long as she could remember. And while it could be difficult to adhere to in certain moments, she was always glad, in the end, when she did. Because now, instead of being plagued by should-haves and could-haves, she could simply breathe and—

"Oh, hey, boy," she said, lowering her chin to Scout's level. "I'd say that was a pretty productive few hours of work, wouldn't you? Invoices sent . . . a new client . . . that phone interview with the podcast guy . . . a few tummy rubs for you . . ."

At the mention of his third-favorite thing in the world, Scout rolled over on the concrete stoop and exposed his tummy. And, like the well-trained owner she'd become, Emma answered accordingly.

"I looked up the obituary and the funeral details for Roger," she said, stilling her fingers on Scout's stomach. "And I'm thinking I should go to the wake tomorrow afternoon. What do you think?"

Scout turned his eyes to Emma, clearly waiting to see if the rubs would resume. When they didn't, he rolled over, sat up, and licked her eyebrow.

"Yeah, me, too. But it's smack in the middle of teatime with Dottie and I'm not sure how she's going to take—"

She glanced down at her phone as it vibrated across the concrete and felt the instant smile born from the sight of Jack's name.

"Good morning, Jack."

"It's five o'clock."

"I know. But I figured, since you worked through the night, that you're just now waking up."

"Ahhh. Smart girl."

She watched Scout clamor down the steps, root around in the bushes, and emerge with a tennis ball in his mouth. "Thank you."

"Still free tomorrow evening?"

Her smile grew still wider. "I am."

"Is Scout free, too?"

"I don't know; let me ask." Shifting the phone away from her mouth, Emma waited for Scout to return to her side, ball in tow. "Are you free tomorrow evening?"

Scout dropped the ball in her lap and cocked his head.

Emma wedged the phone between her cheek and her shoulder and snatched up the ball.

"What did he say?" Jack asked, his own smile evident in his tone.

"He's free."

"Excellent. I'm thinking a picnic at Sweet Falls Park? Food for us . . . a tennis ball or a Frisbee for him . . ."

She threw the ball down the steps and then reclaimed

the phone with her hand as Scout took off in pursuit. "It sounds wonderful. To both of us."

"Good. It does to me, too."

"I can pack us up a nice dinner," she said.

"No way. This is my idea, remember? You just bring yourself and Scout. I'll take care of the rest."

"Could I bring dessert?"

The answering silence in her ear didn't last long. "What kind of dessert?"

"My great-aunt Annabelle's brownies."

"I like brownies."

Emma's laugh brought Scout and his tennis ball back to the top of the steps. "Then it's settled. I'll bring Scout, myself, *and* brownies."

"Five thirty?"

"Five thirty is . . ." She slumped against the door at her back. "Actually, would it be okay if we made it six o'clock, just so there isn't any chance I'm late?"

"Sure, but we could do a different evening entirely if that's better for you."

She took the ball from Scout, wiped it on the concrete, and threw it down the steps again. "No. Tomorrow at six would be perfect. That'll give me time to fit in tea with Dottie, make a stop out at Roger Felder's wake, and still get home with enough time to get myself and Scout ready for our—our . . . *picnic.*"

"You can call it a date, Emma. Because that's what it is." His voice fell away for a moment, and she imagined him shifting the phone from one ear to the other. "You're going to the wake?"

"I feel like I should. For Kim."

"You think she'd have gone?"

"I do."

Another beat of silence was followed, this time, by the creak of a chair that suggested he'd stood. "I checked in on her last night, as you know."

Again, Scout climbed the steps, and again, he dropped the ball in her lap. "I know you did. Thank you, again, for letting her call me. I actually went in and took care of her plants and her mail this morning."

"She told me she'd make cookies for the department once she got back home," he said.

"You sound surprised."

"I am. Most people sitting in our jail cell waiting for a spot with the judge to open up aren't thinking about gifting us with cookies."

Emma traced the top of the soggy ball with her finger while Scout panted in anticipation beside her. "I think that's just who Kim is. Always thinking about what she can do for others over taking care of herself."

"I guess, while she was talking to you, she noticed me looking at a picture of Tommy on my phone. She asked me about him afterward, and I told her it was my son and that his mom and I are divorced. Next thing I knew, she was sharing all of these neat things I can do with him when he's with me that I never knew about."

At the feel of Scout's nose on her arm, she tossed the ball down the steps once again. "That doesn't surprise me. I could tell, even before Natalie walked in on Scout and me in the house this morning, that Kim was the consummate mother. Natalie just confirmed it."

"Natalie Felder, Kim's daughter?" Jack asked.

"That's right."

"I talked to her a little the other day, but have plans to talk to her more extensively after the funeral," he said. "The brother, too."

"In case you think otherwise, Natalie knows Kim didn't kill her father," she said, looking up at the wispy clouds slowly drifting across the sky.

This time, the silence in her ear lingered.

Emma squeezed her eyes closed, shook her head, and then opened them onto the newly returned Scout. "I'm sorry, Jack.

I shouldn't have said that. You're doing your job; I'm doing mine. They don't have to have anything to do with each other."

"But they do."

In lieu of another round of fetch, Emma patted Scout into a sit. "They do. But we don't have to bring any of that into our conversations or our date."

"You're right, we don't. And we won't."

"Okay, good. We'll just . . ." The rest of her sentence fell away as her thoughts returned to Natalie and the folder still sitting on the floor behind the front passenger seat of her car. "Actually, is there any way I could give you something for Kim when I see you? Something her daughter brought by the house for her in the hopes it might lift her spirits?"

Seconds ticked by on yet another round of silence that quickly faded to the thud of her heart in her ears. "I'm sorry. I shouldn't have asked that," she said in haste. "I'll just set it aside for when she finally gets—"

"I'll see what I can do, Emma. But no promises."

"No promises. I understand." She sagged back against the door. "Thank you."

"What can I say? I like cookies."

Her answering laugh yielded a lick of her nose and cheek. "And maybe you like Kim a little, too?"

"She's a suspect in a murder, Emma."

"I hear her cookies are pretty amazing."

It was Jack's turn to laugh. "You're incorrigible, you know that?"

"I guess," she said, gliding her hand down Scout's back.

"And true to what you believe, apparently."

"I am." She cupped her free hand under Scout's chin and kissed him between the eyes. "I don't see a point in being any other way."

"Yet you've agreed to a date with me—the guy who locked her up."

Emma dropped her hand to the stoop and stood as her thoughts ricocheted between the man in her ear and her

great-aunt's brownie recipe. "You're right," she said.
"I did."

The silence was back. Only this time, instead of wariness, she felt at peace.

"I'm glad," he finally said, his voice husky.

"So am I."

She licked the last of the brownie batter off the beater and
stuck it into the mixing bowl she'd left to soak in the sink.
"Wow. I think we should make Annabelle's brownies more
often."

Turning, she caught sight of her reflection in the micro-
wave and then dropped her gaze down to Scout. "Or maybe
not, right, boy?"

Scout stood, wagged his tail, and looked at her the way
he always did—with the kind of love that made her heart
melt. "C'mon, Scout, we've got twenty-five minutes left on
the timer. Let's see what we can find out on Roger before
the brownies are done."

The clicking of Scout's nails against the floor changed in
pitch as they left linoleum in favor of the scarred wood
planking that took them down the hallway and into her office. She flipped on the light, pulled back her desk chair, and
sank onto the peach-colored cushion she'd purchased on
sale the previous week. Scout lay at her feet as she typed
"Felder PR" into the search bar and hit Enter. Another press
of the Enter key led her to the welcome page of the firm's
website and the smiling face of its founder and namesake.

She took a moment to really study Roger Felder.

The short-cropped, thinning hair that was beginning to
gray at the temples . . .

The bright blue eyes that lit from within . . .

The wide-mouthed smile that showed no signs of need-
ing to be prompted . . .

The clean-shaven jawline . . .

The freshly pressed collared dress shirt . . .

To the unknowing eye, Roger Felder looked like a nice, upstanding guy—the kind of person you could count on for a good laugh, heartfelt advice, and a steady hand. A *real family man*, as the bio beneath his picture read. But Emma knew differently.

Shaking off the growing sense of disgust that made her want to reach through the screen and throttle the man, Emma willed her attention onto, first, the firm's mission statement and origin story and then, finally, the menu feature.

A click of the Clients tab led her to a slew of businesses, a few of which she recognized as being based in Sweet Falls or some of the surrounding towns. Slowly, she scrolled her way down the list, clicking in and out of a few merely out of curiosity. Halfway down the list, she drew back at the name of a national recording company tied to some of her favorite musical groups.

"Talk about a feather in their cap," she murmured.

Another click, another scroll brought her to a photograph and a backyard patio she recognized as being Kim's. The small, casual gathering appeared to be a barbecue and yielded a number of faces she recognized.

"Kim . . . Roger . . . Reece . . . Brittney . . ." Emma leaned forward, studied the man and woman seated in the center of it all, and found that they matched a picture on the recording studio's own site. Content with the likelihood they were the clients, Emma took in the remaining half dozen or so faces scattered around the yard and then returned her full attention to the party's host and hostess.

Despite the busyness that came with entertaining a group of people at your home, and the added pressure of it being a work-related gathering, Roger and Kim exuded a sense of teamwork that leapt off the screen. Kim was putting out the last of the food plates, Roger was turning off the grill, and the guests were looking toward the many offerings stretched across the buffet table. All of that she could see. It was a moment frozen in time. But so, too, was the way Roger looked at Kim. With nothing but awe and—

The ding of the oven timer tugged her eyes from the screen and sent them—along with Scout's—back toward the hallway. "Mmmm . . . They sure smell good, don't they, Scout?"

A quick yelp of agreement accompanied Scout up and onto his feet. The wag of his tail served as an exclamation point.

"Maybe if you look the other way while I sample one, we can get in a little more fetch before dinner. What do you say?" A second and even more boisterous round of wagging had Emma looking back at the screen, studying Roger's face for a beat, and then closing out of the page and standing. "C'mon, let's go, boy. I've seen enough."

Chapter Twenty-Two

———•✈•———

"This is all rather exciting, isn't it?"

Emma closed and locked her car's passenger-side door and stepped behind Dottie's wheelchair. "Do you think, maybe, it's time to talk about adding another day together? We could make the new one all about stepping away from your books in favor of a little more real-world interaction."

"Don't be absurd, dear," Dottie said over her shoulder. "I *step away from my books*, as you say, every Tuesday afternoon when you come for tea. And trust me when I say that's more than enough real-world interaction."

"Hmmmm."

"Hmmmm?" Dottie asked.

"What you just said. It makes it sound as if you're not enjoying our weekly tea." At the top of the paved ramp leading to the funeral home, Emma veered right toward an empty bench next to an unusually large and ornate birdbath.

Dottie's steely gaze followed Emma around to the bench. "And you make it sound as if I'm spending too much time with my books."

"Touché," Emma said, holding up her hands. "You're right, I shouldn't judge. I guess it just worries me a little when you find going to the wake of a person you've never met *exciting*."

"You never met him, either."

Emma glanced toward the funeral parlor's front door and shrugged. "Which is why your comment took me by surprise. Because while you were saying you're excited, I was second-guessing our being here in the first place."

"Which is why you need to read the books you borrow from me faster than you do."

She tried to keep from rolling her eyes, but she was only mildly successful. "I have a job, Dottie. One I'm trying to make a go of, which means when I'm not working with a client, I'm knee deep in marketing to find new ones. I also have a dog to take care of, a house to maintain, and . . . oh . . . yes . . . *a murder* I'm trying to investigate thanks to you."

"Your point?" Dottie drawled.

"Reading isn't high on my priority list at this moment."

"Perhaps it should be."

"Do you have some sort of ability to infuse my day with three or four extra—and unaccounted for—hours I'm not aware of?" Emma asked. "Because that's about the only way it's going to happen. Because unless your books can do all those things *for* me, they have to come last."

Dottie smoothed the helm of her black skirt down around her shins. "They can help you with the last one."

"Last one? What last one?"

"The last to-do on your list—which, by the way, should really be at the top right now."

"I don't remember the order I . . ." Trailing off, she slumped against the slats at her back. "Dottie, I know you adore your cozy mysteries. And yes, I've enjoyed the two or three I've read so far, but—"

"Do not follow talk of books with a *but*," Dottie corrected her on the heels of a wounded sniff. "Ever."

"Right. Sorry. I didn't mean to offend. But really, with everything going on, I just can't read any faster."

Dottie looked toward the door, swept her gaze across to the parking lot, and finally set her sights firmly on Emma. "But if you would, you'd understand why being here is exciting."

"I'm not following."

"Murderers are known to return to the scene of the crime."

Emma felt her eyebrow arch. "Okay . . ."

"We're tracking a murderer."

"Roger was killed across town. On the living room floor of his condo."

It was Dottie's turn to roll her eyes. And she didn't even try to refrain. "They like to come back to see their handiwork, dear. To see the effect of their crime."

"Okay . . ."

"Where better to see that effect than inside the funeral parlor where their victim's body is laid out for all to see?"

Emma leaned forward. "You think the person who killed Roger will come to his wake?"

"I think chances are very good."

"But that's . . . *crazy*. Sick, even."

Dottie nodded. "We are talking about a murderer, are we not?"

"I guess, but—"

"Good afternoon, ladies."

Together, Emma and Dottie looked up to find Big Max—dressed in head-to-toe black—approaching them from the sidewalk on the southern side of the building. From the slight brim of his flat black cap dangled a piece of sheer black fabric that stopped at the midpoint of his eyes.

Dottie's lips twitched with the same amusement Emma tried her best to nibble away.

"Big Max, hello!" Emma scooted over to afford her eccentric seventy-eight-year-old friend a spot on the bench he didn't take. "This is a surprise."

"I'm here to pay my respects. To"—he pulled a folded

piece of newspaper from his pocket, opened it up, and held it out for Emma and Dottie to see—"Robert."

Emma traded glances with Dottie. "You mean, *Roger*?"

Big Max turned the paper toward himself, leaned in to read the name under the obituary photograph, and nodded. "Yep. Roger. Roger Felder."

Dottie turned the wheels of her chair so as to see both Emma on the bench and Big Max standing alongside the birdbath. "How did you know him, Maxwell?"

"He was married to the cookie lady," Emma said, glancing back up at Big Max. "Right?"

"The cookie lady?" Dottie echoed.

"He means Kim."

Big Max pushed aside the black fabric, revealing a furrowed brow. "But he didn't stay."

"Who?"

Again he looked at the paper in his hand. "Roger."

Understanding, rather than humor, fueled Emma's half laugh, half grunt. "You're right, Big Max. He didn't. And that was his loss. Big time."

When Big Max said nothing, she stood and made her way in his direction. "So that's why you came? Because of the cookie lady?"

"I don't make cookies the way she does, but I'm a good hugger."

"You are, indeed," Emma said, grinning. "And a heck-uva dancer, too."

"I am, ain't I?" Big Max turned in a slow, hypnotic circle and then stopped, his smile fading. "But I think a hug would be better today."

Dottie pinned Emma with a stare and then slowly released it to take in Big Max. "You know she's not here, right, Maxwell?"

"*She?*" Emma parroted, only to turn her attention to Big Max as reality hit home. "Dottie is right, Big Max. Kim—I mean, the cookie lady—isn't here today."

Big Max stepped back, his eyes wide behind the thin black fabric. "Where is she?"

"She's . . ." Emma caught Dottie's quick head shake out of the corner of her eye and let it guide her accordingly. "She couldn't get back in time for the funeral."

"You know where she is?" Big Max asked.

Too late to pull back her answering nod, Emma cast about for the best way to answer her elderly friend's inevitable next question. "She's not able to make any cookies for you at the moment, but she will. Soon."

"I can wait for cookies, Emma. But maybe—because of Roger—she shouldn't wait for a hug."

At a loss for another way to skirt a truth she didn't want to deliver, Emma looked to Dottie for help. Dottie, in turn, motioned Big Max to come closer to her chair. "Right now, Maxwell, Kim is in a place where she can't be hugged. But Emma and I are working to change that."

"I'd like to help, too." Big Max puffed out his chest. "What can I do?"

Emma's eyes traveled back to Dottie. "I don't really think there's anything you—"

"We go inside," Dottie said, waving off Emma. "We pay our respects to Kim's children. We see where conversations lead. We notice everything—including the little things that seem unimportant in the moment. And we talk about it together afterward when it's over."

"I can do that," Big Max said.

"Good. Then let's go." Fingering the reverse button on her chair, Dottie backed herself away from the bench and led the way forward toward the door.

I s that a tear, I see, dear?"

Brushing her fingertips across her cheeks, Emma lowered herself onto a chair next to Dottie. "I'm a nut. Clearly."

"For shedding a few tears at a wake?"

"For shedding a few tears at *this* wake, yes."

Dottie relinquished her view of the receiving line and the open casket in favor of Emma. "Oh?"

"He was a philanderer, remember?" Emma whispered. "He walked out on his wife of thirty years for someone who wasn't a whole lot older than his own kids."

"He was still a person."

"I get that. But to actually cry?" Emma shook her head. "Really?"

"I suspect your tears are more about them."

Emma followed the path of Dottie's arthritis-ridden finger to the front of the room and the pair of twenty-somethings greeting each and every person who lined up to pay respects to their late father. Natalie was starting to wilt, if her sagging shoulders and unfocused eyes were any indication. Beside her, positioned next to the casket, was Kim's son and Roger's mini-me, based on the poster-topped easels placed around the room and bearing photographs from their father's life.

"I wasn't aware you'd met."

Pulling her attention from the siblings, Emma fixed it, instead, on the wheelchair-bound eighty-something to her right. "Who?"

"You and the daughter."

"How did you know we did?"

"There was clearly familiarity between you when we paid our respects."

"Right. We met yesterday," Emma said, looking forward once again. "At Kim's house when I was there to . . ."

Uh-oh.

Realizing her mistake, Emma straightened in her chair and made a show of searching the room. "I don't see Big Max, do you?"

"Why am I just now hearing about this?" Dottie asked, her voice thick with accusation.

"Because I just now realized he's not here." Again, she

scanned the room, her gaze playing across the chairs, the picture boards, the open casket, and, finally, Kim's children as they continued to greet the steady stream of mourners. "I know he was behind me in the receiving line. I know he expressed his condolences to Natalie and Caleb. And I know he was taking time to look at all of the picture boards. But since I've been sitting here talking to you, I've lost track of—"

"I'm not talking about Big Max, Emma. I'm talking about this little revelation about Kim's house."

Her face warming, Emma shifted in her seat. "Kim asked me to water her plants and bring in her mail. No biggee."

"And you didn't see fit to mention this earlier?" Dottie asked.

"I-I didn't think about it, I guess."

"You were in Kim's home, you met her daughter, you went through her mail, and you didn't *think* about it?"

Emma swallowed. Shrugged. "I don't know, Dottie. I guess I didn't say anything about it because there was nothing to say, nothing to share."

"Says you."

"Exactly."

Dottie's mouth tightened with displeasure. "Sometimes, it's while talking about the seemingly unimportant that clues are found. That's basic Sleuthing 101, Emma."

"I must have slept through that class," Emma said, dryly.

"You know how I feel about your bent toward sarcasm, dear."

"Sorry."

"I'm not looking for an apology. I'm looking for dirt."

"I left that with the plants. Figured that was best."

Dottie didn't need to open her mouth in response. The glare she leveled at Emma said it all, and then some.

"Fine. I'll bore you with the details." Emma pivoted her knees toward Dottie's wheel and leaned forward so as not to be overheard by anyone. "I watered all of the plants. I looked at pictures. I gave Scout one of the treats Kim had bought specifically for him. I sorted the mail into two piles—one for Kim, and one to drop off at the office on my way home. And while I was doing that"—she nudged her chin and Dottie's eyes back to the front of the room—"Natalie walked in. We talked. She cried. I stupidly promised her we'll find the real killer and, in doing so, clear her mother as a suspect in her father's murder. She cried some more. She left. Scout and I left. The end. See? Nothing."

"You said *we*?"

She stared at Dottie. "Excuse me?"

"You said *we* will find the real killer?"

"*That's* what you picked out from everything I just said?" Emma tilted her chin toward the ceiling and shook her head. "Seriously?"

"I'm just surprised, dear. Especially since that's—"

Stemming the rest of Dottie's words with a splayed hand, Emma recited the rest. "Something I didn't do in my interview with that reporter from the *Sweet Falls Gazette* in the wake of the arrest in Brian Hill's murder . . . I know. Trust me. I've heard it a bajillion times."

"It's just nice to be acknowledged. Especially when something is really an ensemble effort."

"Can we move on? Please?"

"Of course." Dottie hooked her thumb across her shoulder. "Can you grab my notebook and pen out of my chair bag, please?"

"Why?" Emma asked. "What do you need that for?"

"So we can talk about the case."

Emma lowered her voice to a whispered hiss. "May I remind you that we're sitting in a funeral home?"

"I know where we are."

"Well, then, you must know that this is hardly an appropriate place to be playing detective."

"*Playing?*"

It took every ounce of restraint she could muster not to groan out loud. "Would it be considered elder abuse if I taped your mouth closed for just a little—"

"I thought that was you, Emma."

Startled, she turned to find a now-familiar woman quietly excusing her way around people to reach the empty chair to Emma's left. "Mind if I sit with you for a while?"

"Of course. Please." Emma patted the cushioned folding chair and then motioned the woman's attention to Dottie. "Reece, this is my friend, Dottie Adler. Dottie, this is Reece Newman. She worked with Roger."

Dottie extended her age-spotted hand to Reece. "I'm sorry for your loss."

"Thank you, Dottie."

Reece sank onto the chair, her eyes fixed on Roger's lifeless body. "I still can't believe this is happening, you know? I keep thinking I'm going to wake up and find that it's all just some kind of crazy dream."

"How are you holding up?" Emma asked.

"I thought I was doing okay until I got here and saw"— Reece squeezed her eyes closed, only to open them, seconds later, with a shake of her head. "Actually, if you wouldn't mind, I'd love to talk about something—anything—else for a few minutes, if we can? I think I just need to catch my breath and get my head straight."

"Of course."

Dottie leaned across the armrest of her chair. "I love your dress, Reece. Is that a Lily Vivaldi?"

"It is," Reece said, with a mixture of pride and surprise. "You have a good eye."

"My Alfred bought me one of her designs as a birthday gift one year. I made him take it back when I saw the price."

Nodding, Reece looked down at the tasteful A-line dress and managed a smile. "As would I, if I'd come across this somewhere other than a retail shop on the edge of a rather upscale community near where my father and his bride of the year live."

"It's beautiful," Emma said.

Reece ran her fingers along the kaleidoscope of blues that fanned out from the dress's simple bodice and then discounted it all with a dismissive sniff. "When I bought it, I imagined wearing it to celebrate my big move, not to attend my boss's funeral. But . . . here we are. And"—Reece slumped back against her seat—"here I am. Wishing I could be somewhere, *anywhere* else."

"I saw the Felder website last night," Emma said. "It's really well done and very user friendly. I was quite impressed."

Reece's eyes traveled back to Kim's children and Roger. "Don't be. Brittney couldn't alphabetize her way out of a paper bag without consulting some app on her phone, or even pretend to grasp the importance of writing appointments down on something other than a scrap of paper she'd invariably throw away while trying to neaten up the office. But ask her to make a graphic I was simply too busy to make myself? Or to completely redo a website? Or destroy a thirty-year marriage? *That* she could do, and do well."

Emma traded glances with Dottie, but only briefly. "I'm sorry, Reece. I'm really not trying to bring up upsetting subjects."

"I know. It's silly to think I can even try to think about something else when"—again, Reece looked up at the casket and shook her head. "There's no pretending this away, no matter how much I wish I could."

Emma plucked a tissue box off a neighboring chair and held it out to Reece.

"Even yesterday, when I was contacting the last of the clients I still had to tell about leaving the firm, it all felt so wrong."

"But you were already on a path to do this before Roger's death," Emma reminded her while Reece dabbed at her eyes. "Don't forget that."

Reece balled the damp tissue inside her manicured hand and sniffed. "Thank you. I'm trying not to."

"Are you leaving the area, Reece?" Dottie asked.

Reece's silent shake of her head had Emma turning back to Dottie. "No. Reece is opening up her own . . ."

The words fell away as a chorus of quiet gasps from around the room led their collective attention back to the front in time to see Brittney Anderson step into the line of mourners patiently waiting their turn to speak with Roger's children.

"Speaking of the devil . . ." Reece murmured as her hand whitened around the balled-up tissue. "And I actually thought she'd err on the side of class."

Dottie leaned into Emma. "Is that her? Is that the hussy?"

Emma opened her mouth to answer but closed it as Reece beat her to the punch. "Yes—yes, it is. And look who she brought with her . . . How lovely."

"With her?" Emma echoed, her gaze moving past Brittney to a man with well-groomed shoulder-length hair. "Wait. Who is that?"

"Trevor. Her husband."

Emma drew back. "*Trevor?* Are you sure?"

"I'm sure."

"But I feel like . . . wait. You're right." Emma took in the more expensive suit, the crisp shirt collar, and the presence of actual suit-appropriate shoes and silently applauded the change. "New house, new suit, I guess."

"Meaning?" Dottie prodded.

"Meaning you'd have had a heart attack if you'd seen the suit he wore at their wedding."

Reece's eyes cut to Emma's. "You were at their wedding?"

"No. No. I saw their wedding photo at the open house their realtor—"

Reece held up her hand. "Actually, can we change the

subject again? I just can't. Not today. I want to remember the Roger before Brittney."

"Of course." Emma willed her attention off Roger's mistress and planted it, instead, on Natalie and the portly brunette holding her in a long, powerful embrace.

She tried to make herself look away, to give Natalie the privacy she deserved in what was clearly a needed moment, but like a moth drawn to a flame, she simply couldn't. "Do you know if that's a family member or a friend of Kim's?" she asked.

"Who?"

"That woman. With Natalie."

Reece shifted to afford herself a better view of Kim's children and then pressed her tissue-holding fist to her lips. "That's Celia. From Loving Arms and Guiding Hands. She represents everything that was good about the old Roger— the one everyone loved. I'm sorry. I have to go say hello."

"Of course." Emma tucked her feet beneath her chair to allow Reece easy passage out to the main aisle and then held them there as Big Max lumbered over from the other end of the row to claim the now-vacant seat. "Hey, Big Max. Dottie and I were wondering where you went."

"I was talking to my friend, Celia."

Emma's gaze returned to the front of the receiving line and the woman now kneeling in front of Roger's casket, praying. "You know that woman?"

"We both do," Big Max said, moving his finger between himself and Dottie.

At Dottie's slow, even nod, she looked back at Big Max. "How?" she prodded.

"She lets me help with the games every year. And this time, she said I can be the clown and hand out balloons if I want. Which I do. Very much." Big Max's smile practically lit the room. "I told her I have everything I need to do a good job and that I don't want any pay."

"Are you sure, Maxwell?" Dottie asked. "Because they have a budget for that."

Big Max was shaking his head before Dottie had even finished speaking. "I want them to put that money back toward the group."

"That's very generous of you, Maxwell."

"Wait. What am I missing?" Emma asked. "What kids? What group?"

Dottie's hand came down on top of Emma's. "You've heard of the annual kids' fest at Camden Park every July, right? In fact, I would imagine the posters for this year's event will be starting to pop up around town soon, if they're not up already."

"Sure. I've seen them. It's to raise money for the place where foster kids go while awaiting placement, right?"

"That, and for the older ones who have aged out of the system, yes."

"I've never been since I don't have kids, but yeah, I've heard of it."

"That was one of the groups Alfred faithfully supported," Dottie said. "And it's also how he and Maxwell met the first time."

Emma looked between the pair, pieces of the puzzle that was Big Max beginning to fall into place. Before she could speak, though, Big Max was up and on his feet. "I'm sorry, ladies. I have to go now. I have a lot of things to learn and a lot of practicing to do to be the best clown ever."

Chapter Twenty-Three

<hr>

It was a summer evening for the record books; not too hot, a gentle breeze, and a good-looking man sitting on the other side of a trio of food containers stretched across the navy blue blanket, his fingers working their magic on Scout's exposed tummy.

"Those brownies are incredible, by the way," Jack said. "Reminded me of my childhood for some reason."

Emma lowered herself onto her elbow and inhaled the sweet smell of black-eyed Susans in the park's neighboring meadow. "They're from my great-aunt Annabelle's recipe."

"This is the great-aunt who lived here in Sweet Falls? In the house you're living in now?"

"Her house that is now mine, yes. I found her recipe box tucked into a cabinet shortly after I moved in."

"Well, I for one think you made a very good find." Jack transferred his hand to his own stomach and grinned.

Emma's laugh had Scout rolling back onto his feet and making his way over to her side of the blanket. "I try to make something from Annabelle's recipe box every month now—a dinner, a soup, a bread, a side dish, a dessert, whatever. But those brownies?" She ran her hand down Scout's back. "I've been known to whip up a batch as a pick-me-up a time or two, haven't I, boy?"

Scout wagged his tail in response.

Jack reached beyond the edge of the blanket and plucked up a blade of grass. "What made you need those pick-me-ups?"

Rolling onto her back, she looked up at the lazy summer clouds playing peekaboo with the sun as it made its way west. "Well, for starters, I tended to make a batch when I lost someone I'd considered a tried-and-true client of my home-based travel agency. Of course, once I was down to only two or three people who'd essentially aged out of traveling anyway, I couldn't keep using that as an excuse anymore. There was also the time, last summer, when I thought my sixteen-year-old niece was going to come and stay with me for a few weeks. I planned all of these things we were going to do together and—wham!—she got herself a boyfriend and begged her mother to let her stay in New York, instead. Oh! And before that, when Alfred—Dottie's husband—died, I might have mourned my way through a batch or two, as well."

"I'm sorry."

Turning her cheek toward the blanket, she met and then released Jack's gaze in favor of a sigh. "Yeah, he was something special. A true one of a kind. Oh, and then there was the whole not-wanting-to-admit-failure thing every time my parents or my sister called."

"Failure?"

"They thought I was nuts coming down here to live. They thought I should've just sold Annabelle's house and used the money I'd make to put toward a place of my own in New York. But why would I want to put money toward something when I could just come here and have a place?"

"Makes sense to me," Jack said.

"Well, it didn't to them. In their eyes, living anywhere

beyond the border of New York is akin to living in a third world country. And to do it in conjunction with a business my father warned me would never last despite the handful of corporate clients he'd helped me secure after college? Well . . . yeah. Brownies. Especially over the last six months when the last of those corporate clients were dropping like flies, one after the other."

Jack's laugh hung on the breeze as he scooped up Scout's forgotten tennis ball and hurled it down the hill. "It seems to me that you've made it all work out okay."

"The verdict is still out on that one."

"Why?" He looked back at Emma. "You didn't wallow over the travel agency thing for long. You did something else."

Scout bounded back up the hill, dropped the ball next to Jack's knee, and wagged.

"Uh, hello? Brownies? Lots and lots of brownies?" She pushed off her elbow into a seated position and snatched up the ball. "Trust me, I wallowed. A lot. Scout will tell you. And as for the *something else* you just mentioned, we'll see if it becomes what I need it to be in order to stay here."

A shadow crossed his face. "Is that in question?"

"I don't want it to be. I'm trying everything I can think of to make sure it isn't. But my bank account can only withstand so much before I have to seriously consider falling into the family business so Scout and I can eat."

He followed the ball and then Scout down the hill with his eyes. "Family business?"

"My parents own a few tutoring centers. Extremely successful ones at that. Some of my longest-held corporate clients were connected to parents of kids my mom and dad have worked with over the years."

"And your parents want you working for them in these tutoring centers?"

Her laugh was thin. "Not *for* them. *With* them. They want me to take on a center or two of my own."

"And I take it that's not your thing?" Jack asked.

"It's not. It's their thing."

He took the returned ball from Scout's mouth and threw it again. "Meaning?"

"Maybe it was from watching them while I was growing up, but for as long as I can remember I've always wanted to start my own thing. From the ground up. With my own blood, sweat, and tears—something I could look at and think, *Wow, I did that. Me. On my own.* Not via my mommy and daddy."

"And your sister?"

Emma shrugged. "Trina and I want different things."

"I see." This time when Scout returned, Jack coaxed him down onto the blanket with a few well-placed scratches. "So, out of curiosity, why a travel agency?"

She felt the instant smile his words stirred across her lips. "I always loved going places—family vacations, school trips, visits here to see Annabelle, and my year abroad in college. I loved experiencing new places, new people, new expressions, new languages, all of it. And the thought of helping others experience the same things? It was a dream fit. Or was for a while.

"My older travelers and my corporate clients hung on the longest. But even they eventually came to the realization that I was nothing more than a middleman they just didn't need anymore."

"You can still travel. Closing your agency doesn't change that."

"No, but starting a business from scratch does." She breathed in Scout's pleasure over Jack's ongoing attention and then let her gaze travel out toward the playground and the duck pond beyond. "When Dottie first brought up the notion of this whole friend-for-hire thing, I thought she was nuts. But you know what? She's right. The never-ending obsession with social media stuff has affected interpersonal relationships. And sometimes you have to get outside and you have to interact in person, whether you like it or not. Having someone by your side in those instances just makes it easier for some people."

She took in a pair of ducks making their way across the pond, and beyond them, a woman making use of the walking trail. "Then there's situations like my friend Andy, who likes the peace of mind that comes from knowing he has someone who will pop in on his aging father while he's traveling for work. And now Kim, who just wants someone to help her find a foothold in a life that's been turned upside down by . . ."

"I'm sorry." Emma held up her hands. "We said we'd keep any and all Kim talk out of this picnic. My apologies."

Jack stilled his hand between Scout's ears. "No worries. But it sounds like this new business idea is picking up steam, yes?"

"I'm not sure picking up steam applies when one of my clients was murdered and another is now sitting in jail for a different murder, but maybe it's getting ready to leave the station?"

"If people are smart, it will." Reaching across Scout, Jack helped himself to a second brownie, lifting it in the air briefly. "And if they're not, you could make a killing selling these things."

Emma laughed. "Thank you. Annabelle would be proud."

"Did you and your sister both spend time here?" Jack asked between bites. "When you were growing up?"

"When we were really young, yes. But Trina never liked coming as much as I did and so, eventually, she just stopped."

"Is Trina older or younger than you?"

"Older. By four years." Emma leaned back on her hands as her thoughts traveled back nearly thirty years. "Which means, from the time I was a good four years old, it was just Aunt Annabelle and me for most of the summer. And boy, did we have fun. We came here, to this very park, and fed the same ducks that Scout now likes to bark at."

Jack's eyebrow arched in amusement. "Do ducks live that long?"

"Ha, ha, ha. You know what I mean."

"Just razzing you a little. But you want to know something fun?"

"Sure."

"I used to come to this park on occasion when I was younger, too."

Emma pulled back. "Wait. You've lived in Sweet Falls your whole life?"

"No. I lived out in Morganville. But one of my mom's friends lived in Sweet Falls when I was growing up, and we'd meet her here in the park every once in a while." Jack finished his second brownie and returned his hand to Scout's back. "That's one of the reasons Tommy likes coming here so much. He thinks it's neat that I played here on occasion when I was his age, too."

"You're doing a great job with Tommy," Emma said.

Jack's answering shrug was heavy. "I want to believe that, but I don't know. I mean, I see him what? One night a week? Two weekends a month? A thirty-minute phone call on all the other days? Am I really having any impact?"

Impulsively, she reached across the blanket and covered his Scout-petting hand. "You're having an impact. He's polite. He's kind. He's so gentle with Scout. And the way he looks at you? You're his hero, Jack. Never doubt that. Just keep being it."

She saw him swallow, heard the beat of his answering silence inside her chest, and then felt the warmth of his hand as he turned it beneath hers and squeezed. "I hope you're right."

"I am."

"Thank you."

Reluctantly, she pulled her hand from his and pointed at

the remains of their picnic. "How about I throw this stuff out and we take Scout over to the pond?"

"How about I throw it out and—oomph." Jack looked from the drool-soaked ball in his lap to Scout and, finally, back at a laughing Emma. "What?"

"Scout likes my plan better. So *you* throw, and I'll be back in a minute." With quick hands, she gathered up their empty plates and napkins, made a beeline for the closest trash receptacle, and stopped dead in her tracks as her gaze settled on the tall brunette meandering by on the park's walking path. "Oh, hi. Celia, right?"

The fifty-something woman stopped mid-step and turned back to Emma, her brow furrowed but her smile at the ready. "Yes. Hi. Do I know you?"

Emma stepped forward. "Hi. I'm Emma Westlake. I saw you a few hours ago at Roger Felder's wake."

"I-I'm sorry. My memory is usually better than this."

Emma crossed to the trash container, dropped the picnic remnants inside, and then made her way back to Celia. "No, no, you're fine. We didn't actually meet. You were just pointed out to me as being with one of the organizations Roger took under his wing."

"Oh, yes, Mr. Felder's generosity helped Loving Arms and Guiding Hands in so many ways. Without people like him, we wouldn't be able to always keep our focus where it needs to be—on the children. We'd be running around worrying about how to fund this and that, how to get the word out to find the funding, et cetera, et cetera. It's why I'm so grateful for people like Mr. Felder, regardless of how long they choose to support us."

"How did he find your group, do you know?"

Celia nodded. "I believe that was his wife, Kim. Years ago, when she was leading their daughter's scout troop, she had her troop members volunteer with our Summer Fest. The girls manned game booths, offered face painting, baked things for the first of what has become our very popular bake sale, and helped in all sorts of other ways. The event was always about doing something special for the kids, and we relied on donations from the community to make it happen. Sometimes, we fell short and had to scale things down a little. Sometimes, we managed to raise enough to do a little something extra, like add a bounce house or an inflatable slide on occasion, but it was always a nail-biter up until the end trying to figure out what we could or couldn't do. That all changed after the first year her troop helped out, when we got a check in the mail from Felder PR with enough money to have a bounce house, an inflatable slide, and a small petting zoo that next year. The kids were thrilled. And the smiles?" Celia closed her eyes momentarily. "They were something I didn't ever want to forget. And for ten years we didn't have to thanks to Mr. Felder. Because every December, he sent us a check for the following year."

"Wow. That's very generous."

"You're absolutely right," Celia said. "We were very fortunate to have had his support for as long as we did. And maybe, in time, we'll pick up another donor—or series of donors—that will support us the way Mr. Felder did. Until then, though, we'll do what we can to make next month's Summer Fest as nice for the kids as we can. Just like we used to in those earlier years."

Emma stopped mid-nod. "Wait. If Roger made his donation for the following year's event every December, wouldn't it be *next* year's event that's affected, rather than the one next month?"

"If he'd sent the check in December, yes. But he didn't." Celia's hands lifted with her shrug. "So instead of scrambling for next year's, we scrambled for this year's. But we'll be okay. We're working with a few of the civic groups to see what they might be able to do for—"

"Why did he stop? Do you know?"

"I don't. I tried to set up a meeting with him, several

times, but every time I did, I was told he was not available. Eventually, I stopped trying and used it as a teaching moment for our staff instead: to be grateful for gifts, no matter how long they last, and to have faith that we'll persevere, regardless."

She sat with Celia's words for a moment as she glanced back at Scout and Jack to find both of them waiting for her on the picnic blanket. "I probably should get back to my date, but I'd be happy to help at this year's Summer Fest. I'm not sure anyone wants me painting their cheeks, but my dog loves children, so you can put us to work wherever we can be most helpful."

"And there you go . . . Things may be different, but that doesn't mean they can't be wonderful just the same." Celia reached into her pants' pocket and extracted a business card bearing her name and phone number beneath the familiar purple-and-gold logo. "Why don't you give me a call sometime this week and we can figure out a spot that would work best for you and your dog?"

Emma took the card, traced her finger along the lilac-colored heart, and then popped it into her own pocket. "I'll do that. Thank you."

Chapter Twenty-Four

Hiking her gym bag higher on her shoulder, Emma stepped around the corner and stopped dead in her tracks.

"Whoa." She rubbed her eyes, blinked, and rubbed them again. "You're . . . here. Before me."

Stephanie yawned, long and loud. "Write it down. It isn't likely to happen again in this century."

"So what's different about today?" Emma asked as she led the way to the gym's front door.

"I didn't want to get cheated of the full rundown." Stepping through the door Emma held open, Stephanie fished her hand inside her own gym bag and pulled out the laminated ID card needed to get past the muscular twenty-something manning the center's front desk. "Though, honestly, this five-thirty-in-the-morning stuff is inhumane."

Emma traded a knowing grin with the attendant and, after flashing her own ID, nudged Stephanie toward the locker room. "Might I remind you that you're the one who set the time? And that you just don't actually adhere to it most mornings?"

"No, you may not."

Her answering laugh echoed around them, as did the click and then thud of her locker door as she readied herself for their workout. "Ready to get your sweat on?"

"I'm good with sitting here on the bench and getting the lowdown."

"On?"

Stephanie gathered her hair inside a ponytail holder and—

"Hold it right there." Emma grabbed Stephanie by the shoulder and turned her this way and that under the fluorescent overhead light. "You colored your hair."

Lowering her hands to her side, Stephanie flopped back on the bench, defeated. "It looks awful, doesn't it?"

"No. No. It looks great! I love it!"

Stephanie lifted her hands to her hair, fingered the stray strands around her face. "You sure?"

"Absolutely." She took in the evenness of the rich cocoa color and grinned. "Was this prompted by anything in particular? Or, should I say, any *one* in particular?"

Stephanie looked down at her hands, twisted them around a little, and then shrugged. "He called."

It took everything Emma had not to pump her hand in victory. Still, there was no denying the squeal that accompanied her onto the bench next to Stephanie. "When? Last night?"

"Yes."

"And?"

"My mother got to the phone first."

"Uh-oh."

Stephanie groaned. "Oh trust me, it gets worse."

"I'm listening."

"I'm in the other room and I hear her answer the phone and repeat my name like three times. Then, without covering the mouthpiece, she says, *'An actual man is calling for you, Stephanie. Hurry! Quick!'*"

Emma didn't mean to laugh. The fact that someone farther into the locker room also laughed just made it harder to stop. "I'm sorry, Stephanie. I know that had to be mortifying, but . . . wow."

Stephanie dropped her forehead into her hands and, after a moment or two of silence, flung herself up and off the bench, her cheeks red but her eyes bright with a smile. "But somehow, despite my mother's best efforts, he was actually still on the phone when I peeled myself up off the floor. And we talked for close to an hour. About his work and my work, the house I want to build, his dad, and you."

"That's fantastic. I'm so glad."

"Wait. It gets better."

"I'm listening."

"He asked me out to dinner!"

Emma's answering clap stirred a second one farther back in the room. Giggling, Emma threw her arms around Stephanie and squeezed. "I knew you two would hit it off, and I was right! So, when?" She released Stephanie and stepped back. "When are you going out?"

"Saturday evening."

"Look at you . . . going on a date . . . with an incredibly sweet *and* super-good-looking guy, I might add."

Stephanie pulled a face. "I know. What's wrong with this picture, right?"

"Stop it! Right now!"

"I'm four years older than he is."

"Cougars are in." Emma dragged Stephanie over to the bank of sinks and pointed at the mirrors above them. "Plus, who wouldn't want to go out with a beautiful woman like you?"

"Ha!"

"No, *truth*."

Stephanie's gaze hit on first Emma's reflection and then, finally, her own. "The hair does look pretty darn good, doesn't it . . ."

"So does the person sporting it. Know that. Believe that."

"It's hard when I haven't looked at myself that way in a very long time."

"Well, then, start looking. Because it's true." Emma hiked her thumb over her shoulder toward the door. "So? Shall we get our sweat on?"

Stephanie turned. "Hold up. Now it's your turn."

"My turn?"

"I want details."

Emma grinned. "On what?"

"Don't play coy."

"Oh. Right." Emma crossed to the door, opened it, and pointed at the line of elliptical machines on the other side. "First, we get on the machines. Then I'll share."

"You do realize your early-morning perkiness and over-the-top persistence is more than a little annoying, right?"

She waited for Stephanie to step into the room and then led the way to their first fitness stop of the morning. "I do. I also know you hired me to be exactly that."

"Is it too late to change my mind?"

"On what? Hiring me?"

Stephanie stepped onto the elliptical, keyed in the speed and course Emma directed her to, and pressed Start. "Yes."

"Yup. Too late."

After a few prerequisite huffs and puffs and an added grumble or two for good measure, Stephanie glanced over at Emma. "You know I'm kidding, right?"

"Are you sure?" Emma asked, increasing the level of resistance on her own machine.

"You've changed my life so much already."

"Could I get you to actually write that as a testimonial for my website?" she quipped.

"Absolutely."

She looked over at Stephanie. "I'm not being serious."

"I am." Stephanie released her grip on one of the arms just long enough to gesture at Emma. "When we started this, I was dying on the treadmill after a minute. Now? I'm doing *this* torture device for as long as ten minutes."

"Today we're doing fifteen."

Stephanie stuck out her tongue. "Fine. Ruin the moment."

"You'll thank me later, when it's over and you're feeling all proud of yourself."

"No, I'll curse you for making it so I can't move tomorrow morning."

"I'll take it." Emma felt the resistance increase as they reached a programmed hill and glanced over at Stephanie in time to catch the woman's horror-filled eyes. "C'mon, Steph. You can do it. Keep going."

"Then . . . spill . . . all . . . or . . . I . . . get . . . off," Stephanie said between labored huffs.

And so Emma told her everything about the date with Jack—the picnic, the easy flow of their conversation, Scout's genuine affection for the deputy, and, finally, the way he'd walked her to her car when it was all over and actually swept a piece of hair behind her ear as he said good night.

"I'd . . . say . . . that . . . was . . . a . . . success," Stephanie said as the time inched toward, and then well beyond, the ten-minute mark.

Reveling in the smile born on the memory of her date with Jack, Emma nodded. "It was."

"So . . . I . . . imagine . . . there will . . . be another?"

"I think so. I hope so. He's a busy guy."

"If . . . he's a *smart* one . . . there . . . will . . . be another."

"Awww. Listen to you paying me a compliment," Emma teased her. "I wouldn't expect that, considering."

Stephanie wiped the sweat from her brow with her arm. "Considering what?"

"Considering you're closing in on fifteen minutes as we speak."

Stephanie's gaze dropped to her control panel as her feet slowed to a complete stop. "Whoa. Would you look at that? I made it."

"Congratulations," Emma said as she, too, stopped and stepped off the machine. "Next time, we'll make it twenty."

S cout was waiting at the living room window when she pulled into her driveway just before seven o'clock. Cutting the engine, she waved at him across the top of the steering wheel and then reached back between the seats for her gym bag. She felt around for its nylon handle, only to pull back as her fingers hit on something different.

Surprised, she leaned over and, at the sight of the manila folder on the floor behind the empty passenger seat, let out a groan. "Way to go, Emma," she murmured, closing her hand around its stack of papers and pulling it onto her lap.

She'd meant to give it to Jack to bring to Kim at the culmination of their date, but she'd been in such a euphoric state she hadn't really been thinking about anything other than the feel of his fingers against her skin as he'd tucked her hair behind her ear.

Yet because of Emma's self-absorption in that heady moment, Kim was sitting in a jail cell missing out on something her daughter had thought would lift her spirits. Disgusted with herself, Emma grabbed her gym bag and the folder and headed inside to feed Scout, take a shower, and, then, run the folder over to the station. If she was lucky, Jack would be there to take it. If not, maybe Dottie's receptionist-friend could hold on to it until he was.

Still, on the off chance Jack was there, she took a little extra time in the shower, paired her white shorts with her favorite baby-blue cami, and added a touch of mascara to her eyelashes and gloss to her lips. When she was done, she turned in a little circle in front of Scout. "So? How do I look?"

Scout barked once and followed it up with an emphatic wag of his tail.

"Thanks, boy. You're the best." She bent down, lost most

of her gloss on the top of his fur, and then made her way back downstairs to the folder-topped gym bag.

Setting the bag on the floor at her feet, Emma looked down at Natalie's big curlicue writing and wondered how the young woman and her brother were faring as they prepared for their father's funeral mass. So much grief. So many unanswered questions.

Without really thinking about what she was doing, Emma peeled back the cover and found herself looking down at a handwritten letter from daughter to mother. Picking it up, she began to read.

Mom,

Caleb and I know you didn't do this. You couldn't have. You loved Dad. You always have and, despite his mistakes, always will. We know this.

You've been through a lot and I know my moving out and trying to live my own life hasn't made it any easier. But I love you. You are my rock. You are Caleb's rock. And, I know, you were Dad's rock, too.

Everyone knew he made a mistake in leaving you. Everyone.

And I know, with all my heart, that he knew it, too.

Before he died, he'd been looking through these reminders of what you did for him. The man you helped him to be. The man I'm convinced he wanted to be again. For me. For Caleb. For himself. And, I believe, for you, as well.

Stay strong, Mom.
This will be over soon. It has to be.
I love you to the moon and back.

Xoxoxo,
Natalie

Emma felt a lump of emotion making its way up her throat and did her best to swallow it back down. "You're right, Natalie. It *will* be over soon," she whispered. "Somehow, someway, I will see to that."

Slowly, she returned the letter to the top of the stack, only to push it off to the side at the last minute in favor of the letter underneath it. There, inside the logo of a golden heart cradled in lilac-colored arms, was the same name she'd looked down at on Celia's card less than twelve hours earlier.

LOVING ARMS AND GUIDING HANDS

An odd sensation tickled at her thoughts, but she couldn't put her finger on what it was. Instead, she found her gaze sliding down to the typewritten letter dated December 29.

Dear Roger,

Thank you for underwriting the cost of this upcoming year's Summer Fest at Camden Park. As always, we are humbled by your continued support for our children, and it is because of it that we are able to impact the lives of so many children during such difficult times. We, at Loving Arms and Guiding Hands, are blessed to have your support and we are forever grateful.

Signed,
Celia Granderson
President
Loving Arms and Guiding Hands

Confused, she read the date and the letter a second and third time. "I don't understand," she murmured. "Why would Celia say he hadn't donated when he very clearly did? When she, herself, had written him a thank you—"

Emma closed the folder, grabbed her keys, and headed for the door, glancing back at Scout as she did. "I'm sorry, boy. I have to go. Please refrain from relocating my possessions while I'm gone, okay?"

Slowly, Scout lowered himself to the wood-plank floor and rested his chin atop his front paws, resigned to his fate of being left alone once again. And, like the well-trained pet owner she'd become, she felt her heart twist with guilt.

"Fine. You win. Hide whatever you want. I'll be back as soon as I can. I love you."

Chapter Twenty-Five

D espite the familiar street and the number that told her
to keep watch on the east side of the sidewalk, it still
took Emma four attempts to find her destination. Tucked
between Sweet Falls Bakery and the studio she'd fallen
asleep in during her first (and only) yoga class, the shingled
sign denoting Loving Arms and Guiding Hands' office was
as unassuming as the single door it marked.

With one last inhale of the cinnamon-scented air being
pumped onto the sidewalk from the bakery, Emma pulled
open the door and stepped inside a small, carpeted vesti-
bule. To her right, and mounted on the wall inside a large
frame, was Loving Arms and Guiding Hands' mission
statement written in bold typeface beneath the purple-and-
gold logo that served as their visual brand.

*We believe all children should know the comfort of a
hand held.*

*We believe all children should know the safety of a warm
embrace.*

We believe all children should know the gift of being heard, and seen.

We believe all children should know that they matter.

We believe all children should know the joy of unconditional love.

We believe all children should know the confidence of having someone in their corner as they make their way out into the world.

And we believe that, together, we can give that to all of them.

One child at a time.

Below the frame, etched on a small, rectangular placard, was an arrow pointing toward the carpeted stairwell. She checked the suite number against the one on the business card in her hand and took the steps to the door at the top.

Her entry through the door was met with a faint chime and, seconds later, a woman sporting a shoulder-length crop of white hair and a name tag that read "Barb." "Good afternoon. Welcome to Loving Arms and Guiding Hands. May I help you?"

"Yes, thank you. I was hoping I could have a moment with Celia, if she's in? I'd just like to ask her a quick question."

Barb looked at the wall behind her chair, ran her hand along the series of open cubbies, and then turned back to Emma. "I'm sorry. I thought she might've returned while I was in back making calls, but the black tag in her box tells me otherwise. I don't expect she'll be much longer, but I can't say for certain. She's meeting with a few local businesses about next month's Summer Fest, and there's always a chance one will go longer than expected or, if we're lucky, lead to another avenue worthy of exploration."

"I see."

"Would you like to write her a message?" Barb's vein-ridden yet delicate hand emerged over the top of the knee-high wall with a pad of sticky notes and a pen. "If she's not back before my shift is over, I can leave your note in her box and she'll see it just as soon as she returns."

It wasn't Emma's first choice, but compared to sitting in the room's lone folding chair waiting for however long it might be before the woman returned, it made the most sense. Nodding, she set Celia's business card, along with the letter Roger had received, down on the counter and picked up the pen.

"Isn't that funny," Barb said, adjusting her eyeglasses across her narrow nose and leaning close. "It's just like ours, but in reverse."

Glancing past the pad to the receptionist, Emma followed the woman's gaze to the part of Roger's letter that was hanging over the counter on Barb's side. "I'm not sure who came up with your logo and your color scheme, but it's really good. Makes me think of Loving Arms and Guiding Hands the second I see it now."

"Not exactly a good thing for whoever *that* is, but if it makes you think of us, I guess we'll take it." Barb rolled back in her chair, scooped up a pile of envelopes from a wire basket, and began placing stamps on them. "Especially now. Any exposure is good exposure when you're in need of funding. We're doing our best to work within our changed means, but that hasn't stopped any of us from crossing our fingers for some sort of Hail Mary pass, as my husband Ralph likes to call it. But I don't think it's coming. Not on the scale any of us would like it to."

She watched Barb make her way through the pile of envelopes with the purple-and-gold logo on the return address space and tried to make sense of a conversation she'd clearly missed while writing her note to Celia. "It?"

"Summer Fest." Barb moved on to a second pile, her fingers affixing stamps at an impressive speed. "At this point, I'd be thrilled if we could just get someone to sponsor the s'more station. That, along with the promise of bunnies and baby chicks from a farmer out in Cloverton, will at least be *something* fun for the kids."

"I told Celia I'd be happy to help. And I come with a dog—a golden retriever named Scout. He loves to dispense licks."

Barb stopped stamping and reached for a pad of paper beside the desk phone. "Oh, are you Emma Westlake?"

Emma smiled. "I am."

"Celia added your name to our list this morning, and we couldn't be more thrilled. Thank you! And you saved me a phone call."

"I guess I did." Emma leaned forward against the counter. "Feel free to put me and Scout wherever you see fit. For however long you need that day."

"Celia mentioned your dog." Barb grabbed a pen from a holder on the far side of the phone. "Said maybe we could do a dog-hugging station?"

"Sure, that'll work for us, if you think it would go over with the kids."

Barb made a note next to Emma's name and underscored it twice. "Trust me, they'll be so starved for anything, I don't think that'll be a problem. Any station we can add is one more station than we had a moment earlier."

"We could make it a game of sorts, too."

Barb's eyes brightened. "Oh? What kind of game?"

"Well, Scout likes to hide things." At Barb's quizzical expression, Emma continued. "Mostly my socks, the TV remote, my pens, and my hairbrush but, really, anything that doesn't belong to him."

The woman's laugh stirred one from Emma, as well. "But he's also good at finding things. So maybe we let him hide something—maybe a small toy or a treat—and the child whose turn it is could find it, and keep it. Or I could hide the toy or treat and Scout and the child could find it together." She stopped, considered her idea, and then blew out a breath. "I'm sorry. That probably sounds silly."

"No! It's something; something different!" Barb drew an

arrow next to Emma's name, indicating the need to turn a page. There, she wrote *Hide-and-seek with a dog* and underlined it three times. "We'll talk it out more with Celia, of course, but I think this will be fun for the kids."

"I'm glad."

Barb returned her pen to the holder and her fingers to the task of stamping the rest of the envelopes in the second stack. When she finished the last one, she slid the pile alongside the first and rested her hands atop them both. "I know the difference is subtle, but I like ours better. It's more appealing somehow."

Emma finished writing the final digits of her phone number on the bottom of the sticky note and held it out to Barb. "If you could see that Celia gets this, I'd really appreciate it."

"Of course. I'll go ahead and put it straight into her mailbox now. It's the first place she checks when she comes in." Barb swiveled her chair toward the wall-mounted cubbies, placed Emma's note inside the one marked CELIA, and then looked back at Emma by way of the counter. "That said, I can't help but wish whoever that is had picked something entirely different. For us *and* for them."

"Different?" Emma echoed.

"The graphic, the colors, all of it."

She followed the path forged by Barb's outstretched finger to Roger's thank-you letter. Confusion led her back to Barb. "I don't—"

"You think there'd be a database somewhere that people could check to see what others have done. Then again, maybe the decision to mimic ours was intentional and that's why they reversed the purple and the gold."

Again, Emma looked back at the paper, this time pulling the part of the masthead that overhung the counter on Barb's side back into her own view. There, above Loving Arms and Guiding Hands' name, was the gold-colored heart cradled by lilac-colored—

She darted her gaze to Celia's business card and then over to the mural gracing the wall behind Barb's desk.

Lilac-colored heart . . .

Cradled by golden arms . . .

Confused, she took in the donation letter once again.

Gold-colored heart . . .

Cradled by lilac-colored arms . . .

The difference was subtle. Minute. But it was there.

"When did you switch the colors?" Emma asked, returning her attention to Barb.

"We didn't."

"Are you sure?" Again, she looked from the mural to the business card and, finally, back to Roger's letter. "Maybe before you started working here?"

"I'm a volunteer. Have been for the past twelve years. And yes, I'm sure. We're lilac with gold, not gold with lilac. I should know. I was part of the committee that created it."

She heard the words coming out of Barb's mouth, but they didn't make any sense. Not when . . . Snatching up the letter, she turned it so Barb could—

The ring of the desk phone stole Barb's attention and fixed it, instead, on the name scrolling its way across the narrow identification window. "Oh! Oh! Oh! This is the scout council returning my call! Finally!" Pausing her hand on the receiver, Barb flashed a parting smile at Emma. "I'm sorry, Emma. I hate to cut our conversation short, but I've been waiting for this call all week and we really need their help more than ever this year."

"No, no, I understand. It's just—"

"I'll be sure to have Celia give you a ring just as soon as she gets back."

"Right. Sure. Okay." She looked back down at the paper in her hand and, as Barb took the call, made her way out the door and down the stairs.

Chapter Twenty-Six

Emma looked out over Alfred's prize-winning landscape and willed it to work its usual magic. To calm her worry. To clear her head. To provide a puff of air under her wings. But for the first time, it fell far short.

Meaning, it didn't work. At all.

Not the flap of the cardinal family's wings as they splashed around in the birdbath . . .

Not the sweet aroma of Alfred's confederate jasmine encircling the arbor and the fence beyond . . .

Nor the kaleidoscope of color from the four-o'clocks surrounding the patio with their trumpet-shaped blooms in fuchsia, yellow, and white.

She tried. She really did. But after a while, even Scout gave up his attempts to nuzzle, and lick, and wag, and, finally, whimper a smile or, really, any reaction out of her at all.

"Glenda greeted me after my afternoon nap just now with news that you'd taken over my patio table with a mess of papers, and it's clear she wasn't embellishing."

Abandoning her view of the brown bobbin attempting to crash the youngest cardinal's bath time, Emma scraped back her chair and stood. "Dottie! You're awake!"

"As I always am at two o'clock, dear. You know this." Dottie wheeled her way over to her spot at the backyard table and leveled an inquisitive stare at Emma across the top edge of her glasses. "You also know I start my nap at one. Yet, according to Glenda, you were here precisely at that time."

Shrugging, Emma sat back down. "I wasn't thinking about the time, I guess. And when I realized my mistake, *this*"— she opened her arms to the table and her mess—"seemed as good a place as any to wait."

"For?"

"Your input. Your thoughts. *Your anything.*"

Dottie's gaze lowered to the papers scattered across the surface of her wrought iron table, and still further to the woeful face now panting beside her chair. "I don't know how you do it, Scout. I really don't." With one hand diligently petting Scout's head, the octogenarian plucked a small silver bell from her chair's side pouch and gave it a single ring. Seconds later, Glenda appeared at her side.

"Yes, Dottie?"

"Please bring out some of that wonderful lemonade you made this morning, along with some of those petit fours."

Emma's stomach rumbled, earning her a raised brow from Dottie, Glenda, and Scout. "What?" she countered. "So, I might've sorta skipped breakfast."

"It's 2:00 p.m., dear."

Her stomach rumbled again. "I skipped lunch, too."

Dottie's rolling eyes found their way back to Glenda. "Perhaps a finger sandwich or two for our uninvited guest, as well? And"—Dottie looked down at Scout and smiled—"something special for this young man who has surely gone unfed?"

"Yes, of course," Glenda said, returning to the house.

Emma watched her friend's trusted housekeeper disappear into the house and then pinned Dottie with a grin. "You do realize Scout just played you, right?"

"Played me?"

"Yes. The big eyes . . . the tilted head . . . the gentle paw on your knee . . . the slow, hopeful wag of his tail . . ." Emma dropped her attention to her dog and made a face. "Because Scout never goes without a meal, do you, boy?"

Resting his head atop Dottie's knee, Scout ping-ponged his eyes between the elderly woman and Emma.

"That's what I thought," Emma murmured.

Dottie continued petting Scout, even as her attention returned to the paper bomb exploded across her table. "So, what is this, dear? And why is it on my table?"

With nary a word, Emma picked up and discarded several pieces of paper before she found the one she wanted and held it out to Dottie. "Look at this. Tell me what you see."

"I see paper."

She shook it. "Take it."

Dottie abandoned Scout's head in favor of the paper. "Am I supposed to read this?"

"Yes."

She watched Dottie's eyes slide left to right across each line of the letter, and then waited as they found Emma across the top rim of her glasses once again. "Why do you have a letter written to our victim?"

Again, she sifted through the mess in front of her, this time securing and showing the folder that had held the papers. "Kim's daughter wanted Kim to see the stuff in here. They're things she thought would cheer Kim up. Demonstrate, I think, that Roger may have been coming to his senses where Kim was concerned. At least in terms of recognizing the kind of person he'd been because of Kim."

"Do you believe that?"

"That he was coming to his senses? I don't know. I just know what the daughter said when I saw her at Kim's house the other day."

"So why do you have this instead of Kim?" Dottie asked, looking back down at the donation letter.

Emma let loose a quiet sigh. "I forgot to give it to Jack after our date last night. And then when I—"

"Your date?" Dottie echoed, returning her full attention to Emma.

"Yes."

"Is that why you were in such a rush to get me home after the wake last night?"

She felt her face warming. Tried to cough it away.

"I see."

"Anyway, I didn't realize I hadn't given him the folder until I saw it this morning after the gym. So I went home, got ready to bring it over, and—"

"Did he take you to the Colonnade Room?"

"No." Emma drew in a breath. "Anyway, when I was ready to go, my curiosity got the best of—"

"The outdoor theater in Cloverton?"

She shook her head. "My curiosity got the best of me and I looked. I know I shouldn't have, but—"

"The vineyard for a jazz concert?"

Emma looked up at the sky. Shook her head again. Lowered her gaze to Dottie's. "We ate fried chicken in a park. On a blanket. With—gasp!—paper napkins. Satisfied?"

"You don't have to be so testy, dear."

"And you don't have to be so—so . . ." She cast about for a fitting description. "Judgmental. And old school."

"Proper dates are old school now?"

"Referring to them as proper dates is." Emma kneaded the skin next to her temples. "We talked. We laughed. We shared things about our childhoods and our jobs. We enjoyed good food. We—"

"Fried chicken is good food?"

"As a matter of fact, it is. So, too, were the brownies I made and the wine he brought."

"Did you drink it out of paper cups?" Dottie asked.

"It was perfect, Dottie."

Dottie's lips twitched at the corners, prompting Emma to stop kneading. "You're just being a pill, aren't you?"

"I prefer to see it as keeping you on your toes."

Emma's laugh set Scout's tail wagging. "You're too much."

Again, Dottie looked at the paper. Read a few more lines. "Am I looking for anything in particular?"

"You mean beyond the fact that Celia, the president of Loving Arms and Guiding Hands, specifically told me that Roger didn't send in his usual donation for Summer Fest in December?"

Dottie turned the paper to Emma and pointed at the date. "But it says December, right here."

"I know it does."

"Then clearly he *did* donate."

"She said he didn't."

Again Dottie looked at the paper and then turned it for Emma to see. "But she signed it, right here."

"I know."

"Then I don't understand," Dottie said.

"Wait. It gets better." Emma leaned forward and pointed at the top of the letter. "Look at the masthead. What do you see?"

Dottie's eyes fairly flew across the logo. "I see the Loving Arms and Guiding Hands' name. Why?"

"In particular, the color scheme."

Dottie looked from Emma to the paper and back again. "Tell me this isn't about A Friend for Hire, dear."

"It's not. Look at it."

When a suitable amount of scouring time had passed, Emma located Celia's business card and slid it across the table to Dottie. "Now, tell me what you see on *this*."

"They switched the colors," Dottie said, holding the two side by side. "In the letter the heart is gold, the arms lilac. But in this card, it's the opposite."

"Exactly."

Dottie took in the card and the letter for a few more moments and then lowered them both onto the table. "So why are you showing me this?"

"Because I think something fishy might've been going on. And maybe, just maybe, since these"—she swept her hand toward the paper-strewn tabletop—"were all together in the folder Roger left at his daughter's, he may have stumbled across something."

Dottie leaned forward. "I'm listening."

"Loving Arms and Guiding Hands isn't the only one with a funky thank-you note." She thrust another example in front of Dottie and followed it up with the first of more than a dozen screenshots she'd taken since setting up camp in the woman's backyard. "Do you see the subtle difference in the logo between this donation letter and the one on their website?"

"The colors are different," Dottie said, her voice quiet.

"Exactly."

"Why would they change the colors like that?"

Emma found another letter-to-screenshot pairing and handed it to Dottie. "They wouldn't."

"But they did." Dottie said, looking at Emma once again. "Clearly."

"*Someone* did, yes. I'm just fairly certain it wasn't the organization."

And just like that, the reality behind Emma's words seemed to take root behind Dottie's sage-green eyes. "These signatures? On these donation letters? They're all forged, aren't they?"

"I think they might be." Emma pushed back from the table and paced her way around the patio. "But it's the why I can't seem to put my finger on."

"*I* can."

Emma stopped midway to the birdbath and whirled around. "I'm listening."

"Those donations are a write-off!"

She stared at Dottie. Waiting.

"To help minimize the profits the government can get their hands on, companies can opt to donate to a charity," Dottie explained. "Doing so is a good PR move, of course, but the biggest benefit is that it can decrease their tax liability. Which is something you might want to consider as A Friend for Hire gets bigger."

"Ha! Like that will ever happen!"

"It won't with that defeatist attitude, dear."

She waved off Dottie's reprimand. "You're right. But we're not talking about A Friend for Hire or me right now. We're . . ."

Her words trailed off as Glenda emerged from the house with a tray of food in one hand and a pitcher of lemonade in the other.

"Oh, wow," Emma murmured. "That all looks so good."

And it was true. It was also true that if she'd had a tail she would've wagged it in that moment. Instead, she stepped inside, grabbed the plates and glasses from the kitchen, and fairly chased Glenda back to the table.

When they were settled with food on their plates and freshly poured lemonade in their glasses, Glenda disappeared back into the house. "Wow," Emma repeated, taking a bite. "So, so good."

"I'm glad."

Two bites in, Emma set her sandwich back down, her thoughts running amuck once again. "So, what then? Roger shows a letter to his accountant saying he donated money to a charity and it comes off the bottom line?"

"More or less. In a nutshell." Dottie lowered Scout's treat plate to the ground and watched as he went to work. "But saying he gave something he didn't give would catch up to him at some point."

"How so?"

"When what he claimed didn't match what the organization showed on their taxes."

"How quickly would that happen?"

"I can't say. I would imagine the answer to that would vary." Dottie took a sip of lemonade, looked out over her late husband's flowering bushes and trees. "So, let's play this out, shall we?"

Emma helped herself to another sandwich. "Let's do it."

"We have a bunch of letters, written to Kim's husband, acknowledging his donations to various organizations last year . . ."

"Check," Emma said between bites.

"And, at least in the case of Loving Arms and Guiding Hands, that letter is signed by a woman who specifically said he didn't donate . . ."

She paused the last bite of her finger sandwich just shy of her lips and nodded. "Check."

"Yet the letter said he did . . ."

"Also, check."

"And the letter looks official . . ."

"Save for the variation in the logo's color scheme, yes. Check."

Dottie abandoned her lemonade and petit fours in favor of the donation letters she'd neatly stacked to the left of her spot. One by one she silently reread each one, pausing on occasion to shake her head or murmur something indiscernible while Emma continued eating and drinking.

"And the man tied to all of these supposed donations is now dead," Dottie said as she added the final letter to the pile.

Satiated, Emma threw herself back against her chair. "*Murdered.*"

"Murdered," Dottie reached inside her chair's side pouch for her trusty notebook and pen and opened both. "Stephanie isn't going to be pleased she's missing out on our sleuthing session, but we can fill her in when we're done."

She felt herself nodding, even heard something that sounded like assent making its way past her lips, but really, the only thing she knew with absolute certainty was the bizarre picture beginning to take shape in her head. "Do you think one of these charities found out Roger was scamming the system?"

"And killed him?"

"Yeah . . . I mean, no . . . I mean"—Emma laughed—"What am I saying? I'm not the cozy mystery reader that you are, or the armchair TV detective that Stephanie is. I like playing in the dirt and watching flowers grow. I like baking brownies. I like chasing ducks with Scout. I don't know how to do this whole amateur sleuth thing."

Dottie looked up from the notes she was taking. "Too bad. We're doing it."

"We shouldn't be."

"Speak for yourself, dear."

"Fine. *I* shouldn't be," Emma said, holding her hands up in surrender before dropping them back to the table. "I mean, those donations . . . No one—particularly someone whose job it is to do good work like Celia—is going to take another person's life over not being able to have a bounce castle and a slide at their annual summer event."

"If it was just a castle and a slide, I'd agree. But those things happen by way of money—money they had been getting for years yet, suddenly, weren't."

She met Dottie's eyes. "Celia isn't killing anyone over the money needed for this year's festival."

"Maybe not. But multiply the amount by at least five or six and *someone* might."

Emma glanced at her friend. "This was the first time in ten years he didn't come through with the donation."

"For them." Dottie swept her pen-wielding hand at the stack of donation letters. "And maybe, based on these, for all of them."

"What? You're saying one rep from each of these organizations came together and killed him?" Emma pushed back her chair and stood. "C'mon. Even *I* know that's way too far-fetched."

"But what if one of the groups threatened to report him for false donation claims or"—Dottie tapped the pen atop the stack—"forging signatures?"

She crossed to the edge of the patio, inhaled the aroma of confederate jasmine, and then turned back to Dottie. "There's one problem with your theory."

"And what is that, dear?"

"He's the one who's dead, not them." Emma wandered over to the birdbath and felt Scout move in beside her for a closer look. "Which means someone was angry at him, or jealous of him, or wanted to keep him quiet, right?"

"Don't look now, dear, but you're thinking like a sleuth."

Emma reached down and scratched Scout's head. "In terms of anger? Sure, Celia or someone from one of these other charities could've been mad about the sudden cessation of donations. But all of those letters next to you were from six months ago. It seems like the kind of anger that would make a person snap and kill someone wouldn't simmer for that long. It would be more of a knee-jerk, quicker kind of thing, right?"

"Agreed."

"Then there's jealousy," said Emma.

"Not so quick, dear. Others could've been angry at him. Like Kim, or the mistress's husband."

She filtered Scout's ear through her fingers and then turned back to Dottie. "Was Kim angry? Sure. But she also still loved him. And Trevor? He and Brittney are back together, and it appears they were *before* Roger's murder. So that doesn't fit, either."

"Sound thinking." Dottie turned her notepad to a clean page and readied her pen. "That leaves us with keeping him quiet."

"No. We skipped over jealousy."

"True. But you already discounted the mistress's husband."

Emma considered Dottie's comment and found that it made sense. "Okay, moving on . . . What could the owner of a PR company in Sweet Falls, Tennessee, get himself into that would make someone murder him just to keep him quiet?"

"Maybe something with a client?"

"I saw his client list. That wouldn't make sense." Slowly, aimlessly, she found herself back at the table, looking down at the stack of donation letters next to Dottie's elbow. "For some reason, I keep coming back to the fact that Roger went through these on his daughter's kitchen table and left them there. Even allowing for the possibility that he left them on her table by mistake, why—if he was doing something illegal—would he choose to go through this kind of stuff in his daughter's apartment? It doesn't make sense.

"*Unless* he wasn't afraid," she added. "Because he didn't do anything wrong."

"Someone did," Dottie reminded her.

"Agreed. Someone did." Grabbing the stack of letters, Emma flipped through them, one by one, the sight of Roger's name in every salutation sending an uneasy shiver down her spine. "What if the person intended to be fooled by these letters was Roger himself?"

"I'm not following, dear."

It was a wild idea, sure, but it was one she couldn't shake away, no matter how hard she tried. "What if Roger *thought* he made all of these donations, but he really didn't?"

"He'd be a fool," Dottie shot back.

"And I'd agree. *If* he knew."

Dottie pointed her pen at Emma. "The money would still be in his account."

"Not if someone went to all this trouble"—she held up the stack of letters and gave it a little shake—"to show a donation that didn't happen."

And just like that, the crazy idea that had been playing hide-and-seek with her thoughts since before Dottie woke from her nap flipped on the proverbial light bulb behind the octogenarian's eyes. "Oh, Emma . . . These supposed donations, added together, would be a nice sum of money for anyone. The kind of money you could actually do something with."

Pulling the stack to her chest, Emma nodded. "Like securing a loan you might not otherwise be able to get."

Dottie's answering and very un-Dottie-like squeal brought Glenda running. A firm shake of her snow-white hair sent Glenda back inside. "It was the mistress, wasn't it!" Dottie said, taking pen to paper.

"Makes sense to me. Brittney worked at Felder PR, she redesigned the company's website, she was amazing with graphics from what Reece said, and yes, she just bought a new home that is substantially nicer than the one she had before."

"And!" Dottie declared, lifting up her pen. "You said she and Roger had some sort of falling out, didn't you? Maybe that's what ended their affair. He'd caught on to what she was doing and confronted her. And then she either got angry or scared, and killed him!"

Hearing it from Dottie's lips shored up what she knew in her heart was true. It all fit. Perfectly.

"We did it, Dottie." she said, as she gathered up the rest of her things. "We figured it out."

"You sound surprised."

Emma paused, her hand on her tote bag. "I am."

"*I'm* not. We make a good team. You bring the pieces we need, and I put it together."

Scout's ears perked up at the sound of Emma's laugh. "*You* put it together? Uh . . . no. Did you not hear how this just played out? How I'm the one who suggested Roger wasn't privy to the fact he hadn't donated to his favorite organizations? How you're the one who said he'd be a fool for not knowing? How—"

"Don't gloat."

"I'm not gloating. I'm setting you straight."

Dottie rolled her eyes. "Fine. Take all the credit. It gives me someone to point at when Stephanie gets all indignant that we solved this murder without her."

Touché.

"Fine. We solved it together. By complete accident. Over finger sandwiches—which were to die for, by the way—and petit fours and freshly squeezed lemonade."

Dottie's eyebrow inched upward, along with the corners of her mouth. "*That's* what you're going to tell Stephanie?"

"Oh. Right. Drat." Emma looped the strap of her tote bag around her shoulder and summoned Scout to her side. "We solved it together. By complete accident. There was absolutely no food involved."

"Much better, dear. Now go get Kim out of that jail cell."

Chapter Twenty-Seven

❦

Emma looked up at the click of the door and watched as Kim's expression ran the gamut from curiosity to surprise to, finally, tired joy at seeing a friendly face.

"Emma, what a nice surprise." Glancing back at the uniformed deputy who'd escorted her into the interrogation room, Kim nodded, said "Thank you," and made her way over to the tiny metal table and the empty chair opposite Emma's. "I assumed you were going to be my attorney, with yet another reason my time in front of the judge was being delayed."

"Nope."

Kim's tired smile faltered. "Did something happen? Is it the kids?"

"Nope. They're okay. Missing you, of course, but hanging tough."

Relief flooded the woman's pale face as she sagged back against her chair. "Thank heavens. I've been so worried about them."

"Understandable. But at least as far as what's going on with *you*, you don't have to be any longer."

Lifting her full attention back onto Emma, Kim pulled a face. "I don't understand."

"Your kids. They don't have to worry about you anymore."

Kim's brows dipped in obvious confusion. "I'm not following."

"You." Emma motioned toward the woman and then outward to include the room as a whole. "Being here. In this place. It stops today. Anytime now, actually."

Kim glanced back at the deputy and then leaned forward across the table. "Is something happening with the judge?"

"I would imagine so. Which means I can drive you home just as soon as they sign whatever papers need to be signed. And then, after you take whatever time you need to mourn Roger's loss and to help Natalie and Caleb do the same, I'm ready—as you can see—to get to our list."

With a gentle shove, she scooted the pile of papers at her elbow across the table to Kim. "I found a few cooking class opportunities you might enjoy and one of those paint-and-sip pottery places that scream 'girl time.' I've also picked a date for our first book club meeting, which we'll do at my house."

Kim looked through the pile of colorful printouts and then back up at Emma. "This looks amazing. All of it. But—"

"No. No buts. We're doing this." She shot her hand into the air and then reached into the tote bag Jack had allowed. "Oh, and look what I found. It's that dessert squad thingy."

Kim took the sheet Emma held out and quietly scanned it from top to bottom while Emma continued. "I'm thinking we shoot for September to head up there. That way, we'll have a book club meeting or two under our belt and if we want to open the trip up to anyone besides just the two of us, we can. Your call. No pressure, either way. This is your list. Your life to reclaim."

"I-I don't understand."

Emma pointed at the printouts she'd hastily assembled

in her home office after calling Jack and before heading over to the station. "Those are some of the things on that list we talked about—your get-back-to-living bucket list, remember? The baking classes, starting a book club, traveling to Ohio to find that dessert squad food truck, all that stuff you want to do. We can do it now. All of it."

"I can't do anything right now," Kim said sliding the papers back to Emma. "Not until this whole mess is resolved. Somehow, someway."

Emma intercepted the papers and pushed them back to Kim. "It *is* resolved. Jack is interviewing Roger's real killer as we speak. Which means, once he's done, I'll be driving you home, or to see Natalie, or Caleb, or wherever it is you want to go first."

"Are you serious?"

"I am."

"For real?"

"For real."

"Who?" Kim asked, planting her hands atop the table. "Who killed him?"

Again, Emma reached into the tote, only this time, she pulled out her phone. "Brittney killed him."

Kim's answering gasp echoed through the windowless room. "Brittney?"

"Yes."

"Why?"

"I don't know for sure. Jack will fill us in when he's done, but from what I can tell, Roger came to realize she was skimming money from the company's account and—I imagine—threatened to press charges. So she killed him."

Kim stared at Emma, clearly waiting for more. And, since there really wasn't anything else to say, Emma tapped her way into her phone's album, called up the picture she'd snapped of the bogus donation letters, and handed it to Kim. "Scroll left. There's a ton."

"What is this?" Kim asked as she moved from one letter

to the next, her fingers enlarging each shot while her lips silently read each word. "These are the annual thank-you letters from the groups we—I mean, *Felder PR*—supported each year."

"They *look* like them, yes. But they aren't real."

Kim's eyes snapped to Emma's. "What do you mean?"

"At first I didn't see it. But now that I have, it's all so obvious." She leaned forward, pointed at the letter depicted on her phone's screen. "See the group's logo? The colors are either reversed or simply wrong. And it's like that with all of the letters."

At Kim's confusion, Emma pressed on. "Brittney pocketed the money Roger thought he was donating at the end of last year. And to throw him off the scent, she crafted bogus acknowledgment letters from all of the groups. It worked, I imagine, for a while—long enough to get her into a nicer house, anyway—but I'm guessing when Roger's books and the various charities' books didn't match, the truth came out. Once it did, he likely confronted her and she snapped."

Kim scrolled through the pictures again and again, her expression unreadable. "And you think it was *Brittney* because why?"

"Because she was good with graphics. Because she handled the books. Because—"

"Did you say Brittney was handling the books?" Kim asked, looking up.

Emma nodded.

"Brittney didn't touch the finances, Emma. Reece did that."

"Not anymore. Reece said he turned that over to her after he left you."

"No. Roger may have fallen for the pretty face, but he was a consummate businessman." Kim scrolled through the pictures, stopping to expand each and every letter once again. "And while he may have temporarily tossed me aside for something younger, he would never have jeopardized his business in that way. Not to mention the simple fact that math was not Brittney's thing."

Emma stared at Kim. "Maybe he knew that when he was *with you* but he obviously changed his mind once she got her hooks in him."

"No. He couldn't."

"Why not?"

"Because our divorce wasn't official yet."

"Okay . . ."

"Which means my stake in that company hadn't yet been decided."

"Okay . . ." Emma repeated.

"Which means any change in job responsibilities would've had to have been discussed with and agreed upon by me."

"Okay . . ."

"Only three people had access to the company's financials. Me. Roger. And Reece. That's it."

"But—"

Kim held up her hand. "That's it. Me. Roger. And Reece."

"But Reece said they fought."

"Who?"

"Roger and Brittney," Emma said, looking back down at her phone and then back up at Kim. "And Brittney was back with Trevor!"

Kim closed her eyes.

Emma continued, her reasons for fingering Brittney for the crime pouring from her mouth. "They bought a house together in Walden Brook! How could they do that without some crazy influx of—"

Kim's lashes parted. "So it was true? They actually *had* broken up?"

"Wh-whoa, wait," Emma stammered. "You knew they'd broken up?"

"Roger told me they did, but I didn't believe him. I figured he was lying."

"But how? When?"

"A month or so before his . . ." Kim cleared the building emotion from her voice with a few deep breaths. "A month or so before his murder. He told me he'd been a fool. That he wanted me back. That he wanted our family back. But he was clearly drunk, and I figured it was a moment of guilt."

She stared at Kim. "But your email . . . You told me he'd left you."

"Because he did. For a woman only a few years older than our son."

"But—"

"Him calling me in a moment of drunken guilt that never came again when he was sober wasn't worth talking about." Kim drew in a longer, deeper breath, and let it go slowly. "But what *was* worth thinking about—as painful as it was—were the reasons he'd given for walking out on our marriage and on me. I had changed. I *did* lose myself. Reaching out to you was about changing that. *For me.*"

At a loss for what to say, Emma said nothing, her thoughts racing.

"But hearing, just now, that it was true . . . that he had broken things off with Brittney . . . I don't know what to say." Kim covered her face with her hands. "I was so angry, so hurt. All I could see was that."

"All pretty understandable, if you ask me."

"Was it, though?"

"Absolutely. You deserved better." Emma considered everything she'd heard to that point, her mind's eye narrowing in on the reason she'd come in the first place. "But the money? And the fake letters? And Brittney's big new house . . . It still makes sense."

"If Brittney had access, maybe. But she didn't. And the new house? It goes with the record label, I imagine."

"Record label?" Emma echoed.

"One of Roger's clients got Trevor in front of the right

people in the country music business. And *that* explains the house."

"So, then, if it wasn't Brittney, and it wasn't you, then . . ."

And then she knew.

Reece had access to Felder PR's banking . . .

Reece knew how to make graphics, too . . .

Reece had taken over some of Kim's duties when Kim's parents were ill . . .

Reece had spoken about an argument between Roger and Brittney, an argument that may or may not have happened . . .

And Reece was in the process of fulfilling her lifelong dream to open her own—

"I have a few more clients still to call about my leaving."

"About her leaving, not his death . . ." Emma murmured, only to bolt upright in her chair. "Kim? Do you have some sort of client list at your house? Something with numbers I could call?"

Kim looked a question at Emma.

"I need to ask them all a question. About Reece."

"About Reece?"

Nodding, she brought Kim up to speed on her thinking, and watched as the woman's eyes clouded at the mention of Reece's plan to leave Felder. "Starting a business—especially one with leased space—takes money. It just does," Emma concluded.

"I'm well aware." Kim pointed at Emma's phone. "I'm also well aware of the clients Roger worked so hard to cultivate over the years, many of whom I entertained at my home on one occasion or another."

Emma reached inside her tote for a pen, only to realize she'd had to leave that behind on the desk outside. Instead, she grabbed her phone and opened the Notes app. "Can you give me some of those names?"

"Actually, I know a few of their phone numbers by heart."

"You do?"

Kim's answering shrug was sheepish. "My entire world revolved around my husband and my kids, remember?"

Chapter Twenty-Eight

(Two weeks later)

Emma was just fluffing the final throw pillow when the sudden acceleration of Scout's tail speed, followed by the clicking of his nails on the hallway floor, alerted her to the arrival of her first guest. With one last glance at the various snack bowls she'd set up around the living room, Emma made haste toward the front door.

"Are you ready for our very first book club meeting, Scout?"

At his ever-increasing wag speed, Emma threw open the door to the evening's waning rays. There, standing on her side of the temporary ramp he'd helped create the previous evening, was Jack. Beside him, holding court in her mobile throne, was the woman no doubt responsible for the almost shell-shocked look in the off-duty deputy's blue eyes.

"Dottie! Welcome! You made it!"

"It was touch and go on account of your boyfriend's driving, but yes, I'm here." With a flick of her hand, Dottie wheeled her way past Emma and into the house, stopping just inside the door to trade kisses with Scout before continuing her trek down the hall. "This is . . . *quaint*."

"Quaint." Emma looked back at Jack and grinned. "Your driving, huh?"

Jack raked a hand down his face, the motion doing little to dispel his dazed expression. "You've driven with me. Am I really that bad of a driver?"

"Dottie Adler only complains about people she likes. So if she picked on your driving, it's a good sign."

Jack shook his head. "So being told I drive like an old biddy is a *good* sign?"

"It is . . . But an *old biddy*? How?"

"She's an old woman," Jack said. "I was being extra—"

"I heard that, young man!"

Jack's face blanched, stirring a laugh Emma couldn't have held back if she'd tried. "You're fine." She rested her hand atop Jack's arm. "Trust me. I've been dealing with Dottie Adler for a long time. Her bark is most definitely worse than—"

"Hmmm . . . Well, well, well," Dottie mused as she continued down the hallway, glancing left toward the living room and then right toward Emma's office. "Would you look at that? Emma Westlake has a bookshelf with more knickknacks than books . . . How very *un*-surprising."

Emma looked up at the door frame, rolled her eyes, and then slowly lowered her attention back to Jack. "I know what you're thinking, and yes, I knowingly invited her. Crazy, right?"

"You can't very well host a proper book club on your own, dear, if you don't *read*," Dottie called out.

She motioned Jack to step inside and, at his hesitation, gave him a tug forward. "C'mon in. You're safe. *I'm* officially in her crosshairs now."

"Are you sure?" he asked.

"I'm sure. Come."

He stepped around her and into the hallway, lowering his voice to a near-whisper. "Did you really not read the book you're supposed to be discussing tonight?"

"Of course I read it."

"Then what's she talking about?" Jack glanced over his shoulder as Dottie disappeared into the kitchen as part of her self-guided tour.

"I don't read a book a day the way she does, and I read various genres, not just cozy mysteries. Therefore, in Dottie's eyes, I don't read."

"What *do* you read?"

"Women's fiction, mostly. Sometimes romantic suspense."

"What kind of book are you doing for tonight's inaugural meeting?"

She grinned. "A cozy mystery."

"Smart woman."

Her laugh brought Scout back out of the kitchen for a quick lick of her hand and Jack's calf. "I try."

Glancing toward the still-Dottie-free hallway, Jack leaned away the space between them and brushed a kiss across Emma's forehead. "You look great, by the way."

It took everything she had not to pinch herself in front of him. Instead, she inhaled the aroma that was Jack Riordan and willed that to serve as confirmation that their budding relationship was, in fact, real. "Thank you. And so do—"

Voices on the other side of the now-closed door cut short her sentence and sent her reaching for the door once again. "Quick! Before she finishes critiquing my kitchen and expands her tour to the other rooms! I've got crackers and cheese in the living room."

She followed his gaze from the living room to the still-empty kitchen doorway and, finally, back to Emma. "I don't want to eat your stuff."

"It's the least I can offer after"—she jerked her head toward the kitchen—"you so sweetly volunteered to transport *that*. But hurry. *Quick*."

When he was safely on his way, Emma pulled open the

door, her smile over Jack spreading still further at the spectacle that was Big Max. Dressed in a too-short tan blazer, a pair of baggy denim jeans, and a pale-blue collared shirt, Max Grayben adjusted the glasses he didn't need across the bridge of his nose and the pipe he didn't smoke between his teeth. "I'm here for book club!"

"I see that."

"Do I look smart?" Big Max asked.

"You do."

"Wanna know why?" Straightening the hem of his jacket into place, Big Max stuck out his elbow to reveal an oddly shaped hunter-green scrap of fabric. "Sewed this elbow patch on myself not more than an hour ago."

Emma gave him the *oohs* and *aahs* he sought and silently applauded Stephanie's as she joined them at the front door.

"Wow. Big Max," Stephanie said, smiling. "Aren't you looking mighty sharp this evening."

"I was trying to look smart." Big Max touched his glasses and then removed his pipe to brandish it in front of them. "See?"

"And you do. Like a sharpened pencil ready to . . ." Stephanie cast about for just the right way to link her word choice to his and then flashed a grin of triumph at Emma as she settled on one. "Ace a test!"

Big Max puffed out his chest in pride, then deflated it to normal size in favor of sniffing the air and pointing into the house. "Is that little hot dogs I'm smelling in there?"

"It is indeed."

"Those are my favorite for parties."

"I know." She waved Big Max into the house and directed him toward the living room. "I have a little cup of mustard waiting inside just for you."

"For swirlin'?" he asked, eyeing her from across the upper rim of his glassless glasses.

"For swirlin'."

Satisfied, Big Max disappeared into the living room, leaving Emma and Stephanie alone.

"Is Kim here yet?" Stephanie asked.

"Not yet. But she will be."

"How's she doing?"

Emma considered her answer, shrugging as she settled on the best. "She's doing . . . okay. Knowing Reece is behind bars is definitely a big weight off her shoulders. But having someone try to frame you for murder the way Reece did has unnerved her, for sure."

"I can imagine. I mean, I get the fact Reece was intercepting the donation money to all those places to help get her own business off the ground. And I get the fact she killed him when he figured out what she was doing. But to use one of Kim's scarves to strangle the guy?" Stephanie shivered. "That's pretty diabolical."

"No doubt." Emma released a slow, even breath. "If he hadn't been drinking when she showed up to tell him she was quitting, or he'd called the cops the second he put two and two together rather than confronting her by himself, he might very well still be alive. That's the part Kim is still struggling with—all the what if's."

"I still don't get why Reece framed Kim instead of Brittney," Stephanie mused. "I mean, Brittney got all of Roger's attention during their fling, right?"

"True. And yes, that upset Reece tremendously. She wanted to be Roger's golden girl for her hard work. Instead, Brittney was his golden girl for a very different reason."

"Okay, so why frame Kim? It doesn't make sense."

"From what Jack told me, Reece didn't come from the most supportive homelife. Watching Kim do everything for Roger and Natalie and Caleb ate at her over time. Built up a resentment that, combined with her anger over Roger's preferential treatment of Brittney and her own insatiable need to be successful, just exploded."

"Wow."

"I know."

"And Kim's bucket list?" Stephanie asked. "How is that going?"

"Officially starts tonight. With this book club." Stepping back, she waved Stephanie into the house and toward the living room. "In fact, she's the only one we're waiting on."

Stephanie peeked into the living room, waved at Jack, and then turned back to Emma, her brow furrowed. "Where's Dottie?"

"Taking notes, no doubt, on my kitchen's shortcomings."

"I love your kitchen."

"So do—"

"Emma?"

She popped her head around Stephanie to find Jack staring down at a photograph in his hand, his mouth gaping open. "What's wrong, Jack?"

"Where did you get this?" he asked.

"It was part of a stack of pictures I found in my great-aunt Annabelle's chest." She craned her neck left and right until she had a view of the picture he held. "That's actually me on the swing when I was probably three or four."

His eyes snapped up to hers. "You?"

"I know. Super-cute, wasn't I?"

Again, he lowered his attention back to the picture, his mouth inching upward in a slow yet steady smile.

"Oh. Hey . . ." She stepped all the way into the room. "Do you see that little boy hanging from the monkey bars in the background? Doesn't he look a little like Tommy?"

"He does."

"Crazy, right?"

Jack shrugged, his smile still in place. "Actually, it's kind of cool. A real chip-off-the-old-block kind of thing."

Something about his expression pulled her up short and sent her own gaze racing from the picture to Jack and back again. "Nooo . . ."

His answer came via a second, more elongated shrug. "Yep."

"But . . . *how*?"

"I told you I played in that same park a time or two myself, when I was a—"

"Hello? Emma?"

Big Max looked up from the mustard cup he'd secured for himself. "The cookie lady! She's here!"

Breaking eye contact with Jack, she nodded at Big Max and then headed back into the hallway to find Kim standing just inside the doorway with her copy of their book club selection in one hand and a wrapped plate in the other. "Kim! Welcome!"

"I knocked a few times."

Emma liberated the plate from Kim and planted a kiss on the woman's cheek. "Sorry. I was distracted by my past colliding with my future."

"Excuse me?" Kim said, drawing back.

She waved away her new friend's worry and instead tilted her chin toward the living room. "I'm so glad you're here, Kim. I've been looking forward to this all week."

"Me, too."

"Come. I want you to meet everyone."

Dottie wheeled her way out of the kitchen, Scout close behind. When she spotted Emma and Kim, she stopped. "Kim Felder?"

"Dottie Adler?" At Dottie's nod, Kim stepped around Emma to envelope Dottie's hand in her own. "Emma told me you were one of her cohorts in uncovering the truth behind my husband's murder."

Dottie's left eyebrow arched. "One of her *cohorts*?"

"Yes," Emma said, locking eyes with the octogenarian. "One of my cohorts."

"*You* were the cohort, dear. *I* was the lead."

Emma waved her non-plate-holding hand. "Whoa. Did I or did I not put two and two together on your patio that day?"

"And did you or did you not come up with the wrong answer?" Dottie shot back.

"At first, sure. But—"

"You brought my favorites, Cookie Lady!"

As one, Dottie, Kim, and Emma turned to find Big Max—mustard cup in hand—pointing down at the plate of cookies in Emma's hand, his joy palpable.

"Of course I did." Kim lifted up a corner of the covering, slipped out a cookie, and handed it to Big Max. "The second I heard you would be here, I knew exactly what I had to make."

Emma looked down at the exposed cookies. "Wait. I know these cookies! My friend made them the other day. I can't remember the name he called them, but they were really good! Almost like licorice."

"They're called anisette cookies," Kim said. "Big Max described them to me one day, and I hunted around on various cookie sites until I found them."

Emma held the plate out to Dottie and then Stephanie, and—after catching a glimpse of Jack still looking down at Annabelle's picture—took one for herself. "So, so good."

Scout barked once, twice, and then sat, his eyes ping-ponging between Emma and the cookie plate.

"I think Scout remembers them from my friend's house, too." Emma squatted down next to Scout. "Only they weren't for dogs then, and they're not for dogs now, okay, boy?"

"Rocket liked 'em!"

Startled, Emma looked from Big Max to Scout and back again, her heartbeat slowing. "What did you say?"

"Rocket liked 'em just fine!"

"Who's Rocket, Maxwell?" Dottie asked.

Big Max finished his cookie and then reclaimed his mustard cup. "He was my dog. A long, long time ago."

"Your—your dog?" Emma echoed, her voice barely more than a hoarse whisper.

She heard the squeak of Dottie's wheels as the woman

rolled by, knew Kim and Big Max had followed the octogenarian into the living room, but all that truly mattered in that moment was that her seventy-eight-year-old wildly innocent friend who loved anisette cookies had nodded before he'd walked away.

He'd *nodded* . . .

Acknowledgments

It is true that an author spends an inordinate amount of time in their own head while plotting and then writing a book. We talk to ourselves, we jot notes that are often illegible to everyone else, and we occasionally reach out to people we know with odd questions.

The good news is, all of the mindless talking and note taking and crazy questions culminates in a finished story—just like you're holding in your hands now. If you read *A Plus One for Murder* (the first book in this series) and were anxiously awaiting *A Perilous Pal* to see what happens next with Emma, Scout, and Jack, and the rest of the gang, thank you. Falling in love with a cast of characters the way I have this crew is all the more fun when I know others feel the same.

A big thank-you to my editor, Michelle Vega, and the entire Penguin Random House team who did all of the things that needed to be done for you to have this book in your hands now. A thank-you, also, to my agent who just happens to share my first and last name. Laura, your belief in me and my ability is a blessing. And, last but not least, a huge thank-you to reader and BFF member Terri Skinner King, who was the recipient of a few of my "can this happen" and "what about this . . . and this . . . and this" questions during the plotting of this book.

You can learn more about me and my books by visiting laurabradford.com.